Love Whispers Through the Veil

by Davyne DeSye

Requests for permission to make copies of any part of this work should be mailed to Permissions Department, Illuminus Publishing, PO Box 9206, Colorado Springs, CO 80932.

ISBN: 978-0-9988747-6-0

Cover art by: Julidesign

BOOKS
BY
DAVYNE DESYE

HISTORICAL ROMANCE

The Phantom Rising Series:
For Love of the Phantom
Skeletons in the Closet
Phantom Rising

SCIENCE FICTION

The Aggressor Queen Series:
Carapace
Warmonger (forthcoming)
Aggressor Queen (forthcoming)

Short Story Anthology:
Soap Bubble Dreams and Other Distortions

PRAISE FOR
FOR LOVE OF THE PHANTOM

"I recommend this book to all fans of Phantom of the Opera and to those who believe in unbridled true love."
Readers Favorite – 5-Star Review

***

"THANK YOU to the author for writing one of the best books I have ever read and will love forever."
Nikki Landis, international bestselling and award-winning author of *Sins of the Father*

***

"Enjoyable...kept me turning page after page."
J. Saman, USA Today Bestselling Author

***

"This is an extraordinary book that will not disappoint any fan of the original work."
Bobby Underwood, author of *The Wild Country*

***

"This is a love story unlike many that have been written … The entire book is rich in atmospheric detail, with enough twists and turns to keep me eagerly turning pages."
K.C. Willivee, author of *The Wrong Man*

***

"Bravo! Highly recommended for lovers of historical romance or those simply infatuated with the Opera Ghost and his beloved Miss Daaè."
Jessica Jesinghaus, author of *Mirror, Mirror*

For Josephine Leslie
1898 – 1979

Contents

CHAPTER 1

DAVID

"Have you lost your mind?"

David chuckled in response as he pushed crumpled packing paper into the top of the box in front of him, then laughed aloud when he raised his head and saw Simon's expression and posture: mouth gaping, chin thrust forward, slumped shoulders, and hands – palm-up, held out as if supplicating.

Simon held the posture through David's laughter, then continued, "No? What is it then? You have three months to live and have decided to live them in peace? Or you're not the real David Cartell, but an alien posing as David? What?"

David stretched tape across the top of the box he'd finished packing, pulled an empty box forward and gestured toward Simon. "Can you hand me those books?"

Simon's expression changed to one of exasperation. He straightened to the regal posture he normally maintained, slid a book off the table, and swept it behind his back. "I will not. Not until you explain yourself."

David pulled his glasses off, cleaned the lenses on the front of his T-shirt, replaced them, and held a hand out for the book. "I meant exactly what I said. I quit." The thrill of excitement flashed through him again, as it had when he first said the words aloud in the solitude of his Manhattan loft apartment months ago, as it had just minutes ago when he repeated them to Simon – the only other person he'd told of his decision.

Simon exhaled deeply, returned the book to the stack he'd taken it from and slid one hand into his front pants pocket. "That's not an explanation. If I promise not to yell again, would you do a favor for your agent – and long-time friend, or so I'd like to think – and explain yourself?"

A brief wash of guilt dimmed David's enjoyment of the moment. He had never applied the word "friend" to Simon in his mind, not explicitly. Never *my friend, Simon*. Always, *my agent, Simon*. But in truth, Simon had been his agent from the beginning,

2

swearing, even through the thin times when there were barely any sales, that David had that "something" which would elevate him to fame and fortune. It had been Simon's enthusiasm for David's sculpture that had led to those first sales – assisted, no doubt, by the man's model-perfect good looks and easy charm. But now, through the lens of Simon's casual comment, David realized that Simon was indeed a friend. Probably his only friend. No, they had never met for purely social reasons, but David would find his company enjoyable. He vowed to make the effort in the future.

And to give Simon the explanation he deserved now.

David dropped his outstretched arm, and said, "How about a glass of wine?"

Simon recognized the capitulation. "Hell yes. Yes, please."

Bringing two glasses and a bottle of his favorite Cab Sauv, David settled expansively on one side of a low table that connected the two wings of an enormous U-shaped couch. Simon settled on the other side, immediately sipping from the glass of ruby liquid David offered. Then leaning toward David, Simon said, "Tell me this isn't about Kacey."

LOVE WHISPERS THROUGH THE VEIL

"It's not about Kacey." It was the truth. Mostly. His wife, Kacey, had been the catalyst, without question. After much searching, he had found her – or the detective had – living in LA. With another man. From the pictures the detective had forwarded along with other details of her life, she seemed happy.

It was then that David had realized he was too late. He had labored like a man possessed for five years, driven to become worthy of her. But she had moved on. Not that he could blame her. Five years! The hope he had held out because she had never filed for divorce flickered and died an inglorious death. And so he had decided to quit.

As he mused, David's eyes were directed toward the floor-to-ceiling windows of the penthouse loft, but he saw nothing of the view. He only broke from his thoughts of Kacey when Simon cleared his throat.

"I've made enough money," David continued. Another man might have snorted but Simon only sniffed indignantly. "I've been doing it by the numbers for the last two years, without really feeling the joy of it… and I've made enough money. I'm quitting."

"But–" Simon began.

David held up a hand to silence him. "I've bought a house in the country–"

"What?" Simon jerked forward in his seat and put his wine down with such force that David expected the thin stem of the glass to snap. Defying expectations, the glass remained whole.

David continued, "In New Jersey–"

"New Jersey, for Pete's sake?"

David laughed and took a sip of his own wine before speaking again. "Simon, you asked me to explain and now you're not letting me get a word in."

Simon sighed. "You're right." He sat back, lifted his glass and finished his wine in a single draft. "House. New Jersey. Go on."

David spoke as he refilled Simon's glass. "It's a big old house built in the late 1800's, honestly not what I thought I'd end up with, but walking through, I just had a feeling about it. It's been partially remodeled along the way, once quite recently – modern kitchen and all that. It's even partially furnished from when they used to give tours. In fact…" David rose and left the room, coming back with a file folder. He pulled a picture from the file and held it

5

out to Simon before continuing. "It's fantastic. Built on the top of a high hill, secluded, lots of acreage."

Simon took the large photo from David. Before looking at it, he smiled indulgently and said, "David, I'm glad you're excited about the house, but what I want to know is *why*." Then he lowered his gaze and said, "Whoa. That's not a house, it's a hotel! Not at all what I would have expected you to choose. Ever." He looked more closely at the photo, then glanced up at David. "Must have cost you tens of millions."

"Only five, actually. For the price, I expected rotting floor boards and all that, but it's in good shape over all. I've sent in a cleaning crew and there's a troop of gardeners still working on the gardens and reflecting pool. I have a couple of ideas for changes to the house, but I want to get a feel for it first. There's a top floor atrium that…" David trailed off as Simon rolled his eyes and handed the picture back. "Yeah, okay, I'm excited about the house."

"I'm sure it's great, David. You're moving to this ancient thing in the boonies, and–"

David spoke through a chuckle. "It's only an hour and a half from here. And I'm keeping this loft."

"Okay, I like the sound of that. So, you meant, 'I'll be commuting.' You did not in fact mean… that obscene four-letter word that I cannot bring myself to say."

"Quit."

"Yes, that one."

David sighed. "I'm quitting, Simon. Really. I've achieved more than I hoped, and I'm not having fun anymore. The creation isn't the magic it once was. If anybody was paying attention, they'd realize that my older stuff was the good stuff. Instead of creating, I'm just constructing. All so that somebody can say they have a *David Cartell.*" He delivered the last words with a phony accent meant to sound snooty.

"David, you've singlehandedly redefined modern art metal sculpture. You've…" Simon stood, strode to the large framed photos of various of David's sculptures, and pointed to one after another. A five-story intertwined tower twisting up the inside of an immense hotel inner atrium. A mirrored half-dome centered amidst a downtown metropolis, reflecting curved images of the

7

skyscrapers surrounding it. A thirty-foot kinetic sculpture rising from the middle of a round pool in some faraway park. "Are you really telling me you don't love creating these amazing things?"

"Those? Yes. They're some of my favorites. As you know, not one of them was made in the last two years."

Simon dropped his pointing arm to his side, lowered his gaze and brushed an invisible piece of dust from the lapel of his sport coat. He returned to his seat, his steps slowed with resignation. He put his head in his hands, then raised his gaze to David. "So, you're saying the juice has run out."

"Maybe. Or, I'll take some time for myself, and then start something new." When Simon straightened up and opened his mouth, David spoke over whatever he meant to say. "No, Simon. I'm not just taking a break. I'm done with metal sculpture. Forever. I might – *might* – try something new. Later. A year from now. Or a decade from now. Or never."

Right now, I just need to figure out what to do with the rest of my life. Oh, Kacey.

Simon sighed, then pressed a sad smile to his lips. "You know I consider you one of humankind's greatest living artists.

Rather than being heartbroken, is it all right if I remain hopeful? If I cling to 'maybe,' and 'later,' and 'something new?'"

"Definitely. If any of that comes about, I'll want an agent who is hopeful." David stood and pressed his hand to Simon's shoulder before stepping away.

"*An* agent?" Simon said as he sprang to his feet. "I'd better be the *only* agent who gets a call!"

David laughed at Simon's mock outrage. "Who else could I possibly mean besides humankind's greatest living agent?" He threw an arm around Simon's shoulder and said, "I need a break from packing. How about dinner?"

CHAPTER 2

SARRINAH

SOMEONE HAD INVADED HER house.

My house! Sarrinah leapt from her reclined position and shook her head to clear her mind from the fog of sleep. She moved quickly toward the door of the room, her movements powered by outrage, then stopped to listen. Yes, she could hear distinct and unfamiliar sounds. *How dare any intruder be so bold? It is broad daylight!*

A hint of trepidation – perhaps even fear – intruded on her anger. If only William was here! She could not recall his schedule well enough to know where he was or when he was due home. *Should I wait?* Without remembering any specifics, she knew she should not expect him soon. *I cannot wait.*

And this is my home. My *home!*

Gathering her courage, she strode from the salon where she'd been napping and proceeded down the main hall, increasing her speed to run past the grandiose imperial staircase; for some reason, simply glancing toward the wide marble steps made her tremble. As she climbed the servants' staircase at the far end of the building, the sounds from the upper floor became clearer. The trespasser was making no attempt at stealth. She looked into the second-floor atrium only long enough to notice the disarray of boxes scattered across the hardwood floor. *Boxes?*

After only a few more paces, she knew the sounds came from her bedchamber. *How dare this jackanapes intrude on my private sanctum?* She hurried down the hallway toward the noises.

"How dare you?!" The words escaped her before she had taken two steps into the room but again, other than the clutter of boxes on the bed and floor, the room was empty. A whistled tune floated to her through the open doorway to the adjoining dressing room, and she spun toward the sound.

Her mouth fell open as she entered her dressing room. A tall, slender man stood just to one side of the couch in the center of the room, back to her, whistling without concern. Far from being properly dressed, he wore rough worker's clothing of simple blue pants and only a white cotton undershirt, one bare foot tapping in time to his tune. She could see from his cheek that he was not clean shaven, although the trim facial hair was too short to be called a beard. As she watched, he adjusted his crude black-rimmed spectacles with a finger to the bridge of his nose.

"I insist you leave these premises at once!" Under normal circumstances, she would never raise her voice, but this violation was inexcusable. Then she noticed what she had not in the first moment of her outrage: Every wardrobe door and drawer stood open – open and empty. He must have removed all her clothes and shoes. "And return what you have taken!" She straightened her back and lifted her chin, ready for his reaction. When he turned toward her, he would not question that he was facing the lady of the house.

To her utter astonishment, he did nothing at all, except to continue whistling his damnable tune and turning his head to survey the empty cabinetry.

"Do you hear me? You trespass where you are not welcome. I will not hesitate to send for the police." In fact, she should have done so at once, but she could not recall passing any servants in her hurry to discover the intruder. "Sir!" Still, he did not respond.

Perhaps this thief is deaf?

She stepped toward him, then reached to tap his shoulder. She gasped aloud as her finger and then a portion of her hand passed through him. Staggering back, she stared at her open palm. A fleeting bit of memory attempted to intrude on the shock that overwhelmed her, but she pushed it aside and tried to get her breathing under control. The man absently brought his hand up to rub at his shoulder where she had attempted to touch him.

Blinking back tears, she spoke again, her voice now small and questioning. "Hello? Can you hear me?"

This time the man snapped his fingers and turned toward her. Apropos of nothing, he said, "Music. That's what's missing from this picture." He stepped toward her. His expression did not look menacing, but his arms and chest were quite muscular – he could easily overpower her. She raised both hands and took a faltering step backward. Instead of acknowledging her presence, he took another step, and another, and then *passed through her*. Sarrinah cried out in confusion and spun toward him. He stood with his back to her, hand pressed to his forehead as if suddenly dizzy. He shuddered and mumbled something before continuing on into the bedroom. She had experienced no sensation of contact – no pain, no tingling, nothing – as if the man were completely insubstantial.

Or, as if…

Sarrinah threw her head back and loosed a loud, keening cry as the insistent fragment of memory returned to her. She knew now what she had not recalled earlier.

It is not he who is insubstantial, it is I. I am… I am dead. Dead and damned to remain here forever, nothing more than a phantasm.

She turned to pass her eyes once more over the empty drawers and cabinets. The man hadn't stolen her clothes and shoes. They had long ago been discarded, the belongings of a deceased woman. She squeezed her eyes shut and tears fell to both cheeks. Reentering her bedchamber, she made no effort to muffle the sounds of her soft sobs. The man would not hear them.

Yet.

Another scrap of memory flitted to the surface: It was his presence that had awakened her. This was the reason for her feeling of resentment that accompanied her first waking thoughts.

Without his intrusion, she would have remained asleep – or if not "asleep," at least engulfed in the oblivion which kept her from conscious thought. From remembering. But, his continued presence would strengthen her, would make her more substantial, and would – over time – allow him to hear her cries. For cry, she would. She had reason to cry. *I am dead.*

She startled when the man spoke from across the room. "Yeah, this'll work. Perfect music to unpack to."

Unpack. So he meant to stay.

Sarrinah had time for no more thought before a cacophony of noise engulfed the room. She clapped her hands to her ears. "What 'music' is this?" she shouted – unheard, of course – but she wondered if even a living person could be heard above the relentless thumping sound. The man bent to the small, black contraption he had been toying with and the noise increased in volume, seeming to come from all directions at once. Then, performing some odd jig, he rounded the large canopied bed and crossed once more to the dressing room.

Sarrinah fled the unbearable sounds, stopping only long enough to attempt to close the bedroom door behind her. Her hand passed through the wood and she nearly growled in frustration as she escaped down the rear stairs and ran back to the salon near the front of the building.

The salon door was closed, but – now knowing her true nature – she stepped forward and passed through the door. *Odd that I did not notice moving through it as I left, but I must have done so.* Here the "music" was indistinguishable except for the barest suggestion of the beat. She paced the room, angry, and made more so by her frustration at being unable to act on it. This stranger had trespassed, not only upon her house, but upon her peaceful oblivion. And now he had driven her to the far front of the house with his abominable noise. She could not even close a door to escape it.

Worse, he meant to stay!

She paused in her relentless path as another thought came to her. *It will be the worse for him should he stay.* She had driven others from her house as she gained strength from their presence, she was sure of it. She would drive him away as well.

And then she would endure the time it took for her to weaken again, to fade, to fall into the sleep that kept her from the knowledge of what she was.

Dead. And clearly damned for it because, though dead, here I remain. I don't want the memories to return. I don't want to understand why.

Tears now flowing, Sarrinah threw herself to the couch to weep with abandon… then cried out when she passed through it, bracing herself for a painful impact. Instead of crashing to the floor, she floated – in a reclined position, yes – to all appearances *within* the couch. Her splayed arms – including the sleeves of the dress she wore – were visible to her where they extended beyond the frame and cushions, but not the parts of her body that shared the space with the couch. She sobbed aloud, rose to her feet, and stepped away from the couch. Too distressed to question how she had risen to her feet, how she had moved away, she crumpled once more to the floor. Burying her face in the skirts of her afternoon dress, she released tears of despair without a thought as to whether they would – or could – stain the fabric. One thought circled through her mind as she wailed aloud.

He must leave my house!

CHAPTER 3

DAVID

"You've done a fantastic job. Better than I hoped, really," said David. He followed the master gardener from the south yard toward the front of the house where he could see the reflecting pool that led to the main entrance. Late afternoon sunshine dappled through the trees that lined both sides of the long pool, creating shimmering yellow-orange sparks on the water.

"I'd like to take your kind words personal, but 'twas the team of us what did it," Finn answered in a thick Irish brogue David found charming. Despite the modesty of his response, the diminutive man pulled his shoulders back and lifted his chin in pride. The man turned away to look once again toward the south yard and large living room terrace, then brought his gaze back to the front of the house, toward the reflecting pool and the long driveway that flanked it. David could not help but smile as he watched the man admiring his own work.

18

When Finn's gaze returned to David's face, he removed his cap and ran fingers through his white hair, his tanned cheeks coloring in embarrassment for so obviously appreciating the gardens he had tamed. "It were a labor of love, sir, and I'm pleased you're pleased. I worked here some years ago, and have never forgotten the harmony of how each part fits with the other."

David's smile widened. "I *am* pleased." He held a hand out, and Finn quickly replaced the hat he had been squeezing between both hands to shake David's. "I'm also glad to hear you considered it a labor of love. Could I persuade you to stay on permanently as head groundskeeper? You'd have complete freedom to choose the people who'd work for you as well as how many you'd need."

To David's surprise, Finn swallowed with what seemed trepidation, his eyes flickering over the façade of the building before him. David spoke quickly, hoping to avert a rejection of his offer. "I can be generous in your pay, I assure you."

Finn cleared his throat, met David's eyes, then looked away again. He shifted from foot to foot. Finally, ducking his head and removing his cap once more, he said, "I don't mean to sound insolent in addressing such a kind offer, but…" The small man's eyes flicked toward the house again, then back to David.

"Whatever it is, just say it," David prompted. "If it's something I can't live with, I'll say so."

Finn huffed up and let his words out in a rush. "I'll not agree to working inside the house. No watering of plants, nor trading of old flower arrangements out for fresh. Naught inside the house. If you leave me to the outdoors – including continuing to meet with me in the pavilion yonder – I'll be happy enough to stay."

David laughed in wonder. "Good grief, why? I don't have a problem with you coming into the house. I don't imagine you'll be tracking dirt in or something just because you're a gardener."

"It's not that, sir. It's…" David waited, curious to hear the reason for the man's anxiety. "It's just that the house is…" Another pause, and David drew his eyebrows together, unable to imagine why Finn was so nervous. "I'll say it plain. The house is haunted, sir."

David loosed a quick burst of laughter, then quickly stifled it, not wanting to humiliate the man. Even so, he could not help smiling as he spoke. "Local legend, is it?"

"No, sir," Finn said, his expression exuding sincerity. "I mentioned I've worked these gardens before – when I was a tad younger. I can tell you, I've heard the wailing woman meself."

"Wailing wom–" David suppressed his smile. He removed his glasses and polished the lenses on his shirt, using the brief moment to compose himself well enough to meet Finn with equal earnestness. Replacing his glasses, he said, "Finn, I've been in and out of this house for a month or more, and I've been here for the last three days and nights without leaving. I assure you I haven't heard, or seen, anything strange." In response to Finn's dubious lift of an eyebrow, he finished, "At all."

"All the same, I won't be going in there. If that's what you're asking of me, I'll be sorry to leave these gardens, but leave I will."

So Finn was superstitious. Fine. He was still a phenomenal groundskeeper and David wanted him to stay. "If I were to agree that you never have to enter the house, would you help me find someone who could handle whatever indoor plants and flower arrangements I do end up getting?"

"I'd be willing to get you a man or woman with the know-how to do the job," Finn responded, then with a glance at the second floor windows, "but I canna' promise they'll stay."

David was certain he'd kept his amusement from his face, but in response to something Finn saw – or thought he saw – in David's expression, the man's face reddened again, and he looked toward his feet. "I'm sure you think I'm being foolish, but I've warned you now." Lifting his chin, he continued with some passion, "The decent thing would've been to warn you before you bought the place, but no seller, nor real estate person, is going to do that."

"You're likely right there," David answered, hoping to alleviate the man's uneasiness. Then: "Okay, I accept your condition. I promise that you will never be expected to enter the house, and the rest of my offer remains as stated. Will you agree to stay on? You don't have to answer right away if you need time to think it over."

Finn turned in place as he cast his gaze once again to the trees, lawns, gardens and fountains he could see, his affection for the grounds shining from his eyes. Then he nodded his head and extended his hand. "Don't need time to think. If you can stand to live with her, and I can stay well away from her – out in the sunshine where no proper ghost goes a-wandering – I'll take the job."

David grinned in response to Finn's hesitant smile. "Excellent. If you can meet me tomorrow, say ten in the morning – in the pavilion, of course – we'll finalize the details."

With Finn safely on his way, David chuckled as he entered the house. "Haunted. I love it. This house is turning into a better and better bargain as the days go by. I get this incredible place with the legend of a ghost thrown in, no extra charge." He laughed as he passed through the entry foyer and down the main hall toward the huge double staircase. As he ascended, he raised his voice and said, "No offense, ma'am, but I don't believe in ghosts. I prefer to use my imagination on other things." At the second landing, he bowed deeply as he imagined men might have when this house was first built, then rose with a flourish. "But, for the sake of being polite, David's the name. Sculpting's the game."

His high spirits fled with the final sentence.

No, it's not anymore, is it?

After a heavy sigh, he descended a step and sat on the landing. He looked right and left at the twin stairways that curved upward to the second floor with their latticed iron balusters, raised his eyes to the sparkling central chandelier, and finally lowered his gaze to the glossy wood floor of the main hall below him.

"I did it, Kacey, my love. Too late, I know. Too late for us, and certainly too late to bring back…" His throat closed around the last words. *Our baby. The baby girl I killed.* Kacey had, of course, denied his fault in what had happened. Even so, David's grief and guilt had driven her away.

He cleared his throat to loosen the lump that had settled there. He tried to conjure the image of Kacey coming toward him up the rich burgundy carpet runner that highlighted the white marble stairs, but could not do it. She was not a part of this place. No longer a part of his life. And she was happy now. She had moved on. He would not disturb her current happiness by reawakening memories that haunted him still.

He loosed a bitter laugh and said, "There I was chuckling at Finn, when I've got ghosts of my own." After casting his gaze around once more, he pushed to his feet in a sudden determination to finish unpacking his bedroom, at least.

He was nearly to the second floor when he heard a door slamming. The sound seemed to come from the lower floor. After a frozen moment, he lowered the foot that hovered over the next step, turned and descended to the hall.

"Hello?" He bellowed the word toward the main entrance, then turned and repeated his call in the direction of the dining room at the back of the house. Hearing no response, he said in a lower voice, "Why am I yelling? I'm the only one in the house – unless I have a burglar, and they're not going to answer." Raising his voice again, he said, "Are you?"

He was halfway to the front entrance – he intended to check for open windows that might have allowed the wind to blow a door closed – when he stopped and laughed aloud. "Oh, no, wait! It's the *ghoooost*," – he elongated the word to make it sound spooky

25

– "right? Geez, David, do you see what happens when you mix an artist's imagination with the power of suggestion? It's been what? Fifteen minutes since Finn mentioned a ghost? Oh and don't forget to throw in some maudlin moping to set the mood." He slapped his forehead with the palm of his hand. "You can't even get it right. Finn didn't say 'door-slamming dame,' he said 'wailing woman.' Do better, man." Laughing lightly, he continued down the hall.

He came alongside the closed door of the salon. "Aha!" As spacious as the house was – more than 60,000 square feet, according to the paperwork – he still preferred open doors to the feeling of being shut in. He opened the door and stepped in to the salon to check the windows. All closed. "Nope. Okay, note to self: get a door stop for the salon room door." After 120 years, he didn't expect that every door in the house was still perfectly balanced. As a temporary measure, he lifted a small round vase from a nearby table and used it to prop the door open, then returned to the main hall.

Talking to himself again, as he often did, he said, "Now, if you can finish getting your clothes arranged, it'll be grilled cheese sandwiches and a movie. Tomorrow, you've got to get serious about settling in here." Mounting the stairs, he thought of Kacey again, imagined her just ahead of him on the stairs, smiling and reaching a hand toward him. He pursed his lips and blew out a long, low whistle. "Then, you have to find something to do or you're really going to lose it."

CHAPTER 4

SARRINAH

THIS DAY HAD GONE better for Sarrinah than most. The intruder had been roaming the gardens with the gardener – for hours – and blessed silence reigned throughout her home.

Having peacefully explored the main floor, she passed along the second floor hallway from the personal residence wing toward the guest wing. Once finished there, she would investigate the third floor. Many things had changed from what Sarrinah recalled of her house – some improvements, some not, and some frankly baffling. She slowed to a stop as she approached the main staircase which divided the front and rear wings, terrified to be so near it for reasons she could not yet remember.

How long she stayed there, she did not know, as time did not pass for her as sequential moments of consciousness. Sometimes sunrise and sunset seemed separated only by minutes and an indefinable moment of fogginess. But, however much time had passed, she knew the moment the man reentered the house. Not only could she sense the spark of his presence, his laughter rang from below and came to her clearly where she stood near the upper landing. (She knew by now that she did not, in fact, "stand," as her feet made no perceptible contact with the carpet, but she thought of herself as standing.)

Sarrinah sighed, knowing her exploration was at an end. She could, of course, wander her home freely, as the man could not see her. Instead she tried to stay far from him, for two reasons: First, she disliked him – on principle, really, simply because he had awakened her with his invasion of her home. Second, she hoped that by avoiding him and the glow of life force he exuded, she might escape the memories that were returning with her continued consciousness.

She turned toward the rear stairs when the man spoke, his words bring her to a halt. His speaking, by itself, would not have caught her attention as he often talked to himself, but on this occasion, he seemed to be speaking to her.

"No offense, ma'am, but I don't believe in ghosts. I prefer to use my imagination on other things."

Approaching as near as she dared, she glanced through the railing of the upper landing in time to see his ridiculous sham of a bow. Fresh tears welled in her eyes, and she hurried away from the dangerous staircase. Now, not only was she tortured by the memories that were returning to her because of his constant presence, but he was mocking her in her own home as well.

Once on the main floor, she walked the hallway toward the salon. As she again approached the main stairs, she increased her speed to an unladylike dash, glancing toward the man just as he began his ascent from the landing toward the second floor. He would undoubtedly start up his awful noise box once he reached the bedchamber – yet another reason to avoid him. She could not imagine why anyone would torture themselves with such a terrible racket. She and he were clearly opposites; she craving the silence of an undisturbed solitude, and he attempting to banish his… what? loneliness? …with the sound of either his own voice or his "music."

She continued her hurried pace until she reached the salon. As she crossed the threshold, she slowed to a stop, and sighed in exasperation at the open door. She craved at least the semblance of privacy.

Oh, how I wish I could close it, close it, close it!

She reached for the door in the exaggerated motion of slamming it, knowing as she did that the gesture was useless. To her surprise, while her fingers passed through it, the door moved in response, as if she had created enough of a breeze with the passage of her hand to effectuate her desire. The door banged shut.

Startled, she backed several steps, blinking toward the door in pleased surprise.

I am getting stronger. This thought came with feelings of victory – she had closed the door! – as well as despondence. *I would rather return to the oblivion of sleep.*

Moving around the room, she once again took in the furnishings, art and knickknacks. She had not noticed on first awakening that they were changed – and arranged differently – from the time when she was a living woman in this house. Thankfully, the décor was artfully arranged and pleasant, retaining

31

the feminine cast such a room should have, it being the room to which she and any visiting ladies retired after dinner.

The salon had also been her favorite room for meeting with friends during the day because it was more intimate than the formal living room; just as the atrium had been her preferred space on the second floor. The atrium's opaque glass ceiling made the room so bright and welcoming, and wide archways in three walls of the room leant a feeling of outdoor openness, even though the room was part of the private residence wing. She had often enjoyed quiet moments there, reading or conversing with William.

William. Her beloved husband, William. She had been practically a newlywed – only one year married – when William brought her here. While all her memories had not yet returned, she now remembered that day with perfectly clarity.

She had been surprised when, upon leaving a friend's house and directing the chauffeur to take her home, the man drove her here instead. On questioning, the chauffeur answered with an enigmatic, "Your husband's instructions, Madam."

As the car approached the main entrance – the driveway was at least a mile long! – she marveled over what she could see of the house and grounds. Alighting from the car, and following the gesture of the chauffeur, she walked toward the imposing door, uncertain what she would say when someone answered her summoning knock.

She had not yet reached the wide rounded steps to the entrance, when the enormous door swung open. Smiling automatically in greeting, she prepared to introduce herself, then recognized her husband, William, as the unexpected doorman.

"Darling," she said, continuing toward him, "Whatever are you…? Whose home…?"

Just as she mounted the final step, he fell to one knee in the grand entry and said, "Yours, my dear, if you like it."

"Like it?" she asked, looking to the interior of the grand home. William rose and took her in his arms. He kissed her on the cheek, then stepped aside to gesture into the foyer.

When she turned toward him, confused by what he might mean and dazzled by what she could see of the inside, he took her elbow and steered her through the doors. "It's a belated wedding gift, my dear. I had it begun the moment you accepted my proposal, but with construction delays and whatnot, it's only just been completed. It's been furnished and decorated so that you wouldn't have to fuss, but if there's anything you don't like, you need only say so and all will be as you command."

"Oh, William!" She threw her arms around him and kissed him, too surprised and delighted to think of appropriate words of thanks. "Show me everything! Absolutely everything!"

She had wept joyous tears that day, but the tears that crept down her cheeks now contained no hint of happiness.

Startled from her reverie by a noise, Sarrinah spun toward the salon door as it opened. The man stepped into the room and she hurried to the far windows, placing as much distance as she could between herself and this unwelcome invader. She wiped at her tears, embarrassed at having been caught in such a compromised state, even while knowing he did not see her, did not know or care that she was there.

After a brief glance around the room and a murmur of nonsensical words, the man took a heavy red glass vase from the side table and used it to prop the door into position before leaving.

Moving to the hallway to watch his retreat, she spoke words only she could hear. "So, I am to have no peace, only misery heaped upon misery?"

Misery. But why? Almost – almost – I wish to understand. And yet, an overwhelming feeling of foreboding warns me that I do not want to remember. Until now, the memories that have returned are of a carefree and fortunate life, with few occasions for sadness, and even then, only the small sadnesses of an otherwise enchanted existence. So, why? Why am I here?

She walked toward the fireplace, gazing at her approaching figure in the mirror above it. She had been surprised when first she saw her reflection, but then dismissed the mystery. *I can see myself, so why not my reflection?* The man could see neither. She had put this to the test on one of the few occasions she was near him by standing behind him as he examined a mirror in the upstairs hallway.

Her hand stole to her smooth cheek as she examined her image in the glass. *I am young, not more than a year older than the age I had attained when William gifted me this house. Could it possibly be true? Did I die at the tender age of twenty-two? How? Disease? Or, no, no, please no… childbirth?*

35

LOVE WHISPERS THROUGH THE VEIL

The thought of having left behind not only her beloved husband, but a child as well, threatened to reduce her to tears once more. She spun away from the mirror, wishing she could collapse onto the nearby chaise lounge. The sight of the open door kindled a new wave of frustration that almost overcame her melancholy. She crossed the room, then bent and tried first to lift, then to push away the heavy glass that blocked the door from closing. Her hand simply passed through it. She stood and feebly mimed slamming the door again, to no avail.

Perhaps I was able to move the door because of my irritation of the moment?

She again swept her hand toward the door, and then kicked half-heartedly toward the vase, but neither action bore fruit. Tears once again wet her cheeks.

I am too unhappy to be truly vexed.

Sarrinah stepped into the hall again, looking down its length and a little upward, as if she could see through the flooring to her upstairs bedchamber from which she could now hear the relentless sounds emerging from the noise box.

I have gone from a life full of joy, to grief and endless tears. Directing her thought toward the man: *The longer you stay, the more you will provoke me from sadness to ire. If anger is what is called for in order to slam doors, Sir, I feel certain – given time – that my irritation will kindle sufficiently to make your life as full of misery as my afterlife. Then, with you gone I can return to…* Tears pricked at her eyes, and her throat tightened around a threatened sob. *…no, not to happiness, nor to peace, but, at least to…*

She could not finish her dismal thought, instead crumpling to the floor of the hall and loosing a pitiful wail of utter despair.

CHAPTER 5

DAVID

SOME THREE WEEKS AFTER arriving with his initial load of boxes – mostly clothes and bathroom necessities, David had finished his move in. There were still various furnishings to be delivered and artwork to be added, but those would come with time. The cleaning staff had been easy to arrange through an agency, and Finn reported that he had acquired the necessary workers for the gardens.

David had also entertained presentations from three different cooks, and had accepted the one who seemed least indignant when David suggested that he might invade "their" kitchen to prepare his own lunches and perhaps occasionally, his own dinners. The man, while being a certified five-star chef with an impressive list of credentials, was younger than David. Perhaps it was his youth that helped him accept the idea of David's unorthodox intrusion into the kitchen.

Now that David felt settled, it was time to begin to make the house his own. Armed with pen and paper, he finished his circuit of the basement floor, having jotted preliminary notes about needed repairs and possible changes. For example, he intended to repair the swimming pool located there, and while he had at first thought to take out the Turkish bath, the tiling and fixtures were too amazing to destroy. He wasn't yet sure what he would do – if anything – with the squash court, gun room, and other various lounge rooms.

He ascended to the main floor, emerging into the entry foyer. As he so frequently did, he stopped to gaze at the foyer ceiling. The painting there had been the first thing to capture his interest in the house. It depicted the remains of an Italian renaissance fresco that had crumbled down, leaving only the corners and edges where partial figures were still visible. The center of the ceiling, where the fresco was missing, was painted in bold modern colors in a square bull's-eye pattern. The jarring juxtaposition of classical with new had rendered David speechless when he first saw it, so hideously did it highlight what had been lost to time. It was that emotional response that he so loved in art – modern or otherwise – and which he felt his latest sculptures failed to evoke.

As he stood gawping upward, the barely audible sound of a woman crying drifted to him – a sound he had heard twice earlier this week.

In response to the mournful voice, David said, "Yeah, I know what you mean. I feel the same way every time I look at it." He expected no answer. He knew the weeping arose purely from his imagination, as spurred by the earnest groundskeeper's talk of the "wailing woman." But, having invented a fictional companion, why not talk to her?

I'd question my sanity, but Agatha Christie had imaginary friends, and no one thought she was crazy.

There was an added benefit to his illusory creation: The thought that he was not the only inhabitant of the grand old house made him feel less lonely – and thus less prone to depressing thoughts of Kacey and the lethargy that overcame him with those memories. The fabricated necessity of putting on a good face for his "roommate" forced him from bed on days when he might otherwise have been content to do nothing but stream one movie after another. And maybe when his brooding over Kacey lessened, his imagination would dispense with the weeping in favor of something brighter.

He left the foyer, walking past the salon and the billiard room opposite it as he had already examined them. The salon had come pre-furnished and did not need any changes, and he loved the billiard room as it was – especially the stamped Italian leather wallpaper. The billiard table and other furnishings were on order and would be arriving soon.

He stopped partway down the main hall and adjusted his glasses to again examine a wall sconce. "These have got to go," he said, jotting a quick note. "Entirely too gothic." Since his first walkthrough of the house, he had not cared for the sconces – they were shaped as arms protruding from the wall, the hands holding torches. His weeks in the house had not changed his opinion.

The rest of his inspection of the main floor went quickly, it being the part of the house kept most preserved when the house was open for tours.

LOVE WHISPERS THROUGH THE VEIL

On his way to the second floor, David's attention was drawn away from his task to the warm smoothness of the polished mahogany handrail against his hand. He continued up another several steps watching his hand and concentrating on the feeling of the wood running smoothly under his fingers. As he did, a familiar tingle spread through his body, exciting him – a sensation he had not felt for years. He dropped his pad and pen to bring both hands to the rail, then ascended several steps, caressing the satiny surface of the wood, while his eyes continued upward following the curve.

"Wood!" he said, and laughed aloud. "I want to work with wood! Yes!" He ran the rest of the way to the second floor, both hands on the handrail as he went, then crossed the top landing to run down the opposite matching staircase, sliding his palms along the lustrous timber.

On reaching the landing again, he slowed and backed to the window, then dropped to sit cross-legged, face lifted, eyes tracing the graceful lines of the mahogany that topped the curved railings of the twin staircases rising to the second floor. "I want to shape wood into beautiful, smooth, warm shapes that cry out to be touched, that attract the hand as well as the eye."

Relief flooded him to mingle with the joy and excitement that already suffused him. Relief, because the magic he had always felt when conceiving and then creating his metal sculptures had not left him after all. His vision blurred as moisture came to his eyes. He closed his eyes and whispered, "Yes," exhaling the word as a long sigh. Then, happy enough to want to scream from the rooftop, he leapt up, recovered his pen and paper, and dashed up the stairs again.

Not stopping at the top, he jogged toward the back of the house, to his favorite room on the second floor: the atrium. He had toyed with several ideas of what to do with the open space, wanting to make the most of the glass ceiling that suffused the room with natural sunlight. Now he knew what he wanted – no – *needed* to do with this room.

"Ta-dah!" he said, flinging his arms out as he walked a full circle in the center of the room. "My studio!"

***

David chuckled from his kneeling position on the floor of the atrium when the door to his bedroom slammed again. A breeze had managed to blow the door closed several times today.

Raising his head, he said loudly, "Well, I'm not opening it again." It was a game he had begun to play – pretending his invented friend was real. Today, he poked fun at himself by pretending that she was "acting up." He laughed again as he bent forward to fit the next rubber mat into place.

He had wasted no time in preparing for the renovations that would transform the atrium into his studio – not that he wanted many renovations, per se. He had no desire to destroy the beautiful room. The hardwood floor, while stained from an ancient leak in the glass ceiling, was salvageable and needed to be protected from the tools and equipment he would need for woodworking. To that end, he had purchased thick rubber matting to cover the floor, as well as a more durable synthetic tile to cover that. Thus far this morning, he had covered a quarter of the room with the rubber matting.

As he placed the next section, the sound of a woman crying began, seeming to come from quite near where he knelt. Startled, he glanced in that direction, before shaking his head in self-admonishment, "Really, David? The game's fine, but now you're jumping? You start *really* believing, and it'll be time to get a shrink."

He had rationalized that the imagined weeping was a mechanism for grieving – for Kacey, for his lost child. By burying himself in work for the last several years, he had repressed and postponed the grieving process. Mourning now – while late in the game – was a healthy and necessary thing. But he knew his "friend" was not real, regardless of the games he may play.

The room dimmed as clouds passed over the sun, which brought his mind to the next problem he needed to tackle: lighting. While the room was often brightly sunlit, he needed lights for when the sun was not bright enough for him to work (or for working at night). He had purchased a tall floor-standing lamp – but recognized immediately that this could not be the only lighting. Nor could he work within a maze of multiple floor lamps. At the same time, he could not attach lights to the glass above him and he loathed the idea of destroying the crown molding. Looking around the room again now, he decided to install several fixtures on the walls near the crown mold – walls would be the easiest part of the room to repair if and when he wanted to convert the room back.

He ate lunch sitting cross-legged on floor of the atrium, proud of the work he had accomplished thus far, in good spirits despite the background sound of soft weeping. As he ate, he searched online for the light fixtures he wanted. Having located the fixtures as well as a local store that delivered, he raised his gaze from his phone and said, "Hush now, I have to make a call." After one last hiccupped sob, the crying stopped. David smiled and said, "Thank you," before touching the dial button.

By the following morning, the rubber matting covered the hardwood and the floor was ready for the contractor installation of the industrial tile that would top it.

"Ready for the lights?" he asked, cocking his head as if waiting for an answer. After waiting an appropriate interval, he said, "Well, I am." Moving his ladder to one side of the fireplace, he climbed toward the twelve-foot ceiling. Using his metal detector, he located the first stud and marked it, then moved his ladder in search of the next. After locating them all, he came back to the first stud and climbed the ladder again, this time with hammer and light fixture in hand. The fixture was a simple one that could be attached with a single nail; the cord he would leave dangling down the wall. Holding the fixture in place, he hefted the hammer to drive the nail in. In the same moment, his bedroom door slammed so violently he imagined he felt the house shake – not possible, of course. And a moment later, another door farther down the hall banged shut.

"Whoa." He was not particularly concerned. Last night, he had opened his bedroom window for a cross breeze and had forgotten to close it this morning. But the timing of the two doors slamming in close succession was startling nonetheless. He lifted the hammer again and pounded the nail. At first, David thought the screech he heard was the nail biting into the ancient wood of the stud and scraping along the nails holding the lathe, but the shriek continued even after he finished.

"Whoa," he repeated. As he climbed down from his perch, the loud wailing transformed into the weeping with which he was so familiar. David walked to the boxes that contained the remaining lights and sat on one of them.

Raising his head and speaking to the air, he said, "We need to talk."

CHAPTER 6

SARRINAH

"WE NEED TO TALK," the man – David – said. Sarrinah knew his name from the many times he spoke to himself.

She was tempted to shriek again in response, her frustration and anger rising again. How dare he destroy her atrium! Instead, she sniffed and attempted to reign in her tears. David had spoken to the air several times recently as if speaking to her, but she always assumed he was carrying on his habit of speaking to himself. This time, there was no mistaking that he was speaking to her. If she could find a way of communicating with him, perhaps she could persuade him to leave her house. Avoiding him within the house had not stopped the memories from returning, so he must leave if she was to have any peace.

"Better," he said as her weeping trailed off. "Thank you." David looked toward his lap as if trying to decide what to say, then straightened, expression serious and as cheerless as she'd ever seen. "Okay, I get that you're sad," he said.

He had such strange colloquialisms, she often had difficulty understanding what he meant when he spoke. *I get that you're sad…* Did this mean, *I understand that you're sad?*

"You're trying to work out some stuff… Kacey, yeah, all the years you missed being with her, the time you're missing with her now. God, I know how much you still love her – you're still dreaming about her, you idiot. And then there's also…" He coughed out a small choking sound. "And there's also…" He brought his hand to his forehead and squeezed as though trying to relieve a headache. "I don't want to talk about that part yet." His voice became hoarse and he stopped speaking.

So, he was not talking to her after all. Sarrinah's eyes welled with tears she released to her cheeks with a blink. Soon, she would begin crying again in earnest.

David cleared his throat loudly and leapt to his feet. Removing his glasses, he pinched at his eyes to clear moisture from them. "Look, I know this is a mechanism to help me grieve, but I'm going about this all wrong." He paced to and fro for a moment and then said. "Okay, I'm going to step back a bit. Distance myself. Let's start this conversation over." He returned to his perch on the box.

Raising his head and speaking to the air again, he said, "I'm David. What's your name?"

Sarrinah hesitated before answering. What if he could hear her? After all, he heard her crying. "My name is Sarrinah."

"Well, I have to call you something. We're friends after all. Not Deborah, not Christine… Michelle. How about Michelle? Yeah, all right."

He hadn't heard her. She could try screaming her name but could not bring herself to do such an unseemly thing.

"Michelle, you seem upset about the atrium remodel. I don't understand why, but maybe it has something to do with fear? You're worried you can't pull off the wood sculpture thing? No, no that's me and I'm not talking about me. I'm talking to you, and you, Michelle, probably aren't a sculptor." He laughed quietly. "So, maybe you're uneasy about messing with this gorgeous room? Yes? No?" He paused between each question as if expecting an answer. Sarrinah did not speak. "Okay, well, I'm just going to go with that one. I'll explain what I'm doing and then maybe you'll feel better. I'm sure it looks like I'm wrecking the place–"

"Yes!" Sarrinah answered with vehemence. David tilted his head as if he heard something, then shook his head as though shooing away a fly.

"–but I'm not. I'm protecting it, don't you see? The rubber mats, sure, they're ugly, but I put them down to protect the floor. If the sculpting thing doesn't work out, or I decide I want to move my studio, I can take them off and still have a gorgeous hardwood floor. Without the protection, I could seriously hurt the floor by dropping a chisel, or scraping it with the metal legs of a band saw, or whatever."

"You're protecting it?" she asked. She glanced around the room. The new flooring was thick and hideous, but was only laid atop the wood. For protection. "Yes, I see."

David clearly did not hear her, as he spoke over her last words. "And the lights. Yes, there's a hole in the plaster wall. But better that – which can be fixed – than drilling into the wood of the crown mold. I'm not even running the power through the walls." David looked around the room, then toward the glass ceiling. "I wouldn't wreck this room. I love this room. It's my favorite room on this floor."

"Mine too," she said, a shy smile coming to her lips. Simply sharing a fondness for the atrium made her look at David in a different light. For all that he had disrupted her miserable existence and made it worse, he did seem to be quite an agreeable man. She almost hated to admit it, but he had a good life force, bright and colorful, without many dark or bent strands. It was also interesting to have him acknowledge her and talk to her, earnestly and kindly. It banished a small bit of her sadness. No one – since her death – had ever spoken to her other than in words of fear, anger or banishment... with the exception of her dear, tortured William, who had spoken to her, begged her, wept for her. She swept those memories aside to keep from dissolving into tears again.

Sarrinah moved toward where David sat turning his head as he glanced around the room.

"So, are we okay now, Michelle?" David waited, then slapped his hands to his knees and rose. He turned back to the box he'd been sitting on and lifted out another light before moving the ladder to a marked spot further down the wall. After climbing, he placed the fixture, lifted the hammer, then lowered it again.

"We're okay, right? No more screeching when I hammer?" He hefted the hammer and said, "Knock twice if you agree." Sarrinah rushed to the wall, and summoning the intensity that allowed her to slam a door rather than having her hand pass through it, she pounded on the wall.

"Oh my g…" David said, head snapping to his right where she stood by the wall. He lowered the hammer and the fixture. Looking toward where she stood, he said, voice lowered, "Dude, you are officially off your rocker." He stared for another long moment, then shook his head and said, "And this is news? You've always been a bit unhinged. So hang your lights."

***

The next month was the most pleasant of Sarrinah's… afterlife? non-life? – no, why try to avoid the word? – her existence as a ghost. Ever since David named her, he spoke to her frequently, engaging in one-sided conversations about many things, sometimes philosophical, often educational, and on topics ranging from music and art to the use of certain tools and machinery.

LOVE WHISPERS THROUGH THE VEIL

She had been pleased to discover that he knew and enjoyed musical composers with whom she was familiar – Beethoven, Mozart, Bach, Chopin – in addition to the "noise" he also liked to play. (She had spent an afternoon in rhapsodic ecstasy when he had caused his music box to produce the music of those artists with a clarity and volume that defied understanding.)

At first, when he spoke to her, she had responded to his questions or asked questions of her own. She quickly became frustrated that he could not hear her and that their exchange could not proceed normally. As such, she stopped responding, instead simply enjoying his discourse and allowing him to choose the path of the conversation.

As the days and weeks passed, time became more concrete for her. The spells of nothingness that separated events or periods of consciousness had reduced until she only "slept" at night, when the house was quiet and David slept as well. She spent many of his waking hours with him in the atrium. It was no longer the beautiful room it had been, with all his equipment and tools, in addition to the blocks and boards of raw, unfinished wood, but she understood now the reason for this. She watched him – sometimes amazed,

54

sometimes amused – as he attempted to relearn a skill which, according to his explanations to her alter ego, "Michelle," he had practiced before engaging in metal sculpture.

She enjoyed his presence even when he did not speak to her, learning about the new world in which he lived. For example, in the evenings, she watched the plays he enjoyed – "movies" he called them – which fantastically appeared in the large frame on the wall of the bedchamber. While she misunderstood many of the social ramifications of the words and actions of the characters in these "movies," she also learned more about his world and the colloquialisms of his language.

With David's attention often focused upon her, she gave up her constant weeping – something upon which he had commented and for which he thanked her. She was not less sad about her miserable fate. His conversations and sometimes incomprehensible actions simply distracted her from her misery.

She had reason to be miserable, she knew that now. And she understood the reason for having been trapped and damned to her ghostly existence because almost all her memories had returned to her. She had not died in childbirth, nor of disease. Instead, she had committed the ultimate sin. She had taken her own life.

This fact was unfathomable to her because the one memory that had not returned was that of the circumstances of her death. From the time before her death, she had memories of felicity, and satisfaction – even excitement over the idea that she may soon be with child. Then nothing, until her first moments of consciousness after her death: William, shedding tears, alone and on his knees in their bedchamber, begging her to explain her suicide. Thereafter, there were condolences to William from friends and family for her inexplicable action in taking her life.

Those were the worst of her memories: Those from that time shortly after her death. William – poor, dear, strong, caring William – had been destroyed by her act, withering in mere months to a shell of his former self. It had almost been a blessing when he left, unable to continue living in the house he had given her and which, together, they had made a home. Had she not already abandoned him in death, his tearful explanation to her as he left the house would have caused her to die of a broken heart.

A tear dropped to her cheek as she once again steeped in her memories of William's last days in their home. She wiped it away and turned her focus outward, on David. He was enjoying luncheon at a table in what she used to call the "secret garden" – a walled garden at the west end of the house, which one entered from the patio off the dining room. (There was another entrance to the garden from the surrounding grounds, but this was used solely by the gardening staff.) She had loved the secret garden when alive and loved it now because only there could she venture outdoors without "leaving" the house – something she was unable to do.

"Michelle, do you know what the secret to great tuna salad is?" David asked around a mouthful of the sandwich he ate. She did not doubt that he knew, as it was his custom to make his own luncheon, despite having the services of a cook.

"I mean, there's your basic. Tuna and mayo. Boring but edible. There are folks who do or don't use onion, do or don't use celery, do or don't use pickle relish – I use them all, by the way." He lifted the sandwich as if showing it to her. "But the secret ingredient is… wait for it." Here he took another bite and chewed, while examining the contents of the sandwich. Swallowing he said,

"It's stone-ground mustard. Just a little, but wow, it makes a difference. Then, if you want to dress it up, sure, you can add a slice of tomato or sharp cheddar, maybe some lettuce, but trust me, Michelle, whatever you do or don't add, it's the stone-ground mustard that makes it great."

Sarrinah sighed. She enjoyed his conversations, even when they were a bit silly – she had never cooked her own meal when alive, and she certainly did not need to now – but she wished he could call her by name. As she had not done in weeks, she spoke aloud. "My name is Sarrinah."

David paused in the act of taking another bite, and with exaggerated slowness lowered the sandwich to the plate. Looking toward where she stood, he said, "Sarrinah?"

CHAPTER 7

DAVID

"Sarrinah?" David repeated. The voice had not sounded inside his head as if supplied by his imagination. In fact, it seemed to come from a few feet away, across the table from where he sat. He was still pondering whether he had heard anything at all when the feminine voice said, "You can hear me?"

David shot out of his seat, bumping the glass-topped table and making the silverware rattle. "Oh, I can hear you all right." His eyes darted left and right while his mind spun toward an attempted rationalization.

"You can hear me!" It wasn't a question this time.

"Yeah, I can hear you. Oh man." The obvious explanation came to mind and he flopped back into his seat. "I've finally flipped my lid, gone around the bend, broken toward bonkers, gone off the deep end. Yep, yep. I'm now officially nuts."

"You're not mad, if that's what you're saying."

"Oh, that's what I'm saying." He panted softly as his eyes searched the space in front of him for… anything that would make sense of what he was hearing. Or thought he was hearing.

"David, you're not mad," the voice said.

Of course the voice knows my name. It's coming from my own mind. His thoughts tumbled over the very real mental illnesses that plagued their unfortunate victims. *I want the voice to stop!*

It didn't. Instead, it seemed to drift around the table, coming nearer to where David sat. "I am but a phantasm damned to spend my afterlife in this place. But I am real. You are not mad."

"Phantasm," David repeated, head turning to follow the sound. "A ghost?"

"Yes, a ghost." This time the voice trembled, as if on the verge of crying.

Crying. Excitement and relief flowed through David. "The gardener's wailing woman! My imaginary friend!" he said. *It's my imagination — on steroids — not mental illness!*

"I beg your pardon?" the voice said.

"Oh, this is rich. This is good." A cleansing laugh burst from him. Speaking quietly to himself, he said, "David, you're just getting better and better at this game." Then raising his voice again, and turning to the side from which he imagined the woman spoke, he said, "Okay, so you're my imaginary friend, Michelle, but grown up. Got it!"

"My name is Sarrinah," the voice answered.

"Yes, of course. It's perfect. Much better than Michelle, I'll agree."

"Thank you, sir."

"You're quite welcome, ma'am. But please, call me David." He laughed again, and standing, bowed and motioned toward the table. "Join me for lunch." If a real woman had been standing there, the gesture might have seemed mocking, but he was only ridiculing himself.

The voice (*in my imagination!* he reminded himself) answered in sad tones. "I regret that I cannot."

This prompted another laugh from David. "Maybe next time," he said. He lifted his plate and silverware. Shaking his head and murmuring to himself as he strode away, he said, "This is more fun, but I'll say it: I think the loneliness is getting to you, buddy."

The truth was, he hadn't felt lonely lately. Yes, he had felt lonely when he first moved to this house, but that had more to do with the depression of no longer having the love of Kacey and not being able to share this place with her. It had little to do with being alone; he had always been an introvert and certainly preferred solitude to the company of strangers. But with the energy and enthusiasm of working at something new, he'd been less depressed, had missed Kacey less. Another part of his not feeling lonely could be attributed to Michelle, to the feeling of having a friend nearby. Before inventing her, he had taken time every day to look through photos of Kacey. Since inventing Michelle, he had stopped this practice, both because he was busy with sculpting, but also because that kind of moping was something to be done in private, not in the company of a friend – even an imaginary one.

So, while your manifestation of the grieving process is odd, to say the least, it seems to be working. You've made up a friend, and now you're not as depressed anymore. Okay. If it ain't broke, don't fix it.

∗∗∗

David sat at his studio workbench gently hand-sanding the fourth coat of lacquer on his latest creation. It was another small one, measuring only about a foot and a half long. The sinuously curved length of thin wood twisted and bent back on itself twice between one end and the other. Had it not curled and arched as it did, it would have resembled an elongated eucalyptus leaf, as it came to a point at both ends.

"It's beautiful," Sarrinah said.

It had been weeks since her startling intrusion on his lunch in the walled garden, and he had become quite comfortable with talking to her. At first, he had reminded himself constantly that she was not real, that he was inventing the conversations. But after a time, he stopped focusing on the impossibility of her existence and what it implied about his mental state (a potentially disturbing topic), and simply enjoyed the companionship and discussions as if she were real woman.

"Yeah, this one I'm proud of," he answered. He had started with the softer woods, basswood and aspen, hand-carving to relearn the art. He had then moved to the harder woods and the power carver. Much of the work he'd done had already been

63

discarded, having served the purpose of refining his skill. This one had been fashioned from Brazilian walnut – the hardest wood he had used thus far. The grain was fantastic, and the gloss highlighted the beautiful curves. "I almost don't want to dump it."

"You can't!" Sarrinah sounded genuinely outraged.

David chuckled. "I worked this piece just to make sure that I could. I'm ready to start a real project now."

"David, please," she said, pleading in her voice. "I would like so much to run my fingers over it and I can't. At least allow me the pleasure of looking at it."

Her reaction was exactly what he hoped to elicit with his wood sculpture and thus transformed this piece from an exercise into a success. His first success with this new art form. Of course he would keep it.

"I could put a base on it. What do you think? Lying down like this?" Cradling the sculpture in both hands, he held it up. Then he turned it to hold it vertically. "Or standing up?"

"Standing up, I think." There was silence for a time and then she spoke in a musing voice. "Upright it seems a cross between a piece of sea grass billowing in the current and the abstract representation of a dryad caught dancing by moonlight."

David chuckled again. "And people say I have an imagination." He examined the wider of the two tapered ends to determine how much he would need to square off for attaching to a base.

"Would you do that for me?" she asked, her voice close to him now, soft and warm in his ear. "Save it simply because I asked?"

"You bet. I'm glad you like it." David shivered at her perceived proximity, then went back to sanding to distract himself from his strange reaction. "Go on with your story."

There was a moment of silence and David imagined Sarrinah thinking back to regain her train of thought.

"That was the day William surprised me with the Stapleton horse. William had asked me to join him riding and I expected to ride my usual mare, although I considered none of the horses to be truly mine. None had struck me as viscerally as the mare I had ridden when visiting with the Stapletons. You can imagine my surprise when, as we approached the stables, there stood our stable hand, holding the reins of Plum Mandy Girl. I was so excited I actually squealed as I ran toward it." Sarrinah stopped speaking and David heard the excited sound of clapping hands. "Oh! She greeted me with the most affectionate whinny you can imagine. Thanks to William's generosity – he was always so generous to me – an afternoon of riding turned into the most sublime of adventures. Plum Mandy Girl seemed to know my every thought and responded so beautifully." Sarrinah giggled, then after a time, sighed. "I miss her. I wonder…" Her melancholy tones faded into silence.

David waited for her to continue, and when she didn't, he switched on the saw. Placing the sculpture on a soft chamois cloth, he slowly pushed the end toward the spinning blade, trimming no more than an inch from what would be the base of the sculpture, then turned the saw off again.

"Have you remembered how you died?" he asked without thinking, then winced internally. When no answer was forthcoming, he decided not to press any further. He himself had topics he did not yet want to face. He turned to look for a scrap of the Brazilian walnut he could fashion into a base. He almost did not hear her when Sarrinah answered.

"I died by my own hand. It is the reason I remain here, tormented."

"Suicide?" David asked in surprise, louder and more vehemently that he meant to. Lowering his volume to speak more softly, he said, "But, that doesn't make sense. You sound like you had a perfect life."

"Nonetheless, that is how I died." Her voice was tremulous and sad. She sounded on the verge of crying, as she had not done for some time.

David put down the sculpture and turned toward her voice which now seemed to hover in the far corner of the studio. "I'm sorry. I'm really sorry. You don't deserve... I mean, you seem like such a nice person, and the stories you tell about your life are so..." He trailed off as the now infrequent thought came to mind that she was a figment of his imagination. *Why would my imaginary friend be a suicide? What does that mean about my frame of mind?*

Sarrinah sniffled before continuing in a low voice. "My dear William. During my life, he lavished such affection upon me, and he could not understand why I would leave him as I did. My death broke his heart, and drove him to near illness."

She sounded so pained that he could not help but feel pity for her, imagined or not. His own reason for heartbreak rose past his defenses and he delivered his answer in a low, tremulous voice. "I can relate. It nearly kills you when someone you love dies." David sat motionless as one particularly painful memory blinded him to his surroundings, a flashback to the terrible day his daughter died.

I don't want to think about it! I don't want to talk about it!

Clearing his throat, he walked to the small refrigerator near the back of the room. Pulling a bottle of water from the fridge, he drank the entire thing down without stopping, finding the near-pain of the ice-cold water sluicing down his throat to be fitting to the no-less-tangible stabbing pain that filled his chest.

As if reading his internal torment, Sarrinah spoke from near where he stood as he panted in the aftermath of swallowing. "I've told you much of my life, much about William. I would hear of your life, should you want to talk of it."

"I don't." David strode quickly back to his workbench.

"It might help…"

"Talking about William hasn't helped you, has it?" His answer was curt and cold, made so by sudden welling bitterness.

Sarrinah loosed a small sound, not quite a sob, but otherwise did not speak.

David instantly felt remorse for the way he had spoken. *Even though you've made her up, you've imagined her as a friend, and that isn't how you talk to a friend.*

"I'm sorry," David said. "I shouldn't have jabbed at you. It's just that…" He sighed and turned, eyes combing the room for the figure of a woman he knew he would not see. "You're right. It probably would help if I talked about Kacey. I need to get it out, right? Keeping it bottled inside isn't healthy." David released another breath, and looking around again said, "Later, okay?" When Sarrinah did not answer, he said, "Are you there?" After the silence had stretched for another minute, he muttered, "Damn it."

Lifting the sculpture, David began hand sanding the rough edges of the newly cut wood, his motions powered by self-directed anger. *Did you need more proof that you need to work through your grief? You need to talk about Kacey! To talk about your pain! Holding onto it is screwing up the only relationship you have left!* The vehemence of the thought brought reality once more to the forefront. He put down the sculpture and dropped his head to hands. *Geez, get a hold of yourself. You're actually starting to believe Sarrinah's real.*

CHAPTER 8

SARRINAH

"Talking about William hasn't helped you, has it?" David's question rang in her mind. The tone in which he delivered the question struck her as a slap in the face might have, but only because he had never spoken so rudely to her before.

No, I suppose talking about William hasn't helped the fact that I am damned to this wretched half-existence. But it has helped me in other ways. I've never been able to speak to someone about my experiences, my feelings. Talking of my time with William has helped me remember the good days and focus less on the pain I caused him.

David was speaking again, apologizing. The tight lines of his jaw had relaxed and furrows came into his forehead as he spoke.

David is so kind. So caring. So like William in all the best ways, which also helps. I'm not alone anymore. I've had the good fortune even in the midst of my torment to have found a friend in this man, a man I am coming to care about deeply.

This thought struck her inner voice silent. It was such an unexpected notion that she could not bring herself to answer when David said, "Are you there?"

She approached where he sat, and reached a hand out to brush against the sculpture he had promised to keep for her. How she wished she could feel the silky smoothness against her fingers. Instead, because she had not summoned the appropriate level of will, her hand merely passed through it. Following the impulse that had brought her so near to him, she raised her hand to brush against the trim beard of his cheek. She stopped herself a mere half-inch from his face.

I never would have done this in life, she thought. *Never to anyone except William, and then only after our engagement to marry.*

The idea of being able to be this close to David without his knowledge thrilled her until another thought came to mind.

I am taking advantage where no advantage has been offered. If I continue, I will become a truly evil entity — something I do not wish to be!

She backed quickly across the room, but did not leave. Being with David was the only meaningful part of her existence, so even though he was now silent, she wanted to watch him work. She did not speak, as was her practice when he was silent. She did not want him to tire of conversation with her, nor did she want him to become aware of her almost constant presence. (She was not with him for all of his waking hours. She did not, for example, follow him when he used the grand staircase, instead using the back stairs. Neither did she invade his more private ablutions. Nor did she sleep in his room – not that she slept at all – instead resting on the couch in the salon.)

As she watched his vigorous motions, she vowed over and over that she would never attempt to touch him again.

***

The following day, David spoke to her from his spot sitting cross-legged on the thick carpet of the library. He had pulled several books from the shelves and piled them in front of him.

"So, which would you suggest I read?" His tone did not reflect any lingering emotion from their maudlin discussion the previous day.

Sarrinah spoke from the armchair in which she sat. (She discovered that she could sit without melting through the furniture soon after discovering she could close doors or move small objects when she summoned the requisite determination.) "I'm not certain I will have knowledge of the books before you, but you can tell me the titles."

"You might have heard of these," David said, with a mischievous smile. "I've picked books I haven't read yet *and* which were published before your death. I only want you to suggest a book you've read. First, you can tell me what you thought about it and when I read it, I'll be able to see if you're right."

"To what purpose? To test my memory or my literary education?" She sat forward in the chair flush with a sudden pique.

"Neither," he answered, smiling growing. "I naturally find you interesting company, and I am testing the depth and breadth of my imagination."

"Imagination? I don't understand you."

David's smile melted away. He settled back, supporting himself with his arms. Looking toward the ceiling, he said, "I did quite a bit of thinking last night."

"And?"

He shrugged and sat forward again. "I haven't focused on it for a long time. But the fact is: You're not real. I've imagined you. I've done a good job, and this is my idea for reminding me of the limitations of my imagination. You see, I'm finding it difficult to remember that you aren't just an elaborate fantasy of my own making."

"But I'm here. I'm speaking to you. Of course I am real."

"You are here because I believe you're here."

Sarrinah rolled her eyes and loosed an exaggerated sigh. "Give me your list of books."

David lifted the first book off the stack. "I tried to pick a variety. If you haven't read any of them, maybe you can suggest a reading list for me. But I thought I'd start with books I already own. So" – he gestured with the book toward her chair – "*Tess of the D'Urbervilles.*"

Sarrinah was happy to recognize the first of the titles he named. "I've read it, but I admit, I found it a bit dispiriting."

David smiled and placed the book on his right side. "Okay, depressing, but it will work for my purposes. Let's see if we can find another that you would prefer."

As it happened, she had read most of the books David had in his stack, including *The Adventures of Huckleberry Finn*, *Pride and Prejudice*, *The Picture of Dorian Gray*, *Emma*, and *Jane Eyre*.

"Okay, take your pick," David said, pushing the three aside that she had not read and spreading the others out in front of him.

"How is it that you have not read these books?" she asked.

"Hey!" David answered, sounding indignant but smiling nonetheless. "I had to look far and wide to find books I hadn't read!"

Sarrinah laughed in response. "I had no intention of insulting you. I asked because these were quite popular in my time. Have they fallen out of popularity?"

"Not at all. No, it's just that I've never been much drawn to Jane Austen or the Brontë sisters and somehow I just missed the others."

"Not drawn to Jane Austen?" Sarrinah feigned the same indignity David had displayed moments ago. "Jane Austin it is then! Your choice of titles!" She laughed again.

David said, "You have a gorgeous laugh."

Sarrinah flushed at the complement, but her pleasure did not last long because he immediately sobered and ducked his head before saying, "And now you see the reason for this little project of mine. I don't mind having an imaginary friend. I just don't want to start believing you're real."

"David, I…" Sarrinah had intended to say, *I am as real as you*, but she wasn't, was she? Or rather, she was real, but not able to be in his world, much as she wished she could be. Yes, his life force made her stronger and more present in his world – he could now hear her speaking – but they could never be together. *I should quit myself of this budding relationship, for my sake and his…*

…but I can't, can I? He came to my house. He woke me.

She could go back to trying to make his life miserable with her weeping, screaming and slamming of doors. She could force him to leave. But, she enjoyed his company and couldn't bear the thought of doing without him now that he had awakened her.

A new frustration rose as she realized that there was no solution to her dilemma. For the first time in her existence, she would not simply be given that which she desired. *I remember a joyful and carefree life, but was my happiness simply the shallow emotion of a spoiled child whose every whim was granted?*

"Well?" David asked, gesturing once more to the books.

David's question brought her to another dilemma. *What should I do after picking a book? Fabricate something so that he'll finally "know" I am imaginary, or prove my reality by telling the truth?* A selfish part of her wanted him to believe she was real, to come to truly know her, but what would be the point? Conversely, would it be better for him to believe himself on the brink of madness? Which would hurt him least?

"I need time to think and remember what I've read, David. I'll choose a book within the week, if that will be acceptable." She struggled to keep her voice as light as it had been at the beginning of their conversation.

Despite her airy tone, his face clouded. "I was hoping to start my project sooner, but…" the smile returned to his face, "it's a date," he said. He stood and placed the books on a nearby table, one next to the other. "If you haven't picked one sooner, we'll meet again, same time, same place, a week from today."

David began whistling as he left the room. Awash in conflicting emotions, Sarrinah hesitated before rising to follow.

CHAPTER 9

DAVID

DAVID STOOD IN THE south opening of the pavilion, looking at a dead and deformed tree on the distant hillock. The crimson outer curtains and the sheer white inner drapes had been tied back; the white drapes billowed in the gentle breeze, tickling his elbow. He glanced down at the sketch pad and his fingers moved rapidly, drawing a smoother, lither representation of the tree that would serve as a model for his next sculpture. The final sculpture would be large – too large to carve in the studio – but his initial model could be completed there. While his eyes darted between tree and drawing, he explained his plans to Sarrinah.

"I'll have to work in the secret garden" – he had adopted her name for the enclosed garden – "and according to the weather. I suppose it's fitting to work at nature's whim since I'm working with wood, one of nature's most awesome creations. So, during the warmer parts of the year, I'll put up a tent of some kind and work out there. Don't worry, it'll be a temporary–"

He was interrupted by the chirping of his phone.

He balanced the pad on the edge of a nearby table and answered, wiping charcoal from his fingers on his jeans as he spoke.

"Simon! Good to hear from you." He chuckled in response to his agent's predictable question and said, "No, I haven't come to my senses. Quite the opposite actually." He laughed again after saying this, uncomfortable with having admitted his fear for his sanity, yet knowing Simon would not suspect the truth of his statement. He turned, eyes flickering over the potted plants and vines decorating the interior of the pavilion. He knew he would not see Sarrinah but having just interrupted his conversation with her, the movement was akin to a reflex. "I…" He sputtered to a stop.

In the archway leading to the secret garden, there hovered a translucent apparition of a young woman in a long, thin-waisted gown the color of deep amethyst. She seemed to be looking into the garden.

"I…" he repeated before lowering the phone from his ear.

81

"Sarrinah?" he whispered, then blinked and shook his head. The illusion did not dissipate as he expected it would. Instead, the woman turned toward him, her long brown hair floating around her shoulders as she moved.

"Oh… my… word," David murmured, his legs suddenly weak. He closed his eyes and turned away, only opening his eyes again to lower himself to a chair. Hearing an indistinct noise, he looked down to his hand were it rested on his thigh and realized that Simon was speaking from the phone held there. He snapped the phone to his ear in time to hear the last of a sentence. "…unless you wouldn't be comfortable with that."

"Whoa, Simon. I need you to start over. I… my service must have cut out," David said. He hoped Simon could not hear the shakiness of his voice.

"*Shoddy service in the boonies, eh?*" Simon answered, then laughed.

"Yeah, I guess," David answered and attempted to chuckle. "What were you saying?" He fought against the temptation to turn toward the apparition that had so shaken him.

"Everybody's asking about you — of course. So, I just wanted to check on you, old friend. Would you mind if I drove out your way so you could show me around that huge pile of bricks you're living in? Although if you'd be uncomfortable with a visitor..."

"No, that'd be great," David answered. "I'd love to see you. Heh heh, I probably need to touch base with the real world." This time, he couldn't stop himself. He turned, then startled and leapt from the chair when he found the woman hovering no more than a six feet away from where he sat, looking at him. In his surprise, he had again missed what Simon had said. "What... what did you say?" he stuttered into the phone.

"I said I can't make it this coming weekend, so how about the following Saturday?"

David stared at the womanly vision, taking in the details of her appearance — almond shaped blue eyes, oval face ending in a pointed chin, high-collared dress — as he spoke into the phone. "What day is it?"

Simon laughed. *"You* are *out of it,"* he said. *"It's Tuesday."*

"Tuesday, right. Sounds good. See you Saturday, right?"

"The second Saturday. Yeah, mid-morning."

83

"Great."

David hung up, turned his back to the apparition and lowered himself to the chair again. Head in his hands, he repeated, "Great." This time the word elongated into a groan.

Although he heard nothing, no rustle of clothing, no footsteps, Sarrinah's excited voice came to him from the direction of the chair facing his. "You can see me! I know you can!"

He sighed and lifted his head just enough to peer from under his eyebrows. The translucent woman sat on the edge of a chair across the low table from him, knees together and tucked to one side. He could indistinctly see through her to the wood of the chair and the crimson upholstery. Her arms were lifted and she was twisting her hair into a knot high on her head.

"Nice… uh… dress," he said and laughed weakly before lowering his head into his hands again.

"Thank you. It was one of my favorites."

When David merely groaned again, she said, "David, please. Look at me. Tell me what you can see of me."

Without raising his head he said, "You are very beautiful. Breathtakingly gorgeous. But then again, of course you are."

"Again, I thank you, but that is not what I was asking. Can you see me clearly? How does my figure appear to you?"

"Your figure?" David asked as he raised his head. Somehow she had secured her hair so that only two wispy tendrils trailed down at each side of her face. His eyes traveled from her eyes to her pink lips, to the high lace of her collar, then down her front, past her breasts to her pinched waist and full hips. "Fantastic."

Her eyes widened in surprise and she turned her head away demurely. Then lifting her chin she met his gaze, and seeming to ignore his previous comment, she asked, "Do I appear substantial to you? As a living person might?"

"No," he answered. "No, I can see the chair behind you, although not clearly."

Speaking quietly, as though to herself, she murmured in eager tones, "To my knowledge, no one has ever seen me. Heard me, yes, but never seen me."

"Yeah, well, I'm seeing you now, which means I'm getting loopier by the minute. Which is bad. Even so, I have to say, you're not hard on the eyes."

"I'm not hard…? Oh, I understand. Thank you. You yourself are a handsome man, David."

"Thanks, I…" He trailed off, unsure of what to say, vacillating between amusement at the inane conversation and horror at the extent to which he had become unhinged from reality. He stood, walked to the open archway and stared out at the acres of wooded landscape sloping down and away from the house.

Sarrinah's voice came from just over his shoulder. "You seem troubled."

"Yep, I'm in trouble all right."

"Why should you be?" When David did not answer, she continued. "We have been conversing for some months now. Why should it so disturb you to see me as well as hear me? Why should anything change?"

"Why?" David asked, incredulous, as he turned toward her. He raised both hands and gestured toward her in an up-and-down motion. "Because I'm seeing things now. Bad enough I was hearing things, but this…"

"David, I tell you again, you are not mad."

David snorted and closed his eyes.

"I have observed how you order your house, how you organize your staff. I have seen you using tools in the creation of your sculpture, as well as manipulating other mystifying instruments about the house. You are far too accomplished and methodical to be mad. Why can you not then accept that I am real, that I am not a figment of your own fancy?" When he did not open his eyes or otherwise respond, she said, "Jane Austen's *Emma*. I choose *Emma*. How much detail do you wish me to discuss before you read it?"

He turned from her and began walking toward the garden entrance at the far side of the pavilion.

Sarrinah spoke from behind him. Her voice was soft and tremulous. "Do you wish to stop seeing me?" she asked.

David spun around and took two quick steps toward her, anxiety nearly choking him in response to a genuine fear for his sanity. "Why? Are you going to do an *I Dream of Jeannie* thing and turn into a cloud of smoke? Or wriggle your nose like Samantha and – poof – disappear?"

"I don't understand your references. But if you wish to stop seeing me, this house is certainly spacious enough for me to avoid your presence. I cannot leave the house, as I have explained, but I can stay well apart from you."

David was surprised to see what looked like tears glistening in her eyes and his anger melted. He astonished himself by asking, "Does that mean I won't hear you anymore?"

"How could you, if we are not in the same room?" she asked. She glided slowly toward him.

She was offering him an escape back to sanity – no more voices and no more hallucinations. But did he want that? And what if he wasn't crazy? Or at least, not the dangerous-to-oneself-or-others kind of crazy? Then again, would he know if he was? Probably every person alive seemed sane to themselves.

Simon. Simon will be here in about ten days. He'll notice if I'm unstable in some obvious way.

Sarrinah stopped her motion toward him and he once again marveled at her beauty. A taunting thought came to mind: *Are you thinking about refusing her offer of disappearing just so you can hang out with your pretty giirrrrlllllfriend?* Then the response: *I don't have a girlfriend. I have a wife.* Had *a wife. And all this is happening because I need to talk it out, talk about Kacey and about my baby girl... I need to find a way to accept or...*

David sighed and his posture crumpled, drawing his shoulders forward and his chin to his chest.

"David, I'll go. I'm sorry. I'm so very sorry. I never meant..." Sarrinah's voice was low, sad, and drifting away from him.

David's head snapped up. "No." Sarrinah was nearly to the covered arcade leading back to the main house, but she turned toward him as he spoke. "Please wait." He took several steps toward her, inhaled deeply and continued. "This is how I see it. One possibility is that I'm off my rocker, in which case I don't see much of a difference between hearing you, and being able to see you as well. The alternative is that you're right – not that I'm putting my money on that option – and I happen to be housemates with a friendly and extremely pretty ghost. Either way, I desperately need somebody to talk to. So, please, if it's acceptable to you, I'd rather you stayed."

The sadness fled Sarrinah's features to be replaced by a smile that nearly dazzled him. She clasped her hands in front of her bosom before dropping them to her sides and delivering a brief curtsy. "Thank you, David. Your invitation is most gracious. I would be delighted."

"Wow," he muttered, transfixed by the vision she presented. For a moment, neither moved nor spoke. His mind railed against the possibility of her existence either as a ghost or as a symptom of his mental illness. *I've got to do something to prove the matter one way or the other.* He said, "Right. Let me get my sketch pad, and tomorrow you can tell me about Emma. I'll need some pretty specific detail from you, because even not having read it, one picks up general knowledge in this day of the internet. The good news is that I haven't seen the movie either."

"There is a movie of Emma?" Sarrinah asked as he came alongside her. "I would so enjoy seeing it."

"Oh geez," David answered in a pretense of lightheartedness, but the laughter that followed was forced.

CHAPTER 10

SARRINAH

THE NEXT MORNING, DAVID seemed strangely shy of her. When she joined him in his studio, he avoided looking in her direction and worked without the conversation to which she was so accustomed. His changed manner infused her with a timidity that made it easy to maintain her habit of not speaking when he did not. An hour of unnatural silence passed during which her anxiety rose and she had difficulty maintaining her composure. Finally, he sighed heavily, put down his tool and turned toward her.

"Here's my thought. I've been driving myself crazy trying to figure you out – why you're here, what I should do about you. But the simple answer is that the whys and wherefores are irrelevant. As I said last night, whatever the situation, I need somebody to talk to about Kacey. If it's okay with you, I think it's about time I get started."

"Of course, David. If it would put your mind at ease, it would be my pleasure." In truth, she was so relieved he was speaking to her, she would have endured almost any subject of discourse. But she also sincerely wanted to help him, and so her answer was quite true.

He began telling her about his wife, Kacey, saying that he knew he needed to "unload his baggage" (a phrase which he also needed to explain). All that day and the next, he had told her of their meeting and courtship, and the happy early days of their marriage, but had not yet touched on the circumstances of her leaving. She knew he was building the courage to approach the painful topic, and she was patient. She enjoyed the implied intimacy of being invited to share his most personal and private agony. His willingness to so candidly share his emotions with her made her cherish his friendship all the more.

Best of all, in the days since appearing to him, not once had he suggested that she was a figment of his imagination. Instead, during intermissions in his discussion of Kacey, he had asked her questions about her current existence, and seemed to accept the answers with equanimity. She was certainly pleased that he had stopped questioning his sanity. On the day she had appeared to him, he had been so distraught she thought he might commit himself to an asylum or otherwise harm himself. She could not think of a more tragic fate for a man she so admired. For this reason, she had spent the third day giving him the most detailed account of *Emma* she could muster in the hopes that his "project," as he called it, would at the very least convince him he was not mad.

Now, after days of conversation, their relationship had once again become easy and natural. As evening fell, Sarrinah entered the library. She arrived before David, having taken the rear stairs, and settled in a chair near the chaise lounge he preferred. He entered soon thereafter, lifted *Emma* from the table where it still lay and strode to the small bar. After pouring a glass of wine, he relaxed into the chaise.

"Why do you insist on using the grand staircase when it takes you out of your way?" she asked. "The atrium – your studio – and the library are both at the rear of the house."

"It's gorgeous, that's why. That'd be reason enough. But also the railings were my inspiration for wood sculpture." He dropped the book to his lap and said, "Why do you insist on using the back staircase?"

"I… I don't know. The grand staircase frightens me somehow. I can't bring myself to go near it." Sarrinah combed through memories of her life, which had all returned to her, with the one exception of how she took her life. "I do recall finding it beautiful, and I recall the exquisite sensation of descending it in a new gown, but now…"

"No new gowns," David said, chuckling. She had explained the day before that she had come to consciousness in the gown she was wearing and had no ghostly boudoir in which to change to another.

"Perhaps," she answered with a small smile, happy to leave off pondering the source of her unease.

David opened the book, then said, "Here we go." He flashed a pained smile at Sarrinah, then put the book down and looked at her more closely. Laying the book aside, he stood and walked to the bank of electric light switches and brought the library to full light. Returning to where she sat, he said, "You're thicker, if that's the right word. I can't see through you quite as easily as before." Sarrinah stood at his gesture. "I thought it might be a trick of the light, but it seems not." He swiveled away to turn off the brighter lighting, then spoke to her over his shoulder. "Can the cleaning staff or the chef see you, or is it only me?"

"I can't tell you. You don't have any full-time servants – none that live on the premises at all. Since the day you first saw me, I have been in the presence of no one excepting yourself."

"Interesting," he said, his brow furrowed. Although he said no more, she could imagine where his thoughts had gone. If he was the only one who could see her, then it was proof he was mad, but if others could see her…

Seated again, he sipped at the wine and began reading. Almost immediately, he laughed and said, "I can see why you liked this book." When she simply looked her question at him, he said, "I imagine you connected with the story after reading the opening sentence." Clearing his throat, he began to read aloud.

"'Emma Woodhouse, handsome, clever and rich, with a comfortable home and happy disposition seemed to unite some of the best blessings of existence and had lived nearly twenty-one years in the world with very little to distress or vex her.' Now tell me that doesn't sound like you."

LOVE WHISPERS THROUGH THE VEIL

Sarrinah hadn't recalled the first line of the book, but she had to admit, it did sound fitting. Although she must have had *something* to distress or vex her. What other reason to take her life? Her expression darkened with the thought but David was now reading and did not notice.

While David read, she walked about the room for a time, looking at the titles of books she did not recognize and wondering which of them David had enjoyed most. Returning to her seat, she watched him read. He was as intent on the content of the book as she could have wished. He was such a dear man.

Sadness washed over her again as she pondered the uselessness of feeling anything for him – not that she could help herself. If only there was a way to salve the pains that wounded them: Her sorrow and guilt for how she left her life and the torment of knowing she was forever damned to this half-life; and his grief for his lost wife and child. To say nothing of his worry over his sanity. Thankfully, that last she at least had some hope of alleviating.

Melancholy swept through her again and she thought: *Not that his believing in me will make it possible for us to be more than dear friends.*

***

The question of whether the servants could also see Sarrinah was seemingly resolved the following morning as the weekend crew of cleaners came to the house. Despite her usual care to avoid the household staff – a habit that had begun from the moment of her waking in her hopes to avoid the return of her memories – Sarrinah stepped out of the salon, and came nearly face to face with two elderly women armed with dust rags, polish and feather dusters. Before Sarrinah could register any reaction in the two women, she spun and reentered the salon, then rushed to the side entrance that led to the formal living room. She threw the door open, dashed through, then pulled the door almost all the way closed. Using the door as a shield, she pressed her ear as close to the opening as she could in the hopes of hearing their reaction. She had heard nothing as obvious as a scream, but perhaps they would speak of what they had seen – if they had seen anything. For a full minute, neither woman entered the salon, but just as Sarrinah was

97

creeping toward the entrance to the main hall, she heard one of the women speaking from the salon. "I'll start with the shelves. You polish the rest of the furniture."

Sarrinah was at once relieved and frustrated. Her relief stemmed from the fact that she had not been visible to the women and therefore had not frightened them, but her frustration far outweighed the relief. If the servants could not see her, David would take this as a sign of his insanity. She vowed not to mention the incident to him.

Later the same day, she was sitting with David in his office near the front entrance of the house when a knock sounded on the door. She rose from her seat opposite him and moved toward the door leading to the salon. She had no fear that the person asking for entrance would see her – the cleaning women clearly had not – but she did not want David to discover that she was only visible to him.

"Stay," he said to her, speaking in a low voice. Then, he called out, "Come in." He ducked his head and returned to finishing some notation on the paper before him. Sarrinah sighed and glided across the room to stand behind where David sat. She did not want to see the disappointment or desperation on his face when he realized the visitor could not see her.

She was surprised when the two cleaning women entered. She was more surprised to see them both stop their forward progress and stare, their eyes focused on Sarrinah's.

They can see me!

She could barely contain her excitement as she envisioned them telling David that they could see an apparition standing behind him, or perhaps – even better – they would address her directly!

David finished jotting his note and spoke without raising his head. "How can I help you?" The women looked at each other, and the smaller of the two backed toward the door. At the sound of David dropping his pen to the desk, their eyes snapped to David and held there as if afraid to look elsewhere. David looked up and seeing that the women had stopped at the entry to the room, he raised his hand and said, "Please. Come in. Have a seat."

The taller, stouter woman swallowed hard and said, "Thank you, no." She backed half a step toward the other woman, as if proximity to her workmate could lend her strength and said, "We've come to tender our resignations. That's all."

"What?" David asked, standing and walking around his desk to approach them. "Why? Are you displeased with the amount of work or the pay?"

The shorter woman's eyes darted to Sarrinah, then back to David, and she spun around and rushed from the room. Her footsteps could be heard clattering through the entrance foyer and, after a brief moment, down the front steps of the house.

The remaining woman ducked her chin and swallowed again loudly – Sarrinah could hear the sound from where she stood behind David's desk – and then said, "No sir... er... um... Yes sir. The work. This house is..." She blinked several times in quick succession, her eyes never leaving David.

Just say it! Sarrinah wanted to shout. *"This house is haunted! There's a phantasm standing over yonder, sir!" If she says half so much, David will have to believe me!*

"This house is... too much work for us, especially at our age," the woman finished. She finally dropped her eyes from her intent focus on David's face to stare at the floor.

"Well, my goodness, I'll tell the service at once to increase the number of–" David began, but the woman interrupted.

"No sir. No. It's our age. We're... retiring. We just can't..." Her eyes were wide as she lifted her gaze to David once more. "We... I..." she stammered, then like the other woman, she spun and hurried away. The sound of the front door slamming reverberated through the house.

When David turned, his mouth still hung open in surprise. "What on Earth?" he asked. "I mean, I understand if they've decided to retire, but just like that? It's like they're late to their retirement party or something. Have you ever seen anything like that?" He looked to Sarrinah then motioned for her to take a seat.

Sarrinah slowly rounded his desk to the offered chair, hesitating before answering. "No, I must say I haven't."

If I tell him they left so precipitously because they saw me, he won't believe me. The words needed to come from them. She was disappointed, but as she seated herself a plan came to mind. *I must first confirm that someone other than David can see me. I'm as sure as I can be, yet it must be confirmed. And then I can only hope that person will say as much to David. Not everyone will be as terrified to speak of what they see.*

LOVE WHISPERS THROUGH THE VEIL

***

Sarrinah had at first intended to seek out other servants in the house: the cook or the various people who were tasked with cleaning windows, or with polishing silver, or those who tended the indoor plants and flower vases. She had been on the verge of entering the kitchen (the cook was the easiest servant to consistently locate) when it occurred to her that if the cook – or any other servants – also left David's employ, she would be harming David rather than helping him. Thus she became even more careful than before to ensure she did not cross paths with any of the remaining servants. However, there was one person who was a stranger to this house and whom she knew would soon be paying David a visit. She would attempt to show herself to this Simon fellow!

David had spoken fondly of Simon, explaining the many years Simon had acted as his agent. Despite his obvious affection for his friend, David seemed to vacillate between enthusiasm for the upcoming visit and uneasiness at the prospect.

"Will you show him your current work?" Sarrinah asked.

"No, I don't think so," he answered. He chuckled and said, "I don't want to raise his hopes. At this point, I'm just keeping my hands busy. I'm not even sure these are saleable."

"Oh, but they are! Or at least I would have been pleased to purchase them during my lifetime. I suppose it's possible aesthetic tastes have changed, but I wouldn't think so."

"Thanks. Just the same…" David's voice trailed off as he applied liquid adhesive to the flat top of a dark piece of African rosewood, then pressed a thicker slab of light-colored Baltic birch to the adhesive. He had explained his plan to carve them together, as a single piece, highlighting the contrasting colors as he sculpted curved edges and smooth-sided holes throughout.

As Sarrinah approached, David raised his head. Tilting his head toward one shoulder, he said, "You know, I'm almost certain now that you're becoming more substantial. When I first saw you, you were standing in sunlight and I could see right through you. In the library, I couldn't be sure because even fully lit, it's not exactly bright in there and I admit, in dimmer light, you've always looked, well, thicker, for lack of a better word, but now – even in here in the studio, you look… more real."

She curled her lips into a coy, teasing smile and said, "Perhaps because I am real."

David only answered with a furrowed brow and a grunt, then returned to tightening the clamps around the two wood pieces, securing them together until the adhesive could dry.

Finally, Saturday arrived. David, unsure of the time of Simon's arrival, flung open the entrance door, then moved to the library to continue his reading of *Emma*. He had not yet commented on whether the book was proceeding according to Sarrinah's description of it, but she had caught him pausing in his reading to throw enigmatic glances in her direction.

Although it was unusual for Sarrinah not to remain in library as he read, she took advantage of his engrossed attention to the book to leave the room. Moving toward the front entrance, she entered the billiard room, determined to wait there for Simon's arrival. Not more than half an hour had passed when she heard the sound of an automobile rounding the reflecting pool, and then footsteps on the gravel drive. The sounds stopped as the footfalls approached the entrance.

"Hello?" The man's accented voice was not loud and was not quite as deep as David's. When no one answered, the man raised his voice. "Hello?"

"Simon!" David's muted voice called out from the library. "Come on in. I'll be right there. Give me a second."

The footsteps tentatively entered the foyer then stopped. Taking a deep breath to give herself courage, Sarrinah stepped out of the billiard room and began crossing the hall toward the salon. She turned toward the entrance where stood a pleasant looking, clean-shaven man in pressed pants and a white shirt, open at the collar. His mouth opened slightly at catching sight of her, then closed. He smiled and nodded his head toward her politely.

"Hello," she said.

"Hello," he answered, smile growing.

She continued her path across the hall, and entered the salon, just as she heard David's footsteps hurrying down the hallway. "Hey buddy!" he called out.

Sarrinah watched from a spot at the far side of the salon as the two men embraced.

Simon lifted his eyebrows, then waved a hand in a gesture that encompassed the house. "Wow, this is quite a place." In response to David's shrug, he smiled and said, "It's great to see you." He cast a look toward where Sarrinah was standing and seemed about to say something when David spoke.

"Have you eaten? I've had a great little brunch set up in the garden and I'm starving. Join me. I'll show you around the place when I'm sure I'm not going to faint from hunger."

Simon laughed. "Sure, I could eat a bite," he said.

Sarrinah followed their progress down the hall by listening for their voices and passing from the salon to the formal living room, from there to the library, and finally into the morning room. She stepped into the arcade leading to the pavilion, and from a position hiding behind one of the arcade pillars, watched them cross the secret garden to the table.

She toyed with the idea of simply approaching the table, but was afraid of what either of their reactions might be. Instead, she snuck from pillar to pillar until she was close enough to hear their conversation. Under her breath, she repeated a whispered plea. *Please Simon. Speak of me. Please.*

CHAPTER 11

DAVID

"MAN, IT'S GOOD TO see you Simon," David said as they seated themselves. He uncovered the food warmers and immediately began building his breakfast sandwich, stacking a toasted English muffin, Canadian bacon, steamed asparagus, and a poached egg, before slathering thick Hollandaise sauce over it all. He topped it with a few dashes of Tabasco sauce, then reached for his cutlery. He looked up as Simon laughed.

"You weren't kidding about being hungry. Are you sure just one of those deluxe versions of Eggs Benedict is going to be enough?"

David smiled as he cut his first bite. "Probably not." He brought the food to his mouth.

"You look fantastic," Simon said. "And here I was worried about you withering away out here with nothing to do and nobody to talk to."

"I've been keeping busy," David said. He gestured toward the house hoping that Simon would assume he'd been working on remodeling. He didn't want to tell Simon about having started with wood sculpture until he was more sure of himself, afraid of disappointing expectations.

"Yeah, I saw that." Simon reached for the fruit platter and began loading fresh blueberries, raspberries and strawberries onto his plate, then drizzled maple cream over the top. While David was still pondering what Simon meant by his comment, Simon raised his eyebrows and asked, "So, who's your friend?"

"Friend?" David repeated.

"Okay, so maybe she's not a friend," Simon answered. "I'm talking about the gorgeous creature who greeted me when I came in. A model maybe? She *was* in strange period garb. I won't lie to you, I'm extremely excited about the idea of you working, but – wow. She's a looker. I'm hoping for your sake that she's at least a friend."

David stopped in the motion of filling his mouth again, fork hovering near his chin before he lowered his fork to the plate. "What are you talking about?"

Simon chuckled. "Hoping to hide her from me, were you? Don't worry, you're in no danger from me – I wouldn't do that to you."

"Hiding… Who are we talking about?"

"The fabulous brunette. Long purple gown. Early twenties. Greeted me as she wandered past me at the entrance." Simon speared a large strawberry as he threw a twisted grin toward David.

"You… you saw her?" David stammered.

Simon raised his eyebrows again and nodded. "So? Who is she?"

David did not answer because the only thought filling his mind for what seemed minutes was: *He saw her. Simon saw her. He heard her speak.* His mind raced through various possible explanations he could give his friend, but he could settle on none that wouldn't sound ridiculous. Finally, he said simply, "Sarrinah." When Simon gestured expectantly with one hand for more information, David said, "Yeah. She's a friend of mine."

"Super."

David turned to look back toward the house hoping to see Sarrinah, then returned his attention to Simon. For a long moment he could only watch Simon eat while his thoughts spun.

The good news is… I'm not mentally unbalanced. But… I've got – no kidding – a ghost living in my house. My haunted house. He suppressed a giddy giggle. He had never believed in such things – in fact had vehemently dismissed such things as impossible. Given his worries of late, the idea did not bother him as much as it might once have. *Now what do I do? Do I–*

His friend woke him from his stupor by speaking. "So, are you working?"

David looked to his plate to cover his momentary confusion at the change of subject. He lifted his abandoned forkful to his mouth and despite his previous decision not to tell Simon about his newest attempt at sculpture, he nodded. With the current chaos of his thoughts, David could think of no other way to maintain an afternoon of clever and intelligent conversation with Simon other than to focus on his work.

Yet, even with the subject of his work broached, his mind spun back to Sarrinah. *If she joins us, I could introduce her, but what happens when he tries to shake her hand?*

Simon smiled and lowered his fork. "And…?"

It took David a moment to pick up the thread of the conversation. He said, "Honestly, I hadn't planned to tell you. I didn't want to get your hopes up."

"Sorry friend. I'm just wallowing in hopefulness over here. Do I get to see what you've been up to? Or are you just going to leave me hanging?" Simon speared another strawberry and shook it at David. "Be careful how you answer. I might decide to stay for a month in the hopes of sneaking a peek when you're sleeping."

"You'd be welcome," David answered. *Although with Sarrinah here…* Then: "But I won't do that to you. I know how you feel about the 'boonies.'" He shot a grin at Simon and said, "When we're done here, I'll take you around the house – the whole tour thing – and we'll finish at my studio. It's upstairs, near the back of the house." As much as he was happy to see Simon, he also couldn't wait for the opportunity to talk to Sarrinah… for the first time without marveling at his imagination or questioning his sanity.

111

The more he thought about speaking to her without that overhanging anxiety, the more exhilarated he became. *A real ghost!* He fought the temptation to turn around to look at the house again, to search the windows for Sarrinah's face.

After brunch, David gave Simon the full tour of the house, including the basement and third floor. Part of the reason for the thoroughness of the tour was David's desire to search the house for Sarrinah. But, despite the exhaustive tour, he never even caught a glimpse of her traversing a far hallway.

As promised, he ended the tour in the studio. "This used to be an indoor atrium. It was gorgeous with terrific light but, in the end, it was really just another sitting room. It's a bit of a mess now with all the raw wood and shavings and saw dust, but–"

Simon interrupted by saying, "Oh my God, David."

David turned to find Simon running his hands over the first of the sculptures he had kept; the one Sarrinah had asked him not to dispose of.

"This is fantastic! Is this what you've been working on?" After sliding his finger along the length of the piece from top to bottom, he asked, "This is really natural wood and not molded plastic or some such?"

David chuckled, pride swelling. "It's wood. That one's Brazilian waln–" but Simon turned away.

"Oh, wow. Oh yes please. Oh David," he said as he crossed the room to the six-foot tall abstract rendition of the dead and deformed tree. David had transformed what, in reality, was the sad image of a carcass into something alive and alluring – but not yet as beautiful as he meant it to be. He strode quickly toward Simon, gesturing with a vague negative motion Simon did not see.

"I haven't finished that one," he said, speaking rapidly. "It only has a single coat of lacquer and it hasn't been sanded yet. It's probably not dry. After that, it'll need at least three more coats of lacquer, with careful sanding between each layer." In truth, the lacquer was probably dry, but he hated the idea of Simon touching it before the piece had attained the smoothness that would make the tactile enjoyment an integral part of its loveliness.

Simon placed one hand in his front pocket and bent the other behind his back as he circled the sculpture with admiring eyes. Then he crossed the room to a table near the fireplace where another finished piece lay. "May I?" he asked.

"Help yourself." As Simon stroked the three-foot-long curling wood form, David said, "That one is designed for hanging on a wall. It has various hangers on the back so that it can be hung in any orientation."

"It's gorgeous! I can't decide if it looks like a crazy, twisted '6' or an abstract of a musical clef," Simon said, once more running his fingers from one end of the curl to the other.

David smiled, shrugged and said, "As you wish."

Simon stepped back from the table, his hands hovering over it as though reluctant to relinquish the warm smoothness. After looking a while longer at the looping sculpture, he turned to David, eyes glowing.

"They're masterpieces, David." When David made a deprecating gesture of dismissal, Simon's expression changed from one of admiration to seriousness. He crossed the room and grasped David's shoulders. "Not a joke. You are amazing." Letting go of one shoulder, he gestured vaguely around the room. "These… these are amazing."

"Thanks, Simon. I–"

"When do you think you can be ready for a show?" Simon put both hands into his pants pockets, backed a pace and winked, smile returning to his face.

Laughter burst from David and his last bit of apprehension about Simon's judgment of his new endeavor evaporated. "How very... Simon of you."

Simon's expression turned to one of exaggerated innocence. "What?"

David threw an arm around his friend's shoulder. "I'll let you know, okay? I've still got a lot of work to do." He began leading Simon from the studio. "But thanks for the confidence boost. I needed that."

**

David attempted to push Sarrinah from his mind so that he could enjoy his friend's visit. He showed Simon around the grounds until lunch, then challenged Simon to a game of pool. Simon did not push David for a timeline for any show, instead updating David about various happenings in the City and suggesting that David might consider a new up-and-coming painter if he needed art for his new home. "And I'm not even pushing one of my own. I don't represent her, more's the pity."

When Simon left, the sun was just kissing the far horizon, and the sky above the reflecting pool glowed like a purple-orange gem.

"I'll keep in touch," David yelled from where he stood at the entrance. "Drive carefully." He waved and watched as the tail lights of Simon's sleek Jaguar XK8 disappeared down the driveway. Then he turned, came inside, closed the door behind him and leaned back against the thick wood.

After listening for a moment, he raised his voice, and called out, "Sarrinah."

"Yes, David," she answered, startling him as she emerged from his office at his right.

He gazed at her approaching form for a long moment. *She was an extraordinarily ravishing woman when she died.*

"Simon saw you," he said.

"Yes. We spoke briefly," she answered. She seemed shy of him, as if worried that he might be angry.

"You're real," he said. "I mean, you're a real ghost."

She nodded.

"You know I'm going to have to Google you now," he said, keeping his expression serious despite the thrill that ran through him at the idea of speaking to a ghost – especially a kind and intelligent one.

Sarrinah ducked her head and after a hesitation said in a small voice, "Is that like performing an exorcism?"

Surprised laughter burst from David. He stepped away from the door and closed the distance between them. "No," he said, still chuckling. "It means I'm going to research your story. I want to find out more about you. I want to learn what history says about how you lived and how you died."

Sarrinah graced him with a tentative smile. "I'm very pleased that you believe me now. And that you don't seem afraid or angry." Her smile grew as he gestured that she accompany him down the hall.

"I need a drink. Join me?"

***

The following morning, Sarrinah found David breakfasting in the formal dining room. He sat at the near end with his back to her, watching the rain fall into the secret garden. He hummed a bright tune that did not fit the murky gloom of the weather. The chair nearest him on the right had been pulled out to accommodate her. (In the days since he first saw her, David had learned that she could not easily manipulate a chair and did not like her having to stand as he ate.) As she approached, David glanced toward the chair and for a brief instant Sarrinah imagined that another figure – one invisible to her – sat conversing with David in a voice she could not hear. She felt an immediate empathy with David's previous apprehension for the stability of his mind.

"Good morning," she said as she neared him.

"Sarrinah! Sit, sit," he said, twisting toward her and gesturing to the chair. Then, before she could sit, he said with excitement, "I found you."

"I beg your pardon?" She laughed as she joined him at the table.

"I couldn't sleep last night, so I looked you up and found all kinds of great stuff about this house, and about you and William, and–" Seeing the cloud that descended over her features at the mention of William, he stopped midsentence. His excitement transformed to an almost breath-stealing sympathy as he realized the callousness of his blurted remarks and recognized her expression as one of heartache and torment – a pain he understood all too well. Without thinking, he brought his hand forward to rest on hers where it lay on the table.

As his hand touched hers, an unimaginable cold engulfed it. The shocking sensation of frost was followed by a horrendous sensation of mucus crawling up his arm. He jerked his arm back with such force he nearly tipped his chair backwards as an unintelligible shout escaped him.

Sarrinah cried out and brought both hands to her mouth, a look of wide-eyed horror marring her usually smooth features. Tears sprang to her eyes and she leapt from the chair to run toward the door.

"Wait! Come back!" David called out. He stood with the intention of following her but the lingering sensation in his hand and arm brought him to a stop. He shook his arm several times, then wiped briskly from his elbow to his wrist as if removing some invisible substance. After flexing his fingers, he lifted his gaze to find Sarrinah standing in the doorway, hands still covering her mouth, tears flowing down her cheeks and onto her fingers.

"Did I harm you?" she asked.

"You didn't do anything at all. I'm the one who reached for you." He glanced down to assure himself that the skin of his hand had not changed in appearance, then manipulated his fingers once more. He tried to smile as he glanced up at her and said, "But I assure you, I won't be doing that again."

CHAPTER 12

SARRINAH

SHAME FLOODED THROUGH SARRINAH. David's touch to her hand – which resulted in the barest tingling sensation for her – had clearly created an abominable sensation in him to have made him react so violently. She had leapt up to run from the room, vowing never to impose her presence on David again, even while sharing the house with him. Yet, when he shouted for her to wait, she stopped to hover in the doorway, helpless to resist his call.

No, not helpless, she chided herself. *I linger here because I wish to. He has no mysterious power over me. I cannot even claim that he has "stolen" my heart. In full awareness of what I have done, I have given my heart to him.*

Before last evening, she had thought of David in terms indicating affection or liking or friendship, but after Simon had gone, she and David had talked long into the night. In the passing of those hours, Sarrinah had felt so happy, so close to David.

Without knowing when her feelings of affection had transformed into something deeper, the thought came unbidden to her mind. *I love him.*

He had spoken so earnestly and kindly to her, apologizing for having doubted her existence. He seemed energized by the final sloughing of his worries over his mental state, and the resulting vitality had made him even more handsome in Sarrinah's eyes. They had laughed aloud as they spoke of *Emma*, as he confessed that she had described the book with an uncanny accuracy. He went so far as to say he was enjoying the book even more than he might have because her closer-to-contemporary viewpoint of several of the episodes in the book had enhanced his appreciation of the story. He had also promised to show her various movie renditions, claiming to be nearly finished with the book and truly enjoying it. He had laughed again and said, "All these years without giving Jane Austen a chance. What a fool I've been!"

It was a small thing. But, even in this, he gave me so much. He transformed his "project" into a shared pleasure. Still more, he has brought me happiness and laughter when I thought the only emotions I would ever experience were sadness, guilt and misery.

Now, instead of banishing her in anger or fear, he called out to her to stay. She watched as he flexed and straightened his fingers once more and melancholy washed through her. *I am truly a doomed creature. Whenever David leaves this house, whether it is days or decades hence, I will surely learn that all the suffering I have endured thus far was nothing to what will follow his absence.*

"Please," David said, "don't go."

Sarrinah wiped at her tears and lowered her hands from her face, but could not bring herself to return his tremulous smile.

"I really do want to talk to you about what I found out about you." He turned as if to seat himself again, then with a dismissive gesture toward the table he said, "I'm finished here. Why don't we go to the salon where you can be comfortable. Unless you'd rather keep that room to yourself?" Again, his infallible courtesy.

"I would be pleased to have you join me in the salon," she answered, once again wiping at her face and trying to suppress in indelicate sniffle.

They walked the main hall to the salon in awkward silence, she embarrassed at having caused him such obvious... what?...

disgust?… and as wary of keeping a distance between them as he appeared to be. The silence continued until she settled onto to her favorite couch, and he sat in a chair opposite her. She felt tears coming to her eyes when David still said nothing, instead meeting her gaze with an enigmatic expression.

"Okay," he said, leaning forward in the chair. "Let's get it out in the open. I'm the one who reached for you. You did nothing to cause me to do it. You didn't hurt me, although I'll grant you that the sensation was… well… creepy for lack of a better word." He lowered his gaze to his hand and shuddered.

"It will not happen again," she said with vehemence, sitting forward to emphasize her words. The fierce protectiveness she felt toward him dried the tears that had begun.

"Thank you for that. And now that's done." He flicked one hand outward in a gesture of dismissal, then checked himself. "Unless you think there's more to discuss?"

"I apologi–"

"No, I wasn't searching for an apology. None is necessary." David sat back in his seat, then bounced forward again. "Although… did *I* hurt *you*? If so, I'm the one to apologize."

124

"I felt almost no sensation at all, David," she answered, in a tone of regret that she was not able to mask. David appeared not to hear it, or attributed it to whatever guilt she was feeling over the incident. "Neither did I feel anything the one other time I touched you. And I assure you, you seemed not to feel anything either."

"Other time?"

"On the day I first discovered you in the house. I attempted to gain your attention by tapping you on the shoulder." She pondered the reason for difference in his recent reaction, then mused, "Perhaps it has something to do with my increased substantiality?"

"Yeah, maybe. But whatever the reason…" He let his sentence trail off and flexed his hand again.

Sarrinah stifled her threatening tears with a series of quick blinks.

"Can we start over?" he asked. When she nodded, he relaxed into his chair. "As I said, I found some information about this house, and about you." She noted that he did not mention William again, no doubt hoping to save her the pain of recalling how her death had affected him.

125

LOVE WHISPERS THROUGH THE VEIL

Dear William. Even without David's mentioning him, she recalled William's warmth toward her and the sorrowful dimming of his life force after her death. Yet, this memory alone did not cause the suffering it once did; her sadness now stemmed from her realization that David now claimed a bigger portion of her heart than William ever had. Perhaps because of her youth when she was with William? (Yes, her ghostly appearance had not changed from that time, but her existence had extended long decades since her death and had been filled with misery.) *Was I too youthful to love with all my heart?* But she did not believe this.

The truth was that she shared a greater intimacy with David than she had with William. David was not constricted by the societal mores that had governed her interactions with William and limited the time spent in each other's presence. While she had found David's behavior and speech inappropriate (and often incomprehensible) when he first came to live here, she thought so no longer. He shared so much more of his heart and his mind with her than William would have found proper. And she had come to cherish that intimacy. She now sought out his presence as hungrily as she had first desperately attempted to avoid it.

She returned her focus to David. He gazed at her with fingers steepled under his chin, his elbows resting on the arms of the chair, clearly giving her time to engage in her musing. Her mouth twisted in a shy smile.

"And?" she prompted. "What did you discover?"

"Everything you've told me checks out – not that that'll be any surprise to you." David rolled his eyes, and spoke to himself. "I don't know why I didn't think to Google you earlier."

Google. What a strange and ridiculous word to have replaced "research."

David continued. "There haven't been that many owners of this house in the last century or so, and it wasn't hard to find who built the house, and when. I found all sorts of details about the original house which you probably already know. I had no idea how extensive the grounds were at the time you lived here."

"Are they no longer extensive?" she asked.

"Only thirty-four acres." Sarrinah could not suppress a gasp as he spoke. "I mean, that's a lot of acreage to a guy from the big City, but–"

"The grounds were nearly twenty times that when–"

127

"I know. It must have been incredible."

Questions swirled through Sarrinah's mind regarding whether the bridle trails or walking paths still existed and which portions of the gardens had been lost, how many fountains, which statuary… Then she laughed. To David's questioning look, she said, "Any outrage on my part is pointless. I cannot leave the house to enjoy the grounds, so it matters not what has been lost over time. You are clearly pleased with the remaining grounds, and what I can enjoy of the surroundings – the view from the windows – is as lovely as ever."

David smiled, whether at her statement or as a way of joining her laughter, she did not know. Then his smile faded and he once again sat forward in his chair.

"I also found out about you. Details about your childhood, and marriage," – she noted that he still forbore mentioning William's name – "as well as…" He stopped and cleared his throat.

"My death," she finished for him.

David nodded with slow, solemn movements. "Yeah. It appears that you…"

When he did not finish, Sarrinah supplied the words. "That I took my own life." The tears she had banished such a short time ago blurred her sight of David's sympathetic expression.

"Do you want to know more? I mean, about how? Would that help you?"

I am beyond help. I have committed a crime against God and nature, and will continue to be punished for it. Is there any point to learning how I accomplished the deed?

Against her intention, she surprised herself by saying, "Yes. I want to know." Gathering strength to withstand what she was about to hear, she blinked to clear her vision.

David leaned forward, almost as though he wanted to reach across the space between them to comfort her. Recalling his reaction to their brief contact, she was grateful a table separated them, even while wishing she could feel his touch. She sighed internally. *It is more than a table that separates us. We are separated by an impenetrable veil.*

"There is good reason behind your fear of the imperial staircase, Sarrinah." His voice lowered to near a whisper. "The article I read said that you threw yourself down it."

129

Sarrinah slumped backward in her chair, body sprawled as flaccidly as if she had fallen there. *Or thrown myself down here.* Warm tears squeezed from behind closed eyelids to chase down her cheeks. While David's revelation did not return memories to her, her imagination supplied images of her broken body bent hideously across the marble stairs, and poor William. William finding her there and filling the house with his sorrow-filled howls. Her mind circled on the imagined scenario trying to make sense of it.

No. It was too out of her character. She could think of no time nor any inciting incident which would have made her want to take her own life. What could possibly have caused her to do such a thing? Without meaning to utter the words aloud, she said, "I can't believe it."

"Good!" David's explosive response startled her back to some semblance of decorum and she straightened to a more proper posture. "I don't believe it either," he continued. "There was a maid who testified to having seen you do it – okay, that's pretty compelling stuff – but then again, she also testified to your 'dark moods,' which I just can't wrap my head around."

Sarrinah tilted her head in genuine surprise. "Dark moods?"

"Right?" David said. He no longer spoke in quite tones and his energy had returned. "Sure, you've been sad since your death – who wouldn't be? – but I haven't heard a single story of your life that allows me to picture 'dark moods.' So, I'm with you. I don't believe it."

David's enthusiasm was infectious. An irrational hopefulness fluttered through Sarrinah. After pressing a tentative smile toward David, reason returned to her and her smile faded. "What difference does it make, David? You may believe it or refuse to believe it, and I am free to do the same. But the deed is history, not some future event we have the hope of preventing. I am what I am for a reason." She sighed deeply and, in an attempt to accept the inexplicable, repeated mournfully, "I took my life."

David sighed, allowing her mood to affect him as surely as his earlier enthusiasm had briefly given her hope. Then, regaining the cheerfulness in his voice, he said, "Sorry, but just I don't believe it. This is a genuine mystery and I'm intrigued enough to look for the answer."

Sarrinah raised her head to meet his bright gaze, then lifted a shoulder in a one-sided shrug that signified any number of questions: *Why? What difference will it make? What can you possibly do?*

"I'll keep looking on the internet to see what I can find. And, I'm going to hire a historian. A history detective!"

Despite David's enthusiasm, Sarrinah could see no point to the investigation. In fact, it would only sadden her to hear more. "I'm afraid I don't see the purpose."

"Listen, not that I'm an expert on ghosts, but don't some of the stories say that ghosts are hanging on in this world because there's something that needs to be done? A mystery to be solved? So, maybe I'll solve it!"

"I don't know about ghosts, David. I only know about my own wretched condition, which will never change, never be 'cured,' never improve." She was unable to disguise the anguish in her voice. "I don't want to know any more. I shouldn't have asked." Misery was a palpable weight within her as she once again pictured William finding her, grotesque and bent, on the stairs. *If I had not asked, I would not have this awful vision of how it must have been.*

Her mind slipped easily from that imagined scenario to her memories of William after her death. His face contorted with pain as he spoke to her afterward. His final words to her, begging her forgiveness as he left the house for the last time. Tears flooded her eyes and she leapt from her seat and spun away from David. "I am what I am, David. I am lost to this world" – *and to you!* – "and nothing will change that." She almost howled the last words over her shoulder as she dashed from the room.

CHAPTER 13

DAVID

ALONE IN HIS STUDIO, David tapped on the straight gouge, careful not to drive too deeply into the wood. He was using the gouge to create subtle divots on his latest sculpture which he hoped would add to the visual as well as the tactile richness of the piece. His mind was only partially focused on his work; the remainder wallowed in grief. He leaned forward and puffed to blow away the small curl of wood he had carved free, then straightened to examine his work. From the corner of his eye he saw Sarrinah enter the studio, and he sighed internally.

Silence. He had had little more than silence from Sarrinah in the three days since he told her about her supposed suicide. (He used the word "supposed" even in his own mind, because after time to think and digest, and a bit more research, he still could not bring himself to believe she had taken her own life.) She spent time in the various rooms he occupied, but spoke little, and then in subdued tones. Unfortunately, her mood infected him and her muteness gave him plenty of time to think, sending him back into the depths of his own torments.

He returned to his work, *tap, tap, tap*, expecting that Sarrinah would once again chose to sit in the far corner without speaking to him. He blew the loose wood fragments away, and then jerked when Sarrinah spoke from over his shoulder.

"David." Seeing his response, she released a low puff of a laugh and said, "I waited until you had lowered the chisel. I didn't want you to damage your work."

David dropped the gouge to the workbench, and turned toward her, chuckling with self-directed humor. "Okay, I'm awake now."

Sarrinah made an attempt at a smile and said, "I did not intend to startle you–"

David opened his mouth in exaggerated disbelief and said, "Yes you did!"

He was rewarded by Sarrinah's light laughter, the first happy utterance he had heard from her in days. "Perhaps I did." She ducked her head shyly and said, "I have missed our conversations." Before David could reply, she raised a hand to forestall any response and said, "I take full responsibility. Learning the details of my death reminded me of the pain I caused and the hopelessness of my situation. I've been indulging in self-pity and in so doing darkened everything around me." Her cheerless smile returned and she bowed her head. "Including you. I am certain you have felt more 'haunted' in these past days than you have since first coming here."

David's own melancholy washed over him again *I have been haunted. But not by you. By the only woman I have ever loved — can ever love — and then lost through no fault but my own.*

Raising her face to meet his eyes, Sarrinah finished, "I apologize."

"Conversation sounds like it might be the right medicine," he answered, "for both of us." David brushed his hands together to dislodge any stray chips of wood. "I'm ready for a break." *From thinking about Kacey*, he thought, but did not say. Sarrinah awarded him with a genuine smile that reached her eyes, and David's mood brightened. He gestured toward the hallway with no particular destination in mind, and as she turned in that direction, he said, "What do you want to talk about?"

Sarrinah did not immediately answer, and he was quite happy to wait for her choice of topic. As they approached the grand staircase – he had a vague intention of going to a comfortable room on the lower floor – he recalled Sarrinah's aversion to using it. In deference to her fears, he hurried past it into the guest wing, and then, on a whim, took the stairs to the third floor, despite the fact that the upper level only contained additional guest rooms and the servants' quarters.

Inspiration struck and he asked, "Would you like to explore the attic? You wouldn't believe all the stuff stored there." He stopped and turned to her. "Unless it'll dredge up old memories and—"

Sarrinah's brittle laughter brought a smile to his face. "You needn't be so careful of me, David. I'm dead after all." David's smile faltered at her last statement, but against his expectations, her face did not darken. Apparently reading the concern in his face, she said, "It is something I have been lamenting more and more lately, but it is not something I can change. That being the case, I have determined to enjoy what can of my existence."

"Which obviously includes my sparkling conversation."

"Precisely. Lead on, fair prince – let's away to the tower." Genuine mirth glittered in her eyes.

David laughed, and the laughter further diluted the renewed grief that had been dragging him toward depression. Eager to hold on to the lightened mood, he raised his arm as though holding a sword above his head and said, "Be careful fair maiden, there be dragons in the tower. Yet, I will keep you safe." He laughed again, feeling ridiculous, but also thankful for the bit of silliness.

On the third floor, David entered a storage closet with the intention of grabbing a flashlight and electric shop light – the few lights that had been strung in the attic were inoperable for a reason he had yet to explore – but then he changed his mind. "Candles?" he asked over his shoulder.

"It would seem appropriate for exploring a dark and abandoned tower."

David emptied a cardboard box of cleaning materials and filled it with a ten-pack of long, white tapered candles, a candelabrum, assorted individual candlesticks, and a long stick lighter. Turning to Sarrinah, he said, "And now onward, toward adventure!"

On reaching the door to the attic stairs, David was almost disappointed that it did not creak on its hinges as he opened it; a squeak or groan would have added to the feeling of adventure. He was grateful, however, for the broad width of the stairs and the fact that the light in the stairway still worked.

At the top of the stairs, David put the box down, placed a candle in its holder, and lit it. Sarrinah giggled as he theatrically threw the door open and stepped in. The huge space was not unfamiliar to him. He had made several previous trips to the attic to search for furniture or art he could use in the main house, and had found at least one treasure in the form of an intricately carved credenza he had installed in the billiard room. Now, he walked to a large sheet-shrouded form, and after pausing to be sure Sarrinah was behind him, whipped the sheet off.

"Ta-dah!" he said, as a colorful head of an Asian dragon seemed to spring toward them in the candlelight. "I warned you there were dragons."

"Oh, David!" she exclaimed, moving toward it, one hand extended. Then drawing back her hand, she said, "The colors haven't faded and the gold gilding… It's so exotic." Smiling she

turned to him. "I've never seen this before, but it's beautiful."

"Agreed. I'm still trying to work out where to put it."

As Sarrinah moved deeper into the attic, David positioned

the candle on a stack of crates and retrieved the box from the

landing. He placed the box on a shrouded table, then put five

candles in the candelabrum and lit them all. Uncovering two nearby

chairs, he pulled them close to the table and arranged them side by

side. After pressing on the seat cushions of each, he called out,

"This one's mine, if you don't mind. It looks a bit more

substantial." He then lit the remaining candles and spaced them

across the top of a large chest across the table from their chairs.

The gloom of the attic was barely alleviated by the candlelight;

when David looked up, he could only make out the barest of

details of the high ceiling rafters – which was probably best,

considering the dust and cobwebs the light did illuminate.

Grabbing one of the candles, he moved toward where Sarrinah had

stopped her exploration.

"What have you found?" he asked as he approached.

Sarrinah was staring down at a stack of paintings leaning against the wall.

"Yeah, I uncrated all the wall art I could find to see if there was anything I might want to use. These were all the portraits, some of which are very nicely done, but because I didn't know any of the people—"

"William's father," Sarrinah said.

"Oh." The portraits were so old, David had not considered that Sarrinah would know the people portrayed. Chagrined, he pulled a sheet from a draped standing mirror and began to cover the paintings.

"No, please. If you move them for me, I may be able to tell you some history of the paintings or who the subjects are." Her voice was timorous but did not seem tinged with the same sadness of the recent days.

David moved the portrait of William's father to the side, followed by the next and the next, listening as Sarrinah either explained what she knew of the people or confessed that she did not recognize the painting. Finally, he reached a portrait that elicited no response from Sarrinah but made him gasp.

Two people were depicted: a man standing behind a seated woman. *Sarrinah!* The artist had captured her beauty and rendered her an ethereal goddess. She wore the barest hint of a smile, and the golden beaded gown she wore, with its low, draping neckline only highlighted the delicacy of her bone structure.

"My God," he said. After another moment of staring, he said, "I've seen this before, of course, but I didn't make the connection. I mean, I hadn't seen you then and once I did, I didn't remember…" Dragging his attention from the woman to the man in the painting, he asked, "William?"

"William," she answered.

The man standing behind Sarrinah in the painting was tall and dressed in a thigh-length coat with a double row of buttons. His hair was short and crowned with a top hat. He sported a mustache and lamb chops beard, which made him look stern, but his eyes were warm and bright, as though he had just stopped laughing to assume his pose. It was difficult to tell if he was handsome – David had never cared for lamb chops – but the merry eyes lead him to say, "He's a handsome man."

"Yes, he was."

Was. Geez, this is ancient history to me, but for Sarrinah... David turned toward her expecting to see tears or melancholy. Instead, her small smile as she looked at the portrait indicated both sadness and affection. In fact, he felt more shaken by the portrait than she appeared to be.

With a slow blink, Sarrinah transferred her gaze to David. "I'm quite all right. If you would like to go through the rest, I am willing."

"I'd rather not," David said, his tone more morose than he had intended. Seeing the portrait of Sarrinah had driven home the reality of her death as well as how long ago it had happened. *Criminy. She's been dead for over a century.* Feeling somewhat unsteady, he went to the chair he had set up earlier and sat. He watched Sarrinah as she crossed the dark attic to join him. In the glow of the candles, she looked as otherworldly as the artist had portrayed in the painting, and yet as real as any other woman would appear in the same dim light. *But she's a ghost. An honest-to-goodness ghost who's been wandering through this same house for a hundred years.* For the first time, David felt he could better understand the depth of her anguish.

"I'm sorry," he said. "I didn't mean to bring up yet another reminder of all you've lost." He dropped his gaze to his lap and focused on the wavering shadows created by the flickering light.

"We both have suffered losses." Her voice was low, but instead of sounding sad, seemed directed toward his own unhappiness.

As much as he meant to respond with, "Yours was worse," her statement – *both have suffered* – brought to the fore the memories he had been wallowing in for days. His mind clicked through a slideshow of images: Kacey laughing; then later, Kacey crying; and later still, Kacey gone impassive. Finally, Kacey closing the door to their small apartment for the last time. He was struck with a wave of self-pity and guilt. "Yeah," he answered without lifting his head.

Sarrinah did not speak for a long moment. Then, "You've heard much of my history," she said, voice gentle. "I think the time has come to hear more of yours."

David's head snapped up. His mouth opened to answer her sharply – *I don't want to talk about me. I don't want to talk about Kacey.*

He exhaled the breath he hadn't known he was holding, closed his mouth and lifted a hand to the back of his neck. *Don't I?*

I'm still grieving, right? I need to talk to somebody. Talking might not help, but at least she's a sympathetic ear. He released a deep shuddering sigh and turned to look at her. "You're right. It's time." Settling back in his chair, he stared into the dancing flames of the candles. He turned his mind away from the beautiful woman at his side and swept into the darkness of his memories.

"Okay, so far you've heard about the beginning of my relationship with Kacey…"

CHAPTER 14

SARRINAH

SARRINAH WATCHED AS DAVID settled back in his seat and stared into the shadows. To a casual observer, he may have appeared relaxed, but his tension screamed across the silence between them. His hands gripped the arms of the chair so tightly his knuckles were white. His thighs, while in a position of repose, clenched until she could see the ridges of his muscles through his pants. The leg farthest from her twitched so regularly it almost approached a tremor.

For long minutes, David said nothing, just looked into the flames of the candles on the table before him and breathed as if each breath was timed and deliberately executed.

"I don't know how to begin," he said.

"Tell me something about your childhood. Once we are conversing, continuing your tale will be less like jumping into icy water and more like talking to a friend." *A friend. I must satisfy myself — nay, rejoice! — that we are friends. Especially as we can never be more to each other, despite my most fervent wishes.*

At her suggestion, the muscles in David's neck slackened and he sank further into the chair. "Mom was great. We were terrific pals," he said, a smile coming to his lips. "Life wasn't easy, but Mom made everything great. She did her best to give me everything a kid could want. Well, except for a puppy, which I nagged her about relentlessly. I know now that we couldn't have afforded to feed it. We were that broke. But still, she was a great mom. I mean, one year when we couldn't afford a Christmas tree, she found a huge cardboard box – like for a refrigerator – cut it open to flatten it, then rolled it into a cone." David's hands gestured as he spoke. His smile widened and he turned his gaze toward Sarrinah, his face alight with the memory. Even without being able to envision the beauty David recalled, Sarrinah could not help but smile. "She painted it green and decorated it. I mean the whole nine yards. She stapled lights to it, and then green sparkly garland. We made homemade ornaments and hung them from the garland. For a finishing touch, we strung popcorn and draped it around the whole gorgeous mess."

Turning his head toward the candles again, he puffed out a laugh and said, "Man, I'm sure it looked terrible, but in my mind, it's the most beautiful Christmas tree I've ever had." His eyes glistened with moisture at the memory.

David's obvious happiness at the remembrance transformed her vision of the tree and created in her a piercing desire to meet the woman – or at least to watch her interacting with her son. "She sounds like a resourceful and caring woman. Do you see her often?"

David's eyes clouded, and in very different tones he said, "She died shortly after…" – he cleared his throat with a choking sound – "…after Kacey left me."

"And your father?" Sarrinah asked, hoping to deflect the subject of Kacey until he was more comfortable, more into the mode of story-telling.

David grimaced. "He left us. But not without doing all the damage he could before he went. He started by spending every dime he made trying to look like he made ten times as much:

upscale clothes, a new car, even a briefcase – although he worked in landscaping and didn't need the stupid thing. It was all about image." He sat forward and blew a long breath out from between clenched lips. "In the end, it paid off for him I guess. He found some rich widow who thought he was charming. Told my mom on the way out the door he never loved her. And didn't have any words for me. Just looked at me and shook his head like I'd disappointed him."

David stood with a sudden jerked motion and paced into the darker part of the attic. After a moment of silence he returned and stood looking at Sarrinah with a strange intensity.

"He's the reason I knew I'd never marry until I knew I'd found *the* one. Someone I loved and would keep loving. I didn't ever want to hurt somebody like he hurt my mom."

Beneath the angry façade, Sarrinah could see the deep injury his father had inflicted and wanted to weep in sympathy. "Or her son," she said softly.

David turned and lowered himself into his chair. He dipped his head so that his face was almost completely shadowed. "Yeah, or her son," he repeated. "I swore no child of mine would ever…"

He trailed off before bringing his hands up to cover his face. "Oh God," he murmured, his words muffled.

"Tell me about Kacey," Sarrinah said. She knew that there had been a child involved and sensed that this was the greater part of David's pain, but his story needed to start with Kacey.

David rocked his head back and exhaled. Directing his eyes once again toward the candles, he began talking in low tones.

"Kacey is beautiful." He directed a brief glance to Sarrinah, made a feeble gesture toward her with one hand, and said, "High cheekbones, like yours, and almond-shaped eyes, too, although hers are hazel-brown, not blue. Not that she looks like you. She doesn't. She's not as tall as you, nor quite as slim." His glance moved down her figure then back up again. "Or at least I don't think so."

He turned away and even in the low light Sarrinah could see that his face flushed with embarrassment. *Is he ashamed that he doesn't remember her figure clearly, or abashed for having scrutinized me in such a manner?*

"Anyway… she has the most delicious café au lait skin, short brown hair. She's a pixie with a come-hither smile and energy enough to go days without sleeping. A real extrovert, too. My opposite there. Ha!" He chuckled and his smile remained for several seconds before fading.

Sarrinah rang her hands together in her lap as insecurity washed through her. No one had ever spoken of her with such passion – at least not in her earshot – and the childish desire to be thought of with such exuberance blossomed alongside a stab of inappropriate jealousy. *She is his wife*, she chided herself. *You are nothing to him.* Recognizing the melodrama of her final thought, she reminded herself, *Not true. You are his friend. You've earned that much. Cherish that, as you cherish him.*

When he continued talking, it was with less enthusiasm. "As I told you when we last talked about Kacey, I was spam-and-canned-peas poor when we met, but that didn't bother her. It was one of the reasons I fell in love with her. She'd never walk out on me like my dad did, chasing the money and crapping on everybody who loves you along the way." David fell silent for long minutes, apparently lost in thought and motionless except for the rise and fall of his chest, the occasional blink of his eyes.

"What happened to cause her to leave?" Sarrinah asked. He had not yet come to the part that pained him so, and Sarrinah felt sure, even if she could do nothing else to help him, she could sympathize and share the burden of knowing the story.

"I… she…" David's voice cracked and he stopped speaking. Tears once more glistened in his eyes. He cleared his throat and said, "She got pregnant. I was as happy as I could be, and so was Kacey – at first. But then…" Again he paused and a tear escaped his eye to roll down his cheek into his sparse beard. He brought his hand up and lifted his glasses to pinch at his eyes in an effort to clear them.

Sarrinah clasped her hands together in a tight knot and fought the urge to rise and go to him. To put her arms around him and murmur soothing sounds, to stroke his hair. She had never seen a man cry until David. She had first seen him cry in the beginning, when he had just come to the house, but then she had been angry and uncaring. To see him so affected now brought her an almost palpable pain. She blinked to clear the sympathetic moisture from her eyes.

"She started asking me if I shouldn't get a short-term job. She didn't want me to give up my art forever – she believed in me – but money became more important to her once she was pregnant. I told her she sounded like my dad. I said it as a joke at first, but as the subject kept coming up, I started getting annoyed. 'I've got a show coming up,' I told her, 'I can't quit this now.' Simon had been working his butt off and had managed to get me into a boutique gallery downtown. I pictured this as my great breakthrough and I was working day and night to get ready for it. I had stars in my eyes."

David loosed a barking sound that was half laugh, half sob. "Every time the subject came up after that, I just asked her 'Aren't you getting enough to eat?' She never answered my question. How could she have? I may as well have said to her, 'This upcoming show is all that matters. Starve for all I care.'"

David's last statement was delivered in the growl of a heartless Scrooge, but Sarrinah knew it was David's guilt that spoke, his self-loathing that caused him to describe the situation in such a bitterly callous manner. Rather than allow him to continue in that vein, she prompted, "She left you because of your poverty?"

"No. I wish to God she had." Another tear fell, and when he spoke again, his voice was choked and trembling, words coming out through lips pursed tight in an attempt to maintain control.

"Instead, she miscarried. She lost the baby. Because I was selfish, I starved my wife and… killed my baby girl." He cried in earnest now, great body-shaking sobs tearing from his throat.

Sarrinah stood and moved away from him, into the darkness, both to hide her own distress, and to distance herself from the man she so wanted to take into her arms, the man she loved more tenderly every day. Every minute of every day. She wept silent tears and watched as David removed his glasses and drew an arm up to cover his eyes. From where she stood, the halo of light where David sat seemed a separate world, a miniature world mere feet in diameter, perhaps something she could reach out and hold in her hand.

We are indeed in separate worlds, and always will be. This thought caused a fresh spate of tears to flood her eyes.

After some time, David began to quiet again, and Sarrinah glided back to her chair beside him. Knowing her words were insufficient, but unable to couple the words with a gesture of comfort, she said, "I'm so sorry, David."

David wiped at his face a final time, replaced his glasses and flashed her a chagrined smile. "Yeah, well. Not as sorry as I am."

154

"You…" Sarrinah stopped, unsure if her statement would upset David further, or help him.

"Go on, you can say it. 'You self-centered, egotistical–'"

"No, I don't believe that of you. What I was going to say was, 'You must know that there are many, many reasons for the loss of a child.'"

"Sure, in 1900."

She forgave David's querulous tone and determined to answer with patience. "I cannot believe women's biology has changed so much as that since my death. And – at least in 1900 – lack of nutrition depleted the mother more than the child she was carrying." David did not answer, but hung his head lower. "Did the doctor inform you that the child – or Kacey – was malnourished?"

"I never saw the doctor. It all happened on one of the days I had buried myself in a friend's garage I was using for a studio then. Kacey swore that malnourishment was not the cause. But, I'm not stupid. It was only after her pregnancy that Kacey began worrying about money. She was worried about the baby." David swallowed and finished, "As I should have been."

"Did she blame you, as you blame yourself? Is that why she left you?"

"No, she didn't blame me. She just managed better than I did with the shock of it. We both were hurt deeply by our loss, but she stopped crying sooner than I did." David puffed out an embarrassed laugh and gestured toward himself. "Heck, I'm still doing it." He sniffed and said, "No, it was my continued depression and guilt that did it. I couldn't work. I blamed myself and my work for what happened. Simon had enough to go forward with the show but I couldn't even attend. I was a mess." David paused, seemingly lost in memories. "She finally said she'd had enough."

After another moment of silence, David inhaled a long snuffling breath to clear his nose, then clapped his hands loudly, startling Sarrinah. He turned the chair until he was facing her, and leaned forward with his arms resting on his knees. As if embarrassed at his display of vulnerability, his voice was strong and steady when he continued.

"So, to wrap up my tale of woe: After she'd gone, I had nothing left. No wife, no child, no will to work. My mother begged me to not give up my art. I promised Mom I would start again when I could, then before I could muster the energy to begin again, she was killed a car accident." David sighed heavily, and ducked his head.

"So, I dove back into my work, for her. For my mom. Too late, of course." Under his breath he murmured, "Always too late, it seems." Raising his gaze to meet Sarrinah's eyes again, and speaking at a normal volume, he said, "At that point, work seemed the only avenue away from self-destruction. With Simon's help, I became the success he always swore I would be. For years, I worked and saved, chasing the money that I didn't have when I'd needed it most. I kept thinking – hoping – that Kacey'd come back, and we'd have another chance. I kept up that hope because she never divorced me. I thought… I thought… I don't know what I was thinking. 'Love never dies' and all that stuff. And it hasn't – for me. I love her still. I always will. But, she's moved on. Found love elsewhere."

"She can't have remarried if she hasn't divorced you, or has the law changed?"

"No, she hasn't married again. But she's with a man." David must have noticed the scandalized look that Sarrinah tried to suppress, because he said, "It doesn't mean what it used to. It's quite acceptable nowadays, believe me."

Sarrinah did not answer as she tried to process and accept David's unconcern, but she could not immediately push aside her negative judgment of the matter – and, unavoidably, of Kacey. *Not fair. Not fair of me to judge Kacey when David has not.*

David stood and cast his eyes around at the darkness encircling them. Then, with an obvious attempt at humor, he said, "Come on. Ghosts may like rattling around in attics, but I'm ready to leave all this darkness behind. Besides, I'm starving." He snatched a candle from the tall chest and blew the others out. Together, they walked toward the open door at the far end of the attic and the stairwell light that shone there.

Once on the landing, David pulled the door closed and turned to Sarrinah. "I'm sorry, that wasn't much of an adventure. But thanks. It did help to talk about it. I don't promise this feeling will last until tomorrow, but it's like… it's like after you vomit. Like 'I feel so much better now.' Doesn't mean you won't be vomiting again later, but for the first few minutes at least, the purge has done you good. Have you had that experience?"

Sarrinah laughed at the ludicrous analogy. "No, I'm quite happy to say I have not, but I take your meaning nonetheless."

David chuckled and blew out the candle. He bowed in mock formality and gestured for Sarrinah to precede him down the stairs. From behind her, he said, "When you said 'conversation,' I'll admit that's not what I had in mind. So, extreme change of subject: Do you know how to make a BOLT sandwich? I have a secret ingredient that I'll let you in on…"

CHAPTER 15

DAVID

"Mmmmmm, that was good," David said as he finished his lunch in the secret garden. He tilted his head back to let the sun shine on his face.

Sarrinah laughed. "I will admit that the various sounds of epicurean pleasure you emit while enjoying food cause me to wish to sample what you are eating, but, in my time, they would have been profoundly frowned upon in polite company."

David joined her laughter as he wiped his mouth with his napkin. "I wouldn't express my delight with such noises in polite company even now." Another thought occurred to him, and he said, "I suppose that means I'm behaving rudely to you. My apologies."

"Not at all David. First of all, I'm quite certain that ghosts are not considered 'polite company.'" Her tone of amusement

160

softened as she continued, "Second, I choose to interpret your informality with me as a sign of your being comfortable with my presence."

The last statement was uttered with touching earnestness, and a shy smile played at her lips, as if she had just made an admission or expressed a hope she had meant to keep secret. Her eyes captured his and he was again struck by how beautiful she was. After a lengthy silence, he broke eye contact and said, "Obviously I am comfortable around you. I just poured my heart out to you, and did the unmanly crying thing…"

"The ability to express your pain did not detract from your masculinity, David. In many ways, it enhanced it by demonstrating you to be a creature of depth."

David met her eyes again, and felt a flush of gratitude and affection. He smiled and lifted his hand to cover hers, then remembered. *Whoa. You don't want to do that. If you've forgotten that, you're way too emotional.*

"Thanks," he said. "And thanks for listening" – he raised a finger into the air, indicating the attic – "up there." He adjusted his position in his chair, suddenly uncomfortable. He was sure Sarrinah would want to reopen the discussion and he was not ready to broach the topic of Kacey or his little girl again so soon.

Instead, Sarrinah smiled, and as if reading his thoughts, she turned her head to look around at the expanse of the garden in which they sat. "We used to play croquet here when the weather was as pleasant as it is today. With the surrounding wall, there was never any danger that a strike would send an opponent's ball down the hill."

David's relief at the change of subject washed through him as a palpable wave of relaxation. *I'm not going to avoid the topic forever, but I need the recovery time. She's one heck of a woman to understand that.* He smiled and sat back in his chair. He mimicked Sarrinah in surveying the garden and his imagination supplied a vision of gowned ladies and sharply dressed gentlemen playing the genteel game. A wistful desire to be a part of that vision made him sit forward with sudden inspiration.

"I'm pretty sure there are croquet sets in one of the basement game rooms. Why don't you teach me to play?"

"Have you never played croquet?" she asked with a surprised giggle.

"Nope."

"It's not difficult," she said, "but at least two are needed to play—"

"I'll take your shots," David said, standing, "Okay?"

Sarrinah rewarded him with another of her infectious laughs as she nodded with obvious excitement, then rose to join him.

***

The light drizzle that had started partway through the croquet lesson changed within seconds to a deluge. David's mouth opened in surprise, and he shook his head violently, much as a wet dog might. "One more shot!" he shouted and ran toward his ball. As he ran, he slipped on the wet grass, and fell to the ground. Sarrinah's giggle changed to loud laughter as David struck a pose of mock indifference, lying in the grass on one hip, upper body raised on one elbow.

He rose, and not bothering to hurry – he couldn't get any wetter – he pulled the hoops and sticks out of the lawn, then collected the mallets and balls. Sarrinah was still tittering with laughter when he joined her in the pavilion. Dropping the bag of equipment to the floor, he ran his hands over his head and down his face to clear off the dripping water. His wet clothes chilled him and his breath came in puffing bursts.

Sarrinah stood not far from him, holding her stomach and giggling. She appeared perfectly dry. His initial surprise at the fact – after all, she seemed so real in so many ways – evaporated in the next instant. *Of course.*

"Nice trick," he said, gesturing toward her, then began unbuttoning his shirt. He bared his chest, then stopped himself just as he was about to pull the shirt off. "Is this okay? I mean, I spent so long thinking of you as my imaginary friend – so no bars to my behavior, thus my appreciative moans while I'm eating – but you're not imaginary. Will I offend you if I…?" He flapped the front of his shirt in his hands.

Sarrinah ducked her head demurely and turned away from him. "This is your home, David, and I would not like you to catch cold. Please, do as you will."

"Thanks," he answered, and peeled the cold fabric from his back. *But I notice you didn't turn away until I said something*, he thought, unable to suppress a chuckle. He went to the low cabinet and pulled out a thick towel and robe. After removing the rest of his wet clothing and chafing his skin dry, he looked toward Sarrinah and found himself wondering if she could remove the gown she always appeared in. *You're perverse, David.* He pulled the robe on, and wrapped his wet things into the towel.

"I'm decent," he said. As he came along side her, he said, "That was the most fun I've had in a long time."

Sarrinah's mouth twisted in a wry grin. "You're a terrible player, David."

"Hey! It was my first time!"

"I must keep that in mind," she answered primly.

David grinned and glanced toward her. He was struck again by how beautiful she was, even in profile (in his experience, people were generally more attractive either face-on or in profile, but rarely from both perspectives). *Her beauty is just a bonus. She's also fun, and kind, and intelligent.* Then because he was conscious of his own nakedness under the robe and had so recently pondered her nudity, his eye traveled from her face to her slender neck above her lace collar, then to her breasts, then lower to her waist and hips. *If she wasn't a ghost, she'd be damned near perfect as a lifetime mate…*

David stumbled as guilt washed through him. *Kacey!*

Sarrinah turned toward him, hands extended as if to support him, then clenched her hands into fists and drew them toward her chest. "Are you unwell, David?" she asked.

"Just staggered by your unkind assessment of my croquet skills," he said. The statement was meant to be funny, but his mind swirled once again with Kacey, and the words sounded grimly serious.

"I was only teasing you, David," Sarrinah said in anguished tones. "You have many skills that—"

"Hah! Got you!" he said, jabbing a finger toward her and managing to smile. *I shouldn't feel guilty for thinking of Sarrinah. It's like feeling guilty for having a dream; it's not real. Or at least, in Sarrinah's case, not real enough. I may as well feel guilty for fantasizing about Marilyn Monroe or Princess Di.*

Sarrinah rolled her eyes and puffed out a short laugh. Apparently getting back into the spirit of playfulness that had dominated their afternoon, she said, "One of the other skills you never acquired is how to dance."

"What are you talking about? I dance!"

"I've seen what you call dance. Bizarre gyrations. At first, I thought you were having a fit."

They were just crossing the border between the arcade and the house proper. David's laughter preceded them down the long hallway. "Oh, that." He chuckled and said, "I do know how to waltz – sort of. Maybe tomorrow I'll let you tell me what I'm doing wrong, but only if you let me tutor you on the finer points of 'bizarre gyration.' Trust me, it can be quite liberating…"

***

The next weeks were some of the best in David's memory. He did not work on his wood sculpture as much as he might have otherwise, but he had lost the desperate need to fill his time doing *something*. Instead, he filled his days with Sarrinah's company and enjoyed her as he had not before.

Part of the magic of these weeks owed to the fact that he was no longer plagued with worries about his sanity – Sarrinah was not the creation of a mind on the brink of madness. Also, and against his expectations, the relief he experienced after his tearful confession in the attic did not dissipate. Yes, he still thought of Kacey, and he would never forgive himself for the loss of his daughter, but having shared the burden with Sarrinah, he was no longer tortured by sad contemplations and bottled up emotions. Instead, he talked to Sarrinah about his feelings, regrets, and memories. Her kindness and empathy at these times acted as a balm to his soul.

But, by far the biggest reason for his happiness was Sarrinah herself. She was so full of joy and verve – and she was contagious. The house often rang with their laughter as they concocted entertainments for each other, or played games that might have been mocked as childish by others. Yet with Sarrinah, David felt neither ridiculed nor ridiculous; not judged, but free.

Not that every moment was filled with frenetic activity. Over the course of two quiet evenings, they watched two movie versions of *Emma*, disagreeing on which version was best. Sarrinah far preferred the 1996 version starring Gwyneth Paltrow, while David enjoyed the modern remake, *Clueless*. He could not fault Sarrinah her preference. In fact, he honored her for her stamina in watching the whole thing because the colloquialisms in *Clueless* left her completely baffled. Her questions regarding liposuction and his attempted explanation reduced them both to tearful laughter.

During those times he did work in the studio, David explained what each tool was used for and how to utilize it, the explanations given at Sarrinah's request. Her thirst for knowledge – not just about his art, but regarding the kitchen appliances and electronic equipment (his outdated iPod was source of real pleasure to her) – seemed endless. Likewise, Sarrinah began teaching him French and also taught him (as best as she could without touching him and without the full complement of dancers) various dances she had learned as a young woman – the march in file, the chassé waltz, the quadrille and the handkerchief chase. He also learned more about the house that he had not guessed; for example, it had never been converted from gas to electricity, having had electricity installed originally – the height of modernity at the time.

There was one bit of business in which he did not involve Sarrinah: he did hire a local historian to search out Sarrinah's history, specifically asking for anything more that could be discovered regarding the circumstances of her death. He was warned that there may not be any more "story" to be discovered, and further, that the proper research could take months or years to conduct.

"Old police records, private family diaries, centuries old employment records won't be found on the internet."

David's response was succinct. "I understand. Just do it."

In answer to the warning that such thoroughness would undoubtedly be costly, David sent a ten thousand dollar advance against costs, and told the man to begin.

David discussed none of this with Sarrinah. Given her current happiness, he had no desire to plunge her back into her morose ruminations on the subject of her death. With all the time they had been spending together, he had come to truly know her and care about her, and – now, more than ever – he could not believe she had taken her life. He wanted the answer (if any answer was possible) to what he considered a mystery. Feeling somewhat guilty at ordering the investigation against her wishes, he rationalized that he need never share the results with her. Then, schooling himself not to expect updates any more frequently than once a month, he put the matter out of his mind.

Today, he and Sarrinah were spending a quiet morning in the library. The curtains were pulled back and tied, flooding the room with sunlight. Sarrinah sat at the opposite end of the couch from David, her body relaxed as she watched David with rapt attention. David had one foot up on the coffee table before them, a book open on his lap.

Once he had completed *Emma*, she had asked which book he would recommend to her. She thought it a hypothetical question because, as she noted wistfully, she could not manipulate the pages of a book. (She told him she thought she could throw open a book cover as the book lay on a table, but did not believe she could do anything more refined then perhaps ruffle the pages back and forth as they might flutter in a strong wind.)

David had been excited at the topic, however. He enjoyed many differing genres but was intrigued at the idea of introducing her to science fiction – one of his favorites. After explaining what he meant by the term, it became obvious that she would have the same difficulty understanding a science fiction story as she had had in understanding *Clueless*, so he had given up the idea. He had turned to the area of library reserved for classics in the hopes of finding something she would enjoy, and there found exactly what he was looking for.

"Have you read this?" he had asked in excited tones. "It was written before your time."

Sarrinah smiled at his obvious enthusiasm and came near to peruse the title. Reading aloud, she said, "*Frankenstein; or The Modern Prometheus.*" Shaking her head, she said, "I have not."

"This is science fiction although I'm sure it wasn't called that then. Interested?"

"Of course, but–"

David interrupted. "I'll read it to you, if you'd like."

Thus far, David had read one chapter (or letter – the book was partly epistolary) each morning. Pointing to a chapter heading at the top of the new page, he said, "We've come to the end of chapter four."

Sarrinah smiled and sighed. "'…when my creation should be complete,'" she said, echoing the last line he had read. "The next chapter promises dread and fascination. I can foresee the consummation of his efforts of creation."

"So, you're enjoying the story?" He didn't really have to ask. She seemed so eager for him to read each morning.

"Oh yes. It is not a book that would have been considered proper for a woman of my time to read. They would have condemned it as 'having a tendency to arouse inappropriate passions,' or something of that ilk. I find myself irrepressibly intrigued and more than a bit horrified – so perhaps they were right in their assessment – but I am enjoying the book."

"Good. I haven't read it in a long time myself and imagining your point of view has made it even better." David put the bookmark in and placed the book on the table. "So, what do you want to do–"

"David," she interrupted softly. She rose and glided away from the couch as if deliberately putting distance between them, then stood for a moment with her back to him. Even while admiring the vision she presented, a brief stab of worry entered his mind. Was something wrong? Was she unhappy? When she finally turned toward him, she was smiling widely and moisture shimmered in her eyes. Her long, glossy brown hair parted over her shoulders like a living cascade.

"Yes?" He stood, certain that whatever she asked of him right then, he would do it.

173

"I want to thank you. For these last weeks. For the time and attention and…," her eyes flashed downward as if shy of continuing, "…and affection you have lavished upon me. I have moments when I forget what I am, when I imagine that we…" She let her statement trail off unfinished.

"Yeah, I know what you mean. I feel the same way." Sudden passion flowed through him and he stepped forward to close the distance between them, then remembered himself. Remembered what she was – something he had repeatedly had to remind himself of for… days? A week? More? In an attempt to lighten the intimacy of the mood, he chuckled and said, "Which is to say, 'Right back at you.'" His use of colloquialisms had become a joke between them. When Sarrinah did not respond with the expected laughter, he grew serious again. "I'm saying thank *you*. I've been having a great time. I feel better than I have in years, in my body and in my mind."

Sarrinah's smile brightened – something he did not think possible – and the joy that shone in her eyes took his breath away. She inhaled and opened her mouth as if to say something, then stopped. Her eyes flashed downward, then back up, and now her smile lessened to timidity. *She's obviously shy of whatever she means to say. Confession? Some thrilling secret?* His pulse accelerated, although with trepidation or eagerness he was not sure. *Whatever you're thinking David, it's stupid. Impossible.* He took a deep breath in an attempt to steady himself.

"What is it?" he asked.

"I must tell you—"

Sarrinah was interrupted by the eight-tone scale of the doorbell – a bell which was amplified throughout the house with wireless repeaters. (David did not employ a doorman, or any other permanent staff, and so needed to be able to hear the bell even if not near the front door.)

Frustrated at the ill-timed interruption, he glanced toward the open library door, then back to Sarrinah, intending to ignore the bell. It rang again.

"Salon? Or should I go upstairs?" Sarrinah asked.

"I'm not expecting anyone," he answered unnecessarily. She knew his staff timetable and schedule of grocery deliveries as well as he did. And he wanted Sarrinah to finish whatever she meant to say. However, she was already moving toward the door, the mood broken. David sighed. "Salon, I guess."

They left the library together and walked in silence down the main hall. At the salon, Sarrinah turned away from him and he followed her far enough to pull the door partially closed. He crossed the entrance foyer, and unlocked the tall wrought iron security door, then the inches-thick main door. He pulled on the handle and the large wooden door swung open silently; despite its thickness and height, it was still perfectly balanced after all these years.

Stepping forward he said, "Can I help y–" then stopped speaking, breathless with shock. He blinked, swallowed, then blinked again at the figure standing on the front stoop. "Kacey?"

CHAPTER 16

SARRINAH

SARRINAH LINGERED AT THE door of the salon for no other reason than to catch another glimpse of David as he walked away.

When I lived, I only thought I understood love, what it meant, how it felt. It is pain and bliss combined! It is obsession. It is greed and selflessness, one balanced against the other. It is the meaning of existence, and the reason for it.

When I lived… Her thoughts inevitably turned to William. He had been sweet, kind, caring – everything she thought she wanted in a husband. She had loved him – that she could not question – but not as she loved David. *I pray William found happiness after he left this house. I hope he found a greater love, as I have.*

She sighed and turned away as David entered the foyer and left her view. Whoever the visitor was, David would not bring them to the salon. Instead of relaxing into a chair to wait for his return, the turmoil of her emotions kept her from being able to settle. She paced the length of the room from the door to the windows opposite, then turned to complete several circuits of the room, as restless as an animal caged.

Normally, she did not begrudge others coming to the house; such visits were either necessary, or pleasurable to David (as when Simon came to call), and she could resent neither a necessity nor someone who brought pleasure to her beloved.

My beloved!

However, this inopportune intrusion only heightened the chaos within her heart. After a week or more of gathering the courage, she had almost said the words, only to be thwarted by this interruption. Not that she had any plan for what she meant to say. She had intended only to lay her heart open to him.

I love you, David!

Yes, she intended to say those words, and many others besides. So many things that she could never have brought herself to say when living – not to a man who had not already expressed his intention and desire to make her his own. To do so would have been scandalous! But David… David was not of her time and she felt certain that he would not be offended or distressed by her confession. She believed this to be so even if he did not share her feelings. If that were the case, he would be kind and understanding. He would forgive her for burdening him with her unrequited affection, she was sure.

But now, she need not entertain such fears!

He admitted he is happier, healthier than he has been in years. I had prayed for but hadn't assumed he had a reciprocal depth of feeling for me! Yet while we were speaking, it became so obvious… By his words, in his eyes, in his every mannerism. Together, we have cured the heart sickness caused by Kacey, and we are free to be truly happy. He can never be healed from the loss of his child, but I do not imagine any parent ever is. What is important is that he can now continue his life, that he has learned to love again, and that he will be with me.

She laughed lightly at the disparity of her emotions between the time when David first came to this house and today. Now, the last thing she wanted – ever – was for David to leave. She wanted to share his life with him!

Sarrinah brought her hands to her mouth and kissed her fingertips, then pressed her hands to her heart.

True, my heart will break when David is no longer with me – dead and buried while I am doomed to continue for all time – but as the great poet observed, "'Tis better to have loved and lost than never to have loved at all." Oh, and I do love you, David. I would not change that for anything, no matter the suffering to come. And until then, we will be together!

Her head rang with the words crying to burst from her: That he had made her happier than she had ever been in life. That he had cleared away the melancholy and sadness that came with her wretched existence as a ghost. That he had granted her wish with his love for her.

As in life, that which I most desired has come to pass. Barring the fact that I am a ghost, I have had the most blessed of existences, and now – with David – I would not wish to be other than I am.

Giddy, but repressing the desire to spin and dance like a madwoman, she crept to the door of the salon to see if she could discern to whom David was speaking. She could hear voices, but not what was being said. No matter. David had not invited the visitor inside, and thus would soon finish his business.

She turned and made her way to the beautiful sculpture David had moved to the salon for her. She raised a hand and brushed her fingers downward to follow the waves and curves. The smooth wood did not feel as her memory and imagination told her it would have when she was living, but there was a sensation, a distinctly pleasant *something* that pushed against her fingers in response to their pressure.

At least now I can tell him the other development which I have thus far kept from him in fear of drawing him closer or causing him to dare too much. Perhaps someday… as I become still more substantial…

As she again stroked the sculpture, she leaned forward and pressed her lips against the smoothness of the curled wood. Closing her eyes, her mind filled with the imagined sensation of David someday returning her tender kiss.

CHAPTER 17

DAVID

"KACEY, IS THAT REALLY you?" Despite the evidence of his eyes, David could not believe she stood on his doorstep. How long had he dreamed of this moment?

She had changed, aged, yes, but the years had been more than kind. Her face had lost the roundness of youth, enhancing her cheekbones, and she seemed more fit than he remembered. He stepped through the door and she watched him with wide and apprehensive eyes, her lower lip caught in her teeth, obviously unsure of his reaction.

Her mouth twitched toward a lop-sided grin. "Hi, David." Her eyes flicked past him to what she could see of the interior of the house, then back to him. She lowered her head and shuffled her tennis-shoe clad feet – strange attire for Kacey, as she almost always wore high heels to compensate for her small stature.

Without raising her head, she said, "If I'm interrupting something, or unwelcome, just say so and I'll go. I only wanted to…" Her sentence trailed off and she flashed her eyes toward him again for a moment.

He pulled his gaze from her to fix on the cab that idled in the driveway behind her.

"Give me a second," he said. He walked around Kacey with slow steps, then skipped down the stairs and stuck his head through the open window of the cab. "What's the fare?"

After paying the taxi driver, he turned toward the house. Kacey was facing him, lip once again trapped in her teeth. Her arms were crossed, hands clutching her elbows as if she was fighting against a chill. She lifted one foot and used it to scratch at her opposite ankle. His eyes drank in every awkward movement.

He approached with methodical footsteps, crossing the driveway, then mounting the steps toward her. His legs trembled as if he were climbing a mountain to approach an ephemeral vision that might disappear any second.

Once reaching the top step, he continued toward her until they were quite close. She bent her head back to look into his face.

"What are you doing here?" he asked, his voice a monotone in his effort to control himself. It was the question he meant to ask – the one that was topmost in his mind – but once the words were out, he realized they probably sounded confrontational, accusatory. "I mean, what can do for you?" Even worse. Cold. He backed a step to put distance between them. "Crap, I don't know wha…" He tilted his head back and after a deep inhale and exhale, he met her eyes again. "Sorry I'm such a freakin' mess."

Kacey laughed but instead of the warm, husky laugh he remembered, it was more high-pitched and hesitant.

She's as nervous as I am.

Kacey opened her mouth to say something, closed it, swallowed and began again. "I…" She looked toward the reflecting pool and the driveway that flanked it. "You didn't have to send the cab away." She returned her gaze to David, and he saw pleading in her eyes. She said, "I wasn't sure you'd want to see me. I…"

David leaned forward and wrapped his arms around her for a brief hug. Stepping back and holding her by the shoulders, he said, "It's okay. Really." His thoughts finished what he dared not say. *You're my wife. I've fantasized about this moment, imagined showing you this house, pictured us together here.* He refrained from embracing her again, from kissing her. They were too long apart and too unfamiliar with each other for him to pretend they still had a relationship. Especially as he knew she was involved with another man.

So, why is she here?

Only one way to find out.

Making sure his voice was gentle instead of challenging, he asked her again, "So, why did you come?"

"I'm not expecting anything from you. I just… wanted to talk. To see that you're okay."

David spoke through numb lips. "I'm okay. I'm better than okay." His eyes locked with hers and his mind spun in a daze. *She's here. She's really here.* His limbs were frozen as he fought against the desire to take her hand, to brush his finger along her cheek.

The silent tableau was broken when she lowered her gaze and bit at her lower lip again. She nodded, pursed her lips, nodded again, and said, "Good. All right." Her eyes flicked toward him then away. "I guess I got what I came for then." She flashed a pained grin, then began fishing in her slouch purse. "I'll call a cab."

LOVE WHISPERS THROUGH THE VEIL

Her words woke David from his stupor. He slapped himself on the forehead and gestured toward the door. "Whoa. No, I wasn't trying to get rid of you. I just meant, 'I'm okay.'" He put a hand to the small of her back, and guided her forward, wondering as he did whether he was taking an unwanted liberty. "Really, I'd love to talk. And I'm not expecting anything from you, either. I'd like to find out how you've been. Please, come in."

Kacey allowed him to lead her, but her unsure posture and hesitant steps screamed of her anxiety. She drifted to a stop only halfway through the foyer. David turned to her to encourage her further, but her face showed astonishment, rather than trepidation. "Wow, David. I mean *wow*."

"You like it?"

A gust of laughter. "What's not to like?" She gestured down the long expanse of the main hallway. David looked down the hallway, seeing it as if for the first time himself: hardwood floors more than twenty feet wide and hundreds of feet long, broken up at intervals with area rugs, large round tables topped with enormous bouquets, sideboards and accent tables supporting statuary, two small sitting areas spaced at long intervals...

David's mind ran through various possible responses, but he settled on the humorous. Speaking in a falsetto, he said, "This old thing? Why, I only wear it when I don't care how I look."

Kacey's throaty laughter rang out, and she slapped his biceps playfully.

David's eyes snapped toward the salon door as he thought of Sarrinah for the first time since opening the front door. She would have heard the laughter. Would curiosity bring her to peer around the door? As much as he would love to introduce Kacey to her – *This is Kacey! This is who I've been talking about all this time!* – he could not envision Kacey taking the introduction well. *Hey, let me introduce you to my ghost friend. Yeah, she's hella pretty, but seriously, she just a ghost, not a girlfriend.* Especially as Sarrinah did not look particularly ghostly any longer.

When he turned back to Kacey she was still smiling, although there was a question in her gaze. "Coffee?" he asked, and began walking toward the formal living room just beyond the salon. Sarrinah would be able to listen to their conversation and later he could discuss it with her, along with the turmoil of emotions he was struggling to keep at bay.

Kacey nodded. After another exclamation of "Wow," and a slow pirouette to take in the huge room, David said, "Have a seat. I'll have the coffee ready in just a second."

"What, no staff? You handle this place by yourself?" There was no judgment in her tone, simply incredulity.

"I have a very part-time staff, cleaning crew mostly. And a chef four nights a week. I used to have them here more frequently, but" – *but for the sake of Sarrinah's freedom to enjoy the house and my desire for her company, which I can't explain to you* – "I realized I didn't need or want them around quite as much." He smiled and said, "Besides, I'm a big boy. I can make coffee."

Minutes later, he returned balancing a tray with silver coffee service and two delicate Victorian cups and saucers which had come with the house. When Kacey's eyes widened, he said, "I like getting the nice stuff out for company." She settled into a large chair and looked up expectantly.

Things certainly have changed. Last time I brought Kacey coffee, we were in a tiny walk-up. The mugs were mismatched, and mine was chipped. The thought came with simultaneous feelings of melancholy for a time long past, and pride at his changed circumstances.

He poured the coffee, then sat back to watch as she added spoonfuls of sugar and as much creamer as the cup would hold without overflowing. *So, that hasn't changed.* His mind flashed to the memory of one of their first dates. He had teased her about how much cream and sugar she put in her coffee and she had joked that her luscious creamy-brown complexion came from the coffee she drank.

Kacey sipped carefully, looking at him over the edge of her cup. "You look great, David."

"Thanks. Retirement suits me I think." He smiled, crossed his ankles, and leaned back to spread his arms across the top of the couch. *What am I doing? Preening? Do I really think after all this time and with no build up, she's going to… what? Leap into my arms again?*

His mood plummeted as the more likely solution came to mind. *She's here to ask for a divorce.* Despite his effort to maintain his smile, his expansive posture deteriorated. He pulled his arms from the back of the couch and dropped his hands to his thighs, then jerked forward and took a long draft of black coffee.

"So, the rumors are true? You've retired?" she asked.

It crossed David's mind to talk about his foray into wood sculpture, but instead he just nodded.

Kacey looked around the room again, then with raised eyebrows, said, "You've done well for yourself. I mean, I've kept track of you, so I knew you were doing well, but… wow."

David flashed her a tight smile. "Thanks." His stomach churned, waiting for her to come to the inevitable crushing request. *Just say it. Just say it and be done.*

The silence between them stretched. Kacey sipped again, then sat back, ruffled her short hair, and crossed her legs. Despite her effort at a relaxed posture, David could see her renewed nervousness in the jiggling of her suspended foot.

"You want to know why I'm here," she said.

David raised the fingers of both hands then lowered them to his thighs again. A shrug of sorts.

"You aren't making this easy on me," she said.

I'm not making this easy on you? You're killing me! David shook his head and exhaled through pursed lips. "Just say what you need to say. I'm not going to wig out on you." Despite his inner turmoil, his thoughts flashed to Sarrinah and her likely amusement with his use of the slang.

"I…" Kacey lurched to standing, walked around to the back of her chair, then turned to look at David. "I've missed you."

David blinked in surprise. He replayed the words in his mind, certain he had misunderstood what she said. A sudden buzzing in his ears almost kept him from hearing what she said next. "I've wanted to come back to you for years now, but couldn't."

David opened his mouth, then closed it again, disbelief and hope warring against each other, tangling his tongue and fogging his mind.

"I left you at a bad time, when I should have been there for you. After that, you started really making it big with your sculpture. What would you have thought of me if I came back to you then? You certainly wouldn't have believed it was for you, just *you*…" Kacey voice cracked and her mouth distorted in the familiar precursor to crying. She rushed around the chair again, dropped into it and covered her face with her hands.

A thousand responses swirled through David's mind, but he could not force the words past his lips.

Kacey sniffled, then wiped at her eyes. "When I heard you were retired, I thought…" She made a noise that was part hiccup, part sniff. "I thought maybe…" Tears cascaded down her smooth cheeks, releasing David from his frozen incredulity.

"Kacey, honey," he said, rounding the table to bring her a napkin.

She took it from him and wiped her eyes, staining the white cloth with black mascara. Gesturing toward him with the napkin, she said in a small choked voice, "Sorry."

"Don't worry about it." He stood beside her chair, unsure what to do, whether to draw her up and into his arms, or pat her shoulder, or return to his chair.

She looked up at him. "I don't know anything about your situation. You know, if you're seeing somebody. And I don't know if you even want to try… anything. To be friends even. I just thought…" Her face crumpled again and she blinked to release more tears.

"Come here honey." He held a hand out to her.

She leapt from the chair and flung herself into his arms, sobbing now, and burying her face against his chest. He could barely understand her as she spoke through her sobs. "You probably still think the worst of me. I mean, it's not like you're suddenly poor. Jesus, this house..."

"I don't think the worst of you." He petted her head and caressed her back as she continued to cry.

Finally, in a tearful whisper, she said, "I just didn't think I could stay away any longer."

David sighed, saddened for the wasted years. "You could have come back anytime. I would have welcomed you with open arms." He tightened his embrace, then bent to kiss the crown of her head. *Don't say it. Don't!* In a low voice, he said, "I've never stopped loving you."

She spoke with her face still buried against his chest, her tones high and childlike. "Really?"

"Really."

"Oh David." Her arms tightened around his waist. His shirt grew warm again with renewed tears.

They stood together for some minutes, David content merely to have her in his arms, to hold her and caress her. After a time, the sound of her crying lessened, then stopped.

"You okay?" he asked.

She nodded against his chest.

"Stay for dinner?" he asked. He released her and stepped back, holding her by her upper arms, gazing into her face hopefully. "It'll give us time to talk."

She nodded and her mouth turned up in a small, shy smile. She lifted the napkin to wipe at the mascara that coated her lower eyelids. David thought the gesture adorable, as it did nothing to remove the mascara that ran in tracks down her cheeks. Even with slightly swollen lids, her eyes were clear, sparkling with trust and gladness. David lost himself in those eyes.

She leaned in for another hug, then backed, sniffled, and said, "I'm sure you've got umpteen gymnasium-sized bathrooms in this place, but I'm just hoping for a mirror and a sink. Is there one nearby, or do you need to draw me a map?"

David's laugh rang from him, and with it, he felt the release of the tension that had cramped through him upon Kacey's arrival on his doorstep. Still chuckling, he patted his chest, then his pants pockets as if looking for something. "I've got the map around here somewhere. But you've got to be sure to bring it back or I won't be able to find the dining room."

Kacey joined his laughter, and slapped at his shoulder. "Seriously?"

"Come on. I'll lead you to the nearest bathroom."

"It's no wonder you look so great. You get all the exercise you need covering the half-mile between each room. No gym membership needed."

David laughed again, not really in response to her comment, but for the sheer joy that suffused him. He took her hand as they entered the hallway, lightheaded, amazed, happy; excited by the familiar-yet-novel sensation of her fingers intertwined with his. When they reached the bathroom, he opened the door for her, then stepped away.

Kacey caught at his arm. "David."

He turned toward her, his smile so big his face hurt. He brought a hand to her smudged cheek.

"I'm not asking for anything but another chance. Let's take it slow, okay?"

"Okay, wife," he answered, nodding agreement to her statement to take it slowly, yet dismissing her statement with the one word. *Wife.*

Her gaze dipped downward. She raised her hand, palm down, her vision following its progress as she stretched it toward him.

Her ring. She still wore his wedding ring.

CHAPTER 18

SARRINAH

As DAVID LED KACEY from the living room, Sarrinah's knees gave way, her back pressing against the slight resistance of the wall as she crumpled to the floor behind the door. Her hands clamped over her mouth, a confusion of powerful emotions swept through her.

David! She managed not to howl his name but could not contain a low moan. She lowered her hands from her mouth to clutch at her chest, her stomach, the pain of her heartbreak quite real to her.

I love you! You love me – I know it to be true! How many short minutes had it been since they had nearly professed their love for each other in the library? And now this?

How could you?

LOVE WHISPERS THROUGH THE VEIL

The accusation – while directed at David – kindled her pain into anger. But not at David. Of course not at David. Her thoughts twisted from the desolation of her heartache to anger and jealousy toward *that woman*. The woman who had so heartlessly abandoned David, causing him such grief, and now resurfaced to destroy his happiness once again. The power of her sudden fury leant strength to her, and she rose swiftly from the floor. Desperate in her need to see their continued interaction, she looked into the living room then dashed across it to the door that led to the main hallway. They were nowhere in sight. She could follow, search them out, but that might anger David. Or would it?

She ducked back into the living room clenching her jaw and her fists until they pained her. *He is mine!*

She conjured the image of Kacey – she could have done so even without catching the brief glimpse of her today, as David had shown her pictures of his wife – and cursed the woman roundly, bringing to mind every vulgarity she could muster. How dare this woman come into her house – *her house* – and attempt to divert David's affection away?

Striding briskly to the salon, Sarrinah punctuated her thoughts with a raised fist or a flinging gesture. *I will make her pay… this is my house, and I will drive her away… David is mine!* Her thoughts turned once again to their interrupted conversation in the library and the sweetness and love shining from David's eyes as they spoke. *He loves me, not you! He practically said as much!*

This last thought brought her sputtering to a halt.

Practically said as much. The thought repeated like an echo in her mind. *But he didn't say it, did he?* With slow steps Sarrinah made her way to the nearest chair on legs now wobbling with renewed weakness. *Yet, how many times has he professed his love for his longed-for wife, for his beautiful Kacey? And he has done so again, today, mere minutes ago. You heard it for yourself.*

She brought her hands up to cover her face as her tears renewed and cascaded to her bosom. *Why, David? Why? She has hurt you and caused you so much suffering. You have only known happiness in this house, with me. What can she possibly give you that I canno…?*

A hiccupped sob escaped from beneath her hands as the incontrovertible answer came even before she could finish the thought.

She is a woman of flesh and blood. She can accept and return your affection as I can only wish to. She can age and change with you as the years pass. She can be a true companion, as I can never be. A fresh spate of tears and a shuddering sigh. *And you never said you loved me. I wanted to believe you loved me. I wanted so much for you to be mine.*

Sarrinah collapsed further into the chair, her sorrow now colored by a cold self-recrimination.

'I wanted.' What a spoiled child I have been — am being. I have proclaimed that, with David and for the first time, I truly understand love. Yet at the first test, instead of considering my beloved and his desires, I am wailing like a babe and declaring 'I want.' And it is true. I want David. I want David to love me. I want to share the whole of his life. But more than this, I want his happiness, even at the expense of my own.

For long moments, Sarrinah's mind was so awash with a miasma of despair and pain that she could string together no coherent thought and she gave herself over to unchecked weeping. Some unknowable time later, the tears finally lessened and she released the last with a tremulous sigh.

I never thought to feel such sadness again. At least not for many, many years, not until the end of David's life. But what right have I to happiness? It is far more appropriate to my condition that I suffer. And so I shall. Kacey can give David what I never can: physical affection.

A traitorous remnant of selfishness fanned an ember of hope in response: *But perhaps I can, with time! I grow more substantial every day!*

Sarrinah quashed the spark to ash. *No. David deserves a living, breathing woman. Someone with whom he can create a family. Even should Kacey leave this house today and never return, he deserves more than I can ever give him. Thus will I prove the truth of my declaration of love. I will farewell David, and then truly begin my existence as a ghost in this house.*

***

The salon had been dark for several hours when Sarrinah was roused from the motionlessness of a wallowing grief by David shouting her name. His exhilaration was evident in the brisk footsteps approaching the salon from the direction of the foyer.

"Sarrinah!"

As David entered the dark room and made his way to a lamp, Sarrinah straightened from her slouched position in the chair. She was smoothing the skirts of her dress over her thighs when the light flared to life.

David's immense smile faltered. "Are you okay? I mean, I don't guess you could be sick…?"

Sick at heart, it is true. "I was… sleeping." Sarrinah attempted to bend her mouth into a smile.

"Oh. I never thought… I'm sorry. We can talk tomorrow." He reached for the lamp to switch it off.

"Nonsense, David. I am quite willing to talk with you now." *This conversation must be had, and the sooner the better if I am to have any peace of mind.* She stood to emphasize her readiness, then moved to the lounge she favored, motioning to a chair opposite. She pressed her mouth into what she hoped was a more convincing smile.

David stood for a moment, looking at her uncertainly, but then his excitement overcame any reluctance, and his smile grew to its original proportions. He flung himself in the proffered chair and leaned forward, hands on his knees.

"That was Kacey. I mean, obviously. What do you think? Did you listen?" The questions were asked rapid-fire and Sarrinah's mouth twitched toward a genuine smile at David's boyish enthusiasm.

"I listened to your conversation in the living room. I thought it inappropriate to listen further. I am happy for you, David, especially as it is evident the rest of her visit went well for you."

David's brow furrowed in what seemed disappointment – that she hadn't listened in on their conversations? or perhaps the tepidness of her response? – but then his expression cleared and he threw himself back into the embrace of the chair.

"Yeah, it did go well. She wants to take it slow and it took everything I had to agree with her. Not that I do. I don't say she should move in tomorrow or anything, but…" David shrugged his shoulders in an exaggerated manner and laughed with real mirth. "She hasn't changed a bit. And she said she missed me. Or maybe you heard that much. Anyway, tonight was just dinner. Nothing fancy, just my spaghetti and cheesy garlic bread – she loved the kitchen, by the way. She's agreed to come back tomorrow night for one of chef's feasts and the grand tour." David punctuated his last words by making quotation marks in the air with his fingers. "We got a lot of talking in and it killed me not to tell her about you, but

I don't want to scare her off on the first night, right?" David chuckled again. "I figure we can–"

"David." Sarrinah swallowed around a tight throat and kept her eyes from watering through sheer force of will.

"Yeah? Oh, sorry. I've just been babbling. I suppose where you're concerned, you'll have your own ideas about how to do this, but I was thinking–"

"David."

David closed his mouth and threw a chagrined smile in her direction. "Right. I'm doing it again. Shutting up now." He pressed his lips together with the fingers of both hands.

Sarrinah gave a soft chuckle. "You're not nearly as handsome with a fleshy duck bill instead of a mouth."

The corners of the duck bill rose into a grin but he did not release his lips.

Clearing her throat, Sarrinah continued. "Kacey need never know about me. I will be leaving you – both – in peace."

The expression of surprise on David's face as his hands fell away and his mouth dropped open was almost worthy of laughter, but she could not manage it.

"What? Why?" David sat forward, palms raised in inquiry. "How? I thought you said you couldn't leave the house."

"Sadly, I cannot–"

"Sadly?" David's explosive repetition was tinged with exasperation or injured feelings.

Sarrinah sighed before continuing. "I cannot leave the house, but as we have previously discussed, this house is quite large enough for three people to live comfortably without ever having to see one another." When David did not respond other than to stare at her with mouth agape, she continued. "And you needn't worry about restricting your – or Kacey's – movement about the house. I am quite adept at moving unseen through the servants' passages and stairways. I will relinquish the salon and–"

"Why? Why are you doing this?" David looked genuinely pained.

Sarrinah sighed again. "David, you are not making this easy on me."

"You're the second person to say that to me tonight. Why is it that just when I feel like I'm the one getting kicked in the teeth,

I'm told *I'm* not making it easy? Well, I'm glad I'm not. So answer my question. Why?"

"First, there is no reason to test Kacey's credulity, or her patience. I have no wish to endanger your renewed relationship." Sarrinah ignored David's eye roll. "Second, you deserve a normal life, and need not be burdened–"

"You're not a burden! You're my friend." Sarrinah opened her mouth but David waved a hand at her and said, "I don't want to hear it. Just listen. I love this house. I did when I first saw it. But now, thanks to you, being here is an important part of my life. *You* are an important part of my life." David panted in his vehemence, only now giving Sarrinah a chance to speak. She could not. Her mind was circling on his words, clinging to the sweet sentiments with a forlorn and useless hope.

"Besides," David continued, apparently having seized on another avenue of argument. He stood abruptly and gestured vaguely around the room. "This is your house – maybe more than it is mine – and I'm not going to allow you to exile yourself in some grand gesture." He nodded once in emphasis of having made his point and dropped to sitting once more.

"David, I…"

"Sarrinah, please. Don't just disappear on me. Don't take my only friend from me on the same night I have gained the hope of winning my wife back."

I'm not your only friend. You have Simon. Sarrinah did not voice the words. It seemed a feeble point even in her own mind.

David lowered his head, then raised it again to look at her with pleading eyes. "Look. Kacey wants to take it slow. Let's do that, you and I. We'll take it slow, and figure out a way for this all to work out. Okay?"

If I had any strength, I would disappear from his life now, this evening, but in the face of his pleading – and my own selfish desires… Racked with sadness and guilt, but also relieved that she would not – yet – need to give up her beloved, she nodded.

David sighed loudly and flopped back into his chair. "Thank you, Sarrinah. You've made me very happy."

Your happiness is all I want, despite the fact that were I not already deceased, this would kill me.

CHAPTER 19

DAVID

"THE END," DAVID SAID, and closed the book. Lost in his own melancholy thoughts, he did not raise his head to look at Sarrinah. Not only had he just closed the book on *Frankenstein*, but also – at least for a time – on the pleasure of these quiet mornings reading aloud to her.

Less than a month since the day Kacey had appeared on his doorstep, she had finally consented to moving into the house. The boxes containing her bedroom and bathroom effects had already arrived, and she would be bringing the last of her clothing in the afternoon. David was delirious over this happy development, but – until he found a way to explain Sarrinah to Kacey – it did put an end to his ability to engage freely with his dear friend.

David was drawn from his musing by Sarrinah's low voice, quoting from the end of the book. "'I shall die, and what I now feel be no longer felt… My spirit will sleep in peace.'" She sighed. "The monster is a vile creature, yet pitiable in the end. I hope his presentiments about the afterlife are true for him. If so, then he is also enviable."

"You can't mean–" David began, but Sarrinah's eyes flashed to his and the challenge there kept him from finishing. Struck anew by the hopelessness of her situation, his throat tightened in sympathy. "I see, yes. I imagine… no, I really can't imagine, can I? I'm so sorry." Swallowing to clear the rasp that had entered his voice, he said, "I know it can't mean anything, but I'm happy you're here."

The challenge in her eyes softened. "That means more than you can possibly know, David."

The sad sweetness of her smile wounded him. Her husband, William, had been a lucky man. It distressed David that Sarrinah – for some incomprehensible reason – had been made to suffer as she did. The silence stretched as they gazed at each other. "I wish there was something I could do, something that could be done, to help you… go." Not wanting her to misinterpret his meaning, he added quickly, "To go wherever it is you should have gone, deserve to have gone."

She shuddered as if in attempt to shake off her melancholy. Her smile changed to a teasing grin and she said, "Would you be rid of me if you could be?"

"No! No, I meant—"

Sarrinah's beautiful laughter rang out, and the room seemed to brighten, as though the sun had emerged from behind a cloud.

What if there is something that can be done? He had hired the historian for his own peace of mind, but… *What if the man could solve the mystery? What if she didn't suicide? What if her reason for being here isn't some aspect of eternal torment, but because of a need that the "truth" about her death be known?* As much as he hoped this was true, he was struck with a pang at the idea of losing her. But how could he do otherwise?

Without thinking further he voiced his thoughts. "What if there is something that can be done? What if—"

Sarrinah's smile fled to be replaced with an emotionless expression. "Nothing can be done, David." She stood and paced away from the couch.

"Hear me out. Hypothetically, what if–"

She spun on him. "Nothing can be done. Why engage in speculation that can only raise false hopes and ultimately add to my misery?"

I hadn't thought of that. That would be cruel.

The tableau held until the clock on the mantelpiece issued a series of soft melodious gongs. Sarrinah closed her eyes in a long blink and released a lengthy exhale.

"Can we agree, I beg you, not to broach this subject again? Not ever? I treasure your desire to assist me, to act the part of my shining hero, but believe me when I say that entertaining a pointless hope will only make my decades… or centuries… or *millennia* even more difficult to endure."

David dropped his head in chagrin.

"Please?" she said.

He nodded. "Sorry."

In a more cheerful voice, she said, "Thank you. Instead of arguing, what I would most like is to enjoy our final hours of freedom before your beloved arrives."

David forced a smile. He hadn't meant to upset Sarrinah, and as glad as he was with his renewed relationship with Kacey, it did mean the end of… *It will be the end of nothing. I'll still have time to hang out with Sarrinah. Just not as much time, and having Kacey back in my life will more than make up for that.* "Your wish is my desire. What do you want to do?"

Sarrinah's answering smile brightened but did not erase the sadness in her eyes. "Perhaps we can decide while strolling the secret garden in this lovely weather."

The secret garden. With a stab of regret, he realized that – until Kacey was on board with the idea of Sarrinah sharing the house – Sarrinah would no longer be able to enjoy the garden. It was visible from both the dining room and the residential wing upstairs, the two areas of the house most likely to be used by Kacey.

Now more than ever, he wanted to find a way to help Sarrinah. He had Kacey back in his life again, and Sarrinah – as much as he would miss her – deserved peace. He rose to join Sarrinah for their walk and made a mental note to check later with the historian for an update.

***

"Hey Baby!" Kacey stood on the front stoop, two garment bags slung over one shoulder and the other hand on the handle of an oversized suitcase. Behind and to the side of her sat six brightly logoed shopping bags stuffed full of shoes. A tower of three boxes stood to the side of the entrance.

David laughed and raised a hand in thanks to the taxi driver who was just reentering his cab. "Let me get those," he said, and stepped forward to take the garment bags from her. He leaned down for a quick kiss then took an exaggerated look around at the bags and boxes. "I didn't think your hotel room was big enough to hold this much clothing."

Kacey laughed as she pulled the suitcase past him to enter the house. "Didn't silly. I went shopping. It's not like that spare room you call a closet won't hold six times this much." Turning back to look over her shoulder at him, she said suggestively, "I got a special something I'd like to show you later." David's pulse increased to match the tick-tick-tick of her ankle-strap high heels on the foyer floor. His eyes moved from her shoes to her taut calves, to her skinny capri pants and up to her shapely rear as it swayed with each step.

She turned and seeing that he hadn't moved from the doorway, stopped, favoring him with a knowing smile and raised eyebrow. "You coming?"

David chuckled at himself and hung the garment bag on the wrought iron security door, then stepped outside to bring the boxes and bags inside. Once again slinging the garment bags over his shoulder and hoisting three bags of shoes, he said, "Right behind you."

He glanced toward the open salon door as he passed, even knowing he would not see Sarrinah. They had parted at his studio when the doorbell rang, she declining to follow him even part of the way to the entrance. Not knowing when they could contrive to meet again, a pall of angst had engulfed him during the long walk to the front door, only to be lifted by Kacey's exuberant greeting.

As he came abreast of Kacey, she flashed a smile at him and said, "I'm so happy, Baby. I've dreamed of this day for so long." She glanced around to the walls, the ceiling, her gaze seeming to encompass the whole of the house. She laughed as her eyes returned to his. "And now I'm here – with you." She stopped and raised her face for a kiss.

"I love you, Kacey," he whispered against her mouth before complying with her unspoken request, all thoughts of his melancholy parting from Sarrinah banished.

Once in the bedroom, David put his load on the bed and turned to get the remainder.

"Come here, mister," Kacey said. She jiggled and danced across the space that separated them, then squealed as she leapt into his arms. "You happy I'm here?"

"Definitely. And sorry for all the time we lost." He leaned in to deliver a soft, slow kiss. "And I do want to talk about, you know, what happened."

Kacey's excited expression did not change. She grabbed his head and kissed him on the nose, then wriggled from his arms. "Yeah, of course, Baby. But not tonight. Tonight we're having fun." She danced back toward her suitcase and began pushing it toward the dressing room. "Would you mind getting the other stuff? Pretty please with a cherry on top? I'll get started with this if that's okay?"

David smiled at her energetic antics. "Yeah. Be right back."

"Thanks Baby. You're the best." She blew him a kiss and pushed the suitcase further then squealed again as she entered the dressing room.

Shaking his head and chuckling, he left her to her fun.

***

David awoke early, the room only just beginning to lighten with the dawn. He smiled at Kacey's sleeping form and kissed her shoulder before rolling out of bed. He slipped on jammie pants and a t-shirt before tiptoeing from the room – not because he eschewed nudity, but because he was going in search of Sarrinah and she would certainly find his nudity improper. He had not caught so much as a glimpse of Sarrinah in the three days since Kacey had moved in. As Kacey often slept in, he might have hours to spend with Sarrinah this morning, reading, talking… anything.

It's crazy to worry about how she's doing, but I am.

He padded down the short hallway to his studio and glanced around hopefully. Poking his head into the hallway to the back rooms, he said, "Sarrinah?" He kept his voice low even knowing that Kacey wouldn't hear him. "Are you here? Sarrinah?"

The next most logical place to look for her was the salon. Instead of taking the main staircase, he took the back stairs hoping to meet her there. On the way to the salon, he called her name as he stuck his head in the various other rooms on the first floor. He was walking briskly by the time he reached the salon, his excitement mounting at the idea of finding her there.

"Sarrinah?"

His enthusiasm deflated as his eyes flashed around the empty room. "Dammit," he murmured and spun to cross the wide hallway to the billiard room.

"David."

"Sarrinah!" He slowed from his jog, and took slow, strolling steps toward the foyer where she stood, smiling shyly, her hands fiddling with her skirt.

"You were in the office?" Approaching with unhurried steps, he was surprised at the warm tenderness in his voice.

"The basement," she answered, turning to gesture to the stairs at the side of his office.

"Is that where you've been hiding?" His smile faded at the thought. The basement seemed an unpleasant substitute for the main part of the house, especially as the lounges there were less comfortably furnished or decorated.

"Or the attic."

His mouth fell open at the appalling idea. Until now, he had imagined her wandering the halls of her beloved home, always just out of sight, or relaxing in the salon. "That's not necessary. This is your home–"

"Your and Kacey's home, David."

He could think of no response because, yes, he did think of it as their house, too. Still, he couldn't stand the thought of Sarrinah spending time in the dark and cobwebby attic. *I've got to figure out a way to talk to Kacey about Sarrinah.*

Sarrinah flashed him a pained smile. "Please don't look so affronted. Basements and attics are the proper venues for ghosts, I should think."

"I disagree," he snapped. Then realizing that his tone was rising toward argumentative – and he did *not* want to argue with Sarrinah – he smiled and said, "Well, in your case, I disagree." He reached toward Sarrinah in an impulse to touch her arm, then dropped his hand to his side. They stood in awkward silence until he gestured to the salon. "Can we talk?"

The uncertainty fell away from Sarrinah's face and she graced him with a genuine smile before crossing the hallway. He followed and took the chair opposite her, noting that even with the early morning daylight silhouetting her, she looked quite solid.

"I've missed you – talking to you," he said.

"Aren't you happy, David?"

"Oh, yeah, ecstatic. Kacey's great."

"Then…?" Sarrinah maintained her smile, but the dazzle had gone out of her eyes.

"I… she…" He laughed and said, "Her interests and mine don't always coincide. Not that they have to. It's just that she's not much of a reader. She's too energetic."

"You are energetic."

"Not to her level, believe me. It's exhausting sometimes." He laughed. "My point is, she's not much of a reader, and I am. As are you. Then, too, she's not much into art–"

"How can she not be?" Sarrinah pointed to his wood sculpture on the side table.

219

"No, I didn't mean *my* art. She's always supported my sculpture – although she's not sure she's crazy about my wood sculpture, to be honest." David chuckled in response to Sarrinah's scandalized look. "Don't misunderstand me. She likes it herself, but she's uncertain about the viability–"

"Oh, David!"

He laughed again. "I'm doing this badly. She's fine with my woodwork. I'm just trying to explain that in some ways she and I are different. She's an extrovert who likes to go out on the town, and I'm a homebody." Then with an impetuous grin, "Which is another way you and I are alike, seeing as how you never go out either." When Sarrinah still looked doubtful of his explanation, he continued. "I'm happy with Kacey. Truly, I am. I'm only trying to explain why I've missed talking with you. You've spoiled me by giving me an outlet for engaging in interests outside of my relationship with Kacey. Does that make sense?"

Sarrinah gave him a hesitant nod.

"I like you, I enjoy your company and I've missed you. That's all I'm saying."

"Thank you. You're very kind. In return I will admit that I have missed your company as well. Very much."

"I'll find a way to talk to Kacey about you. You'd like her. And she'll like you. How can she not? You're by far the nicest ghost I've ever met." David laughed, and Sarrinah giggled at his silliness.

"Very well. I am happy to oblige you. We shall converse. Tell me how you've been." Sarrinah relaxed back into her chair.

"I will. But first, I don't know how long we'll have this morning, so I want to tell you an idea I've had." In answer to her welcoming gesture, he said, "Kacey, as I've mentioned, likes to go out – she's got loads of friends. Any day now, I'm sure, she'll be trying to cajole me into something, but she's also used to me ducking out on these things. So, whenever I know she's due to be out, I'll leave you a note…" – he looked around – "…over there in the left-most cubby of the writing desk. Then, we can meet at the agreed time, instead of me having to roam over the entire house yelling your name. Does that work?"

She looked toward the desk. "Yes. If that's what you wish, David. But you needn't feel you must–"

He interrupted her with a shushing gesture. "Now you're just fishing for compliments. I already said I want to. And this arrangement won't be for long, just until Kacey–"

"I fear you may be overestimating Kacey's ability to accept my presence."

"Nah. She's great. Really. She'll think it's cool. A ghost in the house and all that."

"If you think so, David." She sighed uncertainly, then shrugged to dismiss the topic. Brightening, she said, "Tell me how you've been spending your days."

They talked for an hour before Kacey's voice could be heard coming from the direction of the main staircase. "David? You in the kitchen? David?"

David and Sarrinah both rose swiftly, Sarrinah moving to stand behind the door. "I'll see you soon," David whispered, smiling and winking as he left the room. From the hallway, he yelled, "In the office. Want breakfast?"

CHAPTER 20

SARRINAH

THE RELAXED BUZZ OF pleasure that had suffused Sarrinah during her conversation with David left her in the instant of his shout to Kacey. Unlike David, Sarrinah did not feel confident that Kacey would readily accept Sarrinah's presence in the house, nor did she feel the woman would tolerate David sharing his time and attention. Despite saying otherwise, David's white lie – *office*, rather than *salon* – reflected his own underlying doubt.

Worse, the secrecy of their meeting – including the notes that David intended to leave for future secret assignations while Kacey was out of the house – smacked of gross impropriety. The flash of alarm that crossed David's face when Kacey called to him increased this impression. *I feel I am the hidden mistress of a married man – despite the lack of a physical relationship. It is a situation I would have abjectly rejected when living. I reject it now!*

Yet, could she? Could she deny David when he so clearly sought her out and seemed so pleased by her company? This justification rang hollow, just as it would have done had she been a flesh and blood woman he was seeking to meet outside of his marriage.

Sarrinah rounded the door and peered down the long hallway. She could see nothing of David or Kacey. *They're likely in the kitchen. Or they've gone up. I'll be in no danger of discovery if I linger.*

She walked slowly about the room she loved, focusing on the tabletop vases, the feminine knick-knacks placed artfully amongst the books on the bookshelves, the soft hues of the accent cushions on the lounge and chairs. She passed the writing desk and felt a stab of excitement as her gaze fell on the left-most cubby – *he'll put his notes there* – before the excitement was smothered by a corresponding guilt. Approaching the side table, she lifted a hand to run her fingers along the curled wood carving she so loved, first and foremost because it was beautiful, but also because she considered it David's gift to her. Especially as he had moved it to the salon just to please her. The sensation of the smooth wood sliding under her fingers – a sensation that was strengthening to near normalcy – gave her a sensual pleasure.

And if David is correct? If Kacey accepts my presence here as well as my friendship with David? What then? Her thoughts could proceed no further because she could not make herself believe it possible.

Turning to a different avenue of thought: *What if Kacey's return does not last? What if the incompatibility David hinted at today causes a renewed breach of their relationship?* She suppressed the thrill of hope that coursed through her. Her thoughts spun through various scenarios before arriving at the inescapable conclusion. *Even so, David deserves a living woman to share his life with. For me to imagine or hope otherwise is selfish, even if the greatest of my heart's desires.*

Dropping her hand from the carving and sighing heavily, she walked toward the doorway into the main hall. *I will wait for his note, and I will meet with him as he asked. And at that meeting, I will break with him. He says my friendship makes him happy, but it is a shallow and unimportant enjoyment. Our continued liaison will ultimately lead to his unhappiness.*

LOVE WHISPERS THROUGH THE VEIL

After a quick glance, she crossed the hall to make her way to the billiard room and the hidden door there that led to the servants' stairs.

***

Despite her resolution to restrict herself to the basement (or better still, to the attic), after a week – with only infrequent forays to the salon to check for David's note – boredom overtook her. Before Kacey's arrival, her days had been filled with conversation and activity, affection and enjoyment, so much so that she had stopped wishing for the peace of her previous mindless oblivion. Were it not for her love of David – and the impossibility of achieving mindlessness with two life forces in the house – she would long for it now.

Unable to tolerate another moment of tedium, she came to a decision. Incapable of simply fading away, she would instead take advantage of her increasing substantiality to alleviate her boredom. Being now essentially a material entity made sneaking about the house more difficult because she had a greater chance now of creating a noise – walking on a creaking stair tread, or knocking against a table in her haste to cross a room – but she had also gained the dexterity to affect her surroundings as she never had been able.

Today, having entered the salon to check for a note from David, she crossed to the side door leading to the formal living room, with the plan to go through the living room to the library for a book. Sudden footsteps in the hallway froze her for a breathless moment. Heart beating in her chest, she slid behind the door and pulled it closer to her.

"There you are." David's warm voice. From the sound of it, he had just entered the living room. Was he talking to her? Had he seen her entering the salon? She was on the verge of stepping out of her hiding place and into the living room, when Kacey's voice stopped her.

"Hey Baby. Yeah. Just hanging out."

Lord have mercy! I had no idea Kacey was in the living room. I nearly walked into the room without checking. I must be more cautious in the future!

Kacey again, with an apparently irrelevant comment: "This room is as big as a ball court."

"What are you fiddling with there?" David asked. More footsteps, the unmistakable sound of a kiss, then a chuckle from

David. "A bowl of glass balls? What's so fascinating about these, in particular?"

"I… they're pretty." Kacey's words were without enthusiasm and Sarrinah imagined her shrugging as she said them.

David laughed again. "You're bored. I get it. And I don't blame you. I'm a boring kinda guy."

"Stop! You're not." More kissing sounds.

"Why don't you get out of here? You know I could go a month without leaving the house for more than walks through the gardens, but hey, that's not you. Go see your friends. Have a night on the town, dinner all that. You know I don't mind."

"I don't need to, Baby. Don't want to. I told you, I've changed. I was just trying to give you some space. You were working on your sculpture, so I decided to do some exploring, that's all."

"Well, I'm taking a break. Want some lunch? We can make it a picnic. I still have some of the curried shrimp salad and I'll make up some tea sandwiches…?"

"Picnic sounds nice. I'll hunt us down a blanket." Her voice gained enthusiasm. "And I'll bring my phone and a speaker so we can have music. Maybe we'll dance through wild flowers like crazy people."

David's chuckle. "I'll pack us a cold Chablis."

Their voices moved from the living room to the hallway. A voyeuristic curiosity gripped Sarrinah, for she had not witnessed many interactions between David and Kacey, instead assiduously avoiding them. Holding her breath, she eased her body around the door, and after confirming the living room was empty, dashed across it to listen to their continued conversation. Hearing nothing, Sarrinah peeked around the doorframe, then yanked her head back inside. They were locked in a passionate kiss at the foot of the main stairway, Kacey standing up one step. A surge of bitter jealousy stabbed through Sarrinah, then self-admonishment. She knew they had broken from their embrace when she heard David's heavier footsteps moving down the hall toward the kitchen.

"David?" Kacey's voice.

"Yeah?" Sarrinah heard him approaching once more.

"How's your sculpture going? I mean, what did Simon have to say about it?"

"Not much," David answered. "Why?"

"Well, what does he think about the potential of—"

"I haven't gotten there yet. Right now, I'm doing this for me."

"Sorry, yeah. No, that's great." Silence, then Kacey's voice again, in excited tones that – to Sarrinah – sounded like forced cheerfulness, "Meet you in the kitchen, Baby."

***

Much as she envied the thought of accompanying David on a picnic, Sarrinah was thankful for the hours David and Kacey spent away from the house. Until the unexpected opportunity of their absence, her only plan had been to find a book to read; she needed something to fill her time and draw her mind away her from her ruminations on David. She was determined to break with him – for his own eventual happiness. But, with nothing to do other than to roam the attic (or worse, to sit in the darkness undistracted by the flotsam collected there), her thoughts turned to endless imaginings of how she might still continue to be part of his life. The relentless back-and-forth between heartbreak at the coming loss and hopeful fantasies of the future was maddening.

Rather than being reduced to the tearful, self-pitying woman she had been since her death, she took action.

When she was certain they had gone, she went to the library for the book. She chose *Treasure Island*. She had never read it – it had never caught her interest as it was reputed to be an adventure story for young boys – but David recommended it. She was dashing from the library when the thought occurred that she need not hurry.

Indeed, I need not limit myself to one book. In point of fact... A new plan sprang to mind and she immediately began its implementation.

By the time David and Kacey returned from their outing, Sarrinah was once more ensconced in the attic, one small area of which had been transformed in their absence. Without fear of rousing anyone's interest with the sound of furniture scraping across the floor boards, she had cleared the corner farthest from the door, swept the area free of dust and cobwebs, and dragged a large rolled carpet to cover the area. Once unrolled, it proved stained and contained two large sections that were threadbare, but it would suffice. She added a chair, a side table, and small chest that would serve as a footstool. (She had wanted the rocking chair but was afraid the rocking would alert someone to her presence in the attic.)

Having accomplished this much, she went to the closet on the third floor and collected candles, candlesticks, and one of the magic lighting wands stored there; David had explained the mechanism, but it still seemed a magical device. She dithered for some time over the propriety of taking the carving from the salon – from David's comments, Kacey would not miss it – but decided against going so far.

Satisfied with her efforts, Sarrinah used the remaining time of their absence ordering her alcove to her liking. She pulled aside the heavy drape from the dormer window, and wiped down the glass. *Sunlight enough to read by during the day!* She moved her chair to best take advantage of the light. She even went so far as to lean a pleasing painting of a pastoral scene against a tall wardrobe that conveniently blocked any view of the transformed corner from the attic entry, then used furniture drapes to better enclose and disguise the area. Pleased with the arrangements, she was nonetheless too excited to settle to reading. Instead she explored the attic, randomly opening drawers, cabinets and chests; her search was rewarded with the discovery of a complete deck of cards with which she could play Patience.

She shuffled the limp playing cards as she crossed the dark attic to her alcove. *I should show David how to play. He loves learning new…*

The gloom of the attic returned as she recollected her painful resolution. *I cannot. I must let David go.* The energy that had powered her exertions over the last hour fled between one stride and another. Reaching her alcove, she abandoned the playing cards, sank to her seat, and lifted *Treasure Island* from its place atop the stack of books near her chair. Before beginning to read, her eyes drifted about the small space she had transformed.

My new home. For as long as David may live. A pained sigh. *I love you, David. How much, you will never know.*

CHAPTER 21

DAVID

WHEN DAVID ENTERED THE bedroom, he found Kacey sitting against the headboard, smiling at something on her laptop. "Whatcha doing?"

Kacey transferred her smile to David, closed the laptop, pushed it off her lap and shrugged. "Nothing really. You know, email and stuff." She slid down to prop herself on her side. "Done for the day?"

"Yeah. I need to shower off the sawdust. Don't want to sleep in it." He pulled his T-shirt over his head.

"Mmm. The sight of you makes me hungry." She stretched out on her back, arching and wriggling seductively.

David laughed. "Shower first." At the doorway into the dressing room, he paused. "Sorry for the subject change – and I promise to let you redirect me – but I'm trying to plan for dinner. Are you hungry?"

"For food?" Another wriggle. "Not really."

"Okay... I'll limit dinner to a salad. How about topped with steak and a bleu cheese vinaigrette? It won't take long to fix so we'll have plenty of time for" – he dropped his pants – "other entertainments before dinner."

"Chef's not working again tonight? You really ought to bring him in more. You shouldn't have to cook all the time."

"I like to cook."

Kacey pushed herself to a sitting position. "I know, Baby, and it's a good thing you can. You know I'm useless."

"Not useless." He crossed the space between them to deliver long, slow kiss. He panted in the aftermath and said, "I'll be right out. There's more than one way to cook and your way's a lot more fun."

***

Later that evening, David entered the dining room, two large salad plates in hand, then whistled in appreciation. The chandelier was unlit and the area around the end of the table was covered in dozens of candles of all shapes, sizes and colors.

Candelabras of long white tapers covered the serving buffets and

hutches around the room as well as being placed at intervals the

length of the long dining table. Kacey, wearing nothing but a short

silk robe and high heels, pulled his chair out for him as he

approached.

"You like it?" she asked.

"It's perfect." He kissed her before placing their plates.

Smiling, she slid into her chair, then bent toward the salad.

"Smells yummy."

David reached for his napkin, only then noticing the fancy

fan-shaped folded napkin emerging from his wine glass. "Where'd

you learn to fold napkins?"

"Googled it," she answered. His mind flashed to Sarrinah's

initial misunderstanding of the term and he chuckled. Pulling her

napkin from her glass, she asked, "You like it?"

The question – even once – was uncharacteristic. "Yeah, I

like it." He watched Kacey as she stabbed a forkful of seared filet,

rolling her eyes with an expression of ecstasy as she brought it to her mouth. "What's up, Kacey? 'You like it? You like it?' Twice in two minutes. What are you worried about?"

She lowered her fork and placed her hand on his. Leaning toward him, she said, "I just want you to be happy I'm here, Baby. No second thoughts, you know."

David barked out a laugh, then stifled it when Kacey threw him a wounded pout. "I'm happy you're here. We aren't a couple of teenagers living together on a trial run or something. We've done this before."

"Yeah…" Kacey stretched the word out and left it hanging between them.

But it didn't end well. Is that what she's not saying? Well, I'm not the one who left. David suppressed the defensive thought with an internal shudder. *Or is this her way of warning me? "I'll leave again if you don't stay happy." Or worse yet, does she feel it's her "job" to keep me happy… because she sees me as some fragile person who'll relapse into depression at the drop of a hat? I had good cause!*

David inhaled deeply, surprised at the underlying tone of anger to his thoughts. He pulled his hand from beneath hers, then reached for her shoulder and squeezed lightly.

"I think we should talk about that."

Kacey blinked, her expression blank. David thought back to what had been said aloud and realized that she might not understand the segue.

"I think we should talk about the baby we lost," he clarified.

Kacey softened immediately and brought her hand up to sandwich his against her shoulder. "Let's not go there again, Baby. It's done, we can't change it. There's no point in–"

"I think it's important. First, I want you to know where I was emotionally–"

"We talked ad nauseam about it then." She dropped her hand and rearranged the napkin in her lap, tension obvious in the sudden rigidity of her posture.

"–and how far I've come since then. With the help of a friend, I…" He trailed off as he thought of Sarrinah, her kindness and patience with him. Then, instead of completing his sentence, he softened his voice and said, "Second, I thought we should talk about whether you'd be willing to give it another try."

Kacey's posture relaxed and she met his eyes with a soulful expression. David smiled and leaned toward her, certain he knew her answer, ready for the kiss that would follow.

"Let's give it some time, Baby. Okay?"

David blinked in hurt surprise. "We're not getting any younger–"

Kacey interrupted, caressing his cheek as she spoke. "I know, Baby. I mean, I think it's a great idea – I do – but let's give it some time. Not a lot. Something like six months. Not a lot. I only just moved in. Let's give *us* some time. That's all I'm saying. Okay?"

She's not saying no. And she's right. Given the emotional rollercoaster I've been on, she's right. Even so, he could not completely banish a wounded feeling. He pressed a smile to his face. In a bright tone of voice, he said, "You're right, of course." Abandoning the conversation, he lifted a forkful of salad to his mouth. "Mmm. Oh. Mmm. I got the salad dressing just right."

***

David settled into the couch in his favorite corner of his favorite Manhattan coffee shop. He hadn't been to the City since moving out to the New Jersey countryside, and the frenetic energy of the City-That-Never-Sleeps exhausted him. He watched the crowds passing the large window, noticing – as he never had before – the tense and preoccupied expressions of the seemingly endless pedestrians. Turning away, he cast his eye around the little café, more than ever appreciating the comfortable seating, the proliferation of potted plants, the eclectic artwork, and the relaxed atmosphere. Having concluded his unavoidable banking business earlier than he expected, he planned to visit the Museum of Modern Art before his lunch with Simon, but first – quite the opposite of Kacey in this regard – he needed to shake off the contagious frenzy of the City.

Kacey had taken the opportunity to join him in his trip to the City, albeit to pursue her own errands. Arriving much earlier than expected, he had offered to show her his apartment before going to his appointment. He smiled as he thought of her appreciative response to his Manhattan penthouse loft. "This is yours? All yours? Geez, Baby, this is fantastic!" She had flopped onto the oversized couch, and said, "I don't know how you left this!"

He cocked his hip, brought a hand to his waist, then ruffled his hair in Kacey's characteristic gesture. Adopting a falsetto, he said, "I'm just not the city girl you are."

Kacey laughed and leapt from the couch to slap his arm. "I'm out of here, country boy. Give me a kiss." Chuckling, he obliged. She flipped her purse over her shoulder, pranced to the door, then spun, put her hand to her waist and ruffled her hair. In answer to his guffaw, she stuck her tongue out at him, then blew him a kiss. "I don't think I'll be late tonight. Just a shopping lunch and catching up with old friends. Enjoy your boring bank errand."

Now, sufficiently refreshed after two cups of coffee, he wandered the quiet museum, revisiting old favorites and contemplating the new exhibits. By the time he entered the swanky restaurant Simon had chosen, he felt revitalized, his mind swimming with inspirations and half-formed ideas for additional wood sculptures.

Approaching his friend with enthusiasm, he was taken aback by the sour look Simon wore, and further surprised when Simon did not rise to deliver his usual effusive greeting. He reached a hand out and Simon gave it a perfunctory shake, then gestured for David to sit.

"Good to see you, pal?" David said, his inflection rising, making the statement a question.

"Have you lost your mind?" Simon's expression seemed a mix of concern and anger.

"Favorite question of yours," David answered, grinning. "Why? What's up?"

"You're back with Kacey? Truly?" Simon raised a hand to a passing waiter, then looking to David, asked, "Wine?"

"Sure, whatever you're having."

Simon gestured with a finger between them to indicate two glasses, then said, "The 2013 Gramercy Cellars Cab, please." As the waiter departed, Simon jerked his hand to his wine glass, and finished the last of it. Glowering at David, he said, "Well?"

Speaking in cautious tones, David said, "Gee, that's a heck of a grapevine you've got." Reaching for a slice of warm bread, he continued warily. "Yeah, Kacey's back in the picture. What of it?"

Simon groaned, dramatically squeezing his forehead. "Oh, David, David."

Unsure of how to react, David raised one hand, palm up, in an unspoken question.

"What does she want?" Simon asked.

In an attempt to lighten the situation – David did not want to become angry with his friend, but Simon was treading on dangerous ground – he quirked a one-side smile and said, "I imagine she wants what any red-blooded woman would want with a handsome guy like me."

Simon snorted. "Yeah, your money."

"Simon, I think maybe this is my business, and we probably shouldn't–"

"She came to see me today." Seeing David's open-mouthed expression, Simon continued. "You heard me right. Just waltzed past my protesting receptionist, gave me a hug and kissed my cheek like we were old friends."

"What did she want?"

"A-ha!" Simon raised one finger beside his face in a "Eureka" gesture.

"Well?"

Simon was assisted in drawing the moment out by the waiter approaching with the wine glasses and the requested bottle. After the requisite uncorking and tasting, David repeated his question. "Well?"

"She asked me for my opinion about your wood sculpture. About the *viability* of your new venture – her word. She wanted to know if anyone had shown any interest."

David recalled Kacey posing him a similar question but was utterly baffled that she would approach Simon. Stalling to cover his confusion, he asked, "What did you tell her?"

"I told her there had not been one iota of interest. Not even a nibble." Simon sniffed his indignation and sipped his wine before continuing. "Which is the absolute truth. As you know, I took no photographs when I visited you. You haven't given me a portfolio to exhibit. In fact, I have not mentioned your woodwork to a living soul. You asked for time, and as your friend, I have scrupulously honored your request. She clearly assumed otherwise and I did not elaborate. I simply told her there was no interest."

"You don't know that there will be," David answered, deflating a bit at this possibility. Simon did not reassure him with words, but donned a knowing smile and shrugged.

Despite David's surprise at Kacey's unexpected visit to his friend, he could not accept Simon's bitter judgment of her motivation. Exhaling, he said the first thing that came to mind. "She's just worried about me. She's desperate to make me happy. Yes, that's right" – this in response to Simon's eye roll – "and doesn't want me hurt by an ego-wounding failure."

"David–" Simon began but David interrupted.

"I'm happy, Simon. Leave it alone, okay, buddy?"

Simon sighed, his exasperated expression changing to one of concern. "I'm not just your agent. I'm a friend who doesn't want to see you hurt. Again."

"Yeah, I know. And I appreciate it. I know you don't like her much, but give her a chance, huh?"

Simon bowed his head, then raised it to meet David's eyes. He nodded, then continued rocking his head in a series of nods that decreased in intensity like ripples dissipating across a pond.

"Thanks." David plucked another bread slice from the basket between them, smiled and said, "Still feel like lunch?"

"Of course," then as if only remembering his customary manners, "It's terrific to see you, David." He looked at his watch and said, "I have another hour and a half. Tell me what you've been doing, other than" – cough – "the obvious." He lifted one eyebrow in mock chastisement, then smiled. "More sculpture, I hope?" He raised a hand to signal the hovering waiter. "Oh, and do tell me what happened to that gorgeous creature I chanced to meet when I visited you. If you've broken her heart, I might have to sweep in and console her." Simon laughed.

Tension flowed from David as he joined in the laughter. "Sarrinah, you mean. She's pretty wonderful. And I don't think I've broken her heart." He thought of the sadness that seemed to live behind her eyes of late, and he hoped he was not the reason. He never would have thought of the possibility before Simon's jest. It was a possibility that made him uncomfortable, and doubled his anticipation of spending time with Sarrinah this afternoon.

I hope I beat Kacey home by a couple of hours. He was struck by a pang of disloyalty, then shook off the feeling. *I'm just worried about Sarrinah, that's all.*

CHAPTER 22

SARRINAH

DAVID'S NOTE SAID ONLY that he and Kacey would be gone for the day, and that he hoped to meet with Sarrinah by early afternoon. It seemed to have been penned in haste, for the handwriting was nothing like the neat block lettering he used to make notes on his sculpture sketches. Worse, she was unsure of the meaning.

Were he and Kacey returning together? Was the purpose of the meeting an introduction? Or was Kacey returning later, and this was to be the first of the "secret" meetings?

You do not yet know, my love, but if this is a clandestine rendezvous, it is the last as well as the first.

She didn't know which alternative she hoped for more: If Kacey was part of the meeting, Sarrinah may be able to continue in her friendship with David – albeit while suffering the pain of unrequited love. If she met with David alone, she would call a stop to any further meetings. The pain of being deprived his company would be acute, and made more excruciating by being trapped in the house by her nature and denied oblivion by his life force. Either way, her situation was hopeless.

In the past, she would have attributed her current circumstance to the "torture and suffering" appropriate to her crime. However, with all the time recently available for introspection and reflection, she recognized and accepted that the blame – if blame was the correct word – belonged to the vagaries of the heart. After all, was literature not rife with stories of unanswered affection?

Regardless of her anxieties about the upcoming meeting, Sarrinah did take advantage of their absence and the freedom it afforded her. She spent the morning wandering the secret garden, reveling in the delicious sensation of sun-warmed skin and the velvet of rose pedals against her fingertips. Although she knew the variety of rose to be a fragrant one, she could not discern any scent, but given her delight in the other sensations, this did not dispirit her. And perhaps scent would come with time?

Remembering the humorous spectacle of David caught in the storm during his first croquet lesson, she laughed aloud. She had little doubt that she would – with her increased corporeality – now experience the sensation of rain, but pondered the question of whether she would appear wet as she had not then. Glancing at the cloudless sky, she was happy to see that the question would not be answered today.

As morning turned to afternoon, Sarrinah entered the house and wandered the connecting rooms toward the main entrance. David's note had not indicated a specific time for his arrival, nor where they were to meet, but she did not want to force him to search for her. She settled in the billiard room to wait, but as the hours passed, her rising nervousness led to pacing. Several times, she opened the door to the servants' stairs, having made the decision to escape to the safety of the attic, only to close it again to resume pacing.

When she finally heard the front door latch, she spun toward the sound and ran two steps toward the door – *Finally!* She stumbled to an abrupt halt as dread anticipation flared.

"Sarrinah?"

David's voice. She crept to the door of the billiard room to ascertain if David was alone. *But what does it matter if Kacey is with him?* Whatever the situation, David had asked for this meeting. She lifted her chin and stepped into the hall.

"Sarrin–" then as David caught sight of her, "Ah!" He – apparently alone – quickened his pace toward her and his smile both cheered her and broke her heart. "I'm so glad for this opportunity." When she did not respond, he asked, "Where do you want…?"

"I will go whither you direct me." She smiled to take the sting from the formality of her response.

"Salon? Library?"

"Will Kacey be joining us?"

"No." David's face darkened, and his mouth quirked in apology. "Not this time."

Because he is as aware as I that Kacey will not accept the notion. "Then, I suggest the library. It is farther from the entrance and would afford us more warning of her return."

David made an "after you" gesture. As he came alongside her, she could see in her peripheral vision that he was studying her face. Looking for… what?

"Is everything okay? I know I don't have any reason to worry about you, but I am concerned… that you're all right."

Sarrinah turned toward him and made a sincere effort to smile. Injecting as much cheerfulness into her voice as she could, she said, "You are quite right that you have no cause to worry. I'm happy to see you, of course." Another two paces in silence and she added, "You must tell me of your adventures today."

David snorted. "I wouldn't call them adventures. A meeting with my investment advisors – boring but necessary – and then a visit to a museum." His voice gained more animation. "Wandering the museum was nice, but not really an adventure. After that, I joined Simon for lunch."

"I'm glad for you. I remember Simon."

"And he remembers you. You apparently made quite an impression." David laughed, but the joviality did not last. In a sober voice, he said, "Although…"

Entering the library, she chose a seat near David's favorite chair rather than the couch, where he would likely have joined her. She wanted – no, *needed* – to distance herself physically in preparation for breaking with him. She had, thus far, managed polite conversation, but her mind swirled with how and when she would broach the subject, her stomach twisted, and she had to clutch at her skirt to keep her hands from trembling.

Once David settled, he seemed lost in thought, furrows creasing his forehead. She prompted him to continue with, "Although? You haven't fallen out with Simon, have you?" *Losing two friends in one day... Will I have the strength to do this?*

"Oh, no. It's just... Kacey went to see him this morning."

"How nice that he should see two friends in the same day, though I do wonder you didn't go together."

David's face flushed with an emotion she could not identify. "They're not really friends."

"In that case, why would she approach him?"

"She asked what he thought of my wood sculpture. Simon thinks she's after my money, but I think she was just being concerned about me." He remained quiet and pensive for a moment, then shook his head. "What do you think?"

Sarrinah puffed out a breath of surprise at the question. "I can't possibly know, David. I know nothing about Kacey. I know that you love her and, knowing nothing else, that speaks in her favor."

"Well said, thank you." Shaking off the pall, he said in a brighter voice, "Other than that small disagreement, it was great to see Simon again. Terrific lunch, too. Fresh fish in a white wine caper sauce – yum." Sarrinah smiled at his enthusiasm, knowing how much he enjoyed food and cooking. "He's doing well, and that's important to me. After all, I haven't given him anything in a long while now."

"I hope you will, eventually. Your work is really quite lovely, attractive to both eye and touch."

His eyes flashed to her. "Touch?"

"Or so I imagine, David." Her voice all innocence, she smiled and lifted a shoulder in a shrug. There was no reason to raise his interest in the changes she was undergoing when, after today, she would be gone from his life.

He held her gaze for a long moment, then said, "To answer your question, I do plan – someday – to see if I can make a go of selling some of them, maybe even doing the show circuit if Simon thinks there's a market. But I still feel like… I don't know…" He tapped his temple with a fingertip. "Like I'm not quite there." His smile expanded to its full warmth. "Simon sure would like the idea. He only told me so about forty times today." He laughed and she joined his laughter, happy for the affection he felt for his friend.

Sitting forward in his chair, he said, "But, enough about me. Tell me how you've been, what you've been doing." Then mimicking her earlier question, even to the same inflection, he said, "You must tell me of your adventures today."

She smiled wistfully. "I did rather enjoy the secret garden this morning. The sun was so bright and the roses are in bloom; such a delightful flush of colors. I laughed aloud remembering your croquet lessons." She giggled and expected a similar response from David.

To her surprise, he glanced away, chagrin evident. "Yeah. I know. I feel terrible, I really do. I keep meaning to get things worked out with Kacey, but–"

"David—"

Slapping his thighs with an unexpected violence, and then rising from his chair, he said, "There's no easy or obvious way to do it, so I just need to bite the bullet. I'll talk to her as soon as she gets home, or tomorrow at the latest. You shouldn't have to live like a ghost in your own house – ha ha." Despite his mock laughter, his expression contained no humor.

"David." She watched as he paced in agitation. "David, please sit down." The seriousness of her tone caught his attention. He stopped mid-stride, tilted his head at her in query, then resumed his seat.

There is no better time. Oh, how I hope I can say the words. Without tears or other dramatics.

"There is no need to speak to Kacey, David." *My love.* She wished she could speak the endearment, but the discomfort it would cause him would be cruel.

"But you—"

She held up a hand. "Please let me speak."

He stared, silent, then bowed his head and gestured for her to continue.

"I have discovered a way to leave this house." When David opened his mouth to question her, she again raised her hand. "Yes, I thought it impossible, but I have found the manner in which it might be done. And I am going."

"Why? Where will you go?"

"Does it matter, David?" She shrugged, and forced a smile in the hope that he would not hear the question as an accusation or complaint. "You cannot follow. Nor would you. You have Kacey, and deserve the life you can make with her – a life of growing together over the years, without divided loyalties."

There. I have said it. Now to find a way to gracefully depart.

David sat in stunned speechlessness, lips parted, brow furrowed. After a moment, he swallowed and said, "Are you going…?" He raised a finger to point toward Heaven.

Shall I compound the lie to bring him peace? Instead, with the bitterness of the truth souring her thoughts and twisting her mouth, she said, "No. You must know that to be impossible. I am irredeemable."

"I don't understand why you want–" He sputtered to a stop as she stood. She regretted the rudeness but had been propelled from her seat both by resentment of her fate and the knowledge that she could not withstand any arguments he might pose against her "leaving."

"Wait! What...?" he asked, shock plain on a face gone suddenly pale. Standing abruptly, he said, "You're going now? That's it? You're just...?" His hand slashed toward the door. "What's the hurry? Got a train to catch?"

Sarrinah stifled a bitter laugh, knowing it would only hurt and exasperate him. She would not be mocking him, instead finding a twisted humor in the idea of her catching a train, but he may not understand that. "David, I..." She could not finish, was not even certain of what she meant to say. She swallowed against a tight throat and blinked back tears.

The tableau was broken by the slamming of the front door, followed by Kacey's raised voice traveling down the hallway toward them. "Hey Baby. I'm home. I brought you a present." Sarrinah and David stood frozen, each gazing into the other's eyes, as they listened to the ticking of Kacey's high heels through the foyer, the sound changing as she stepped onto the first carpet, then off it again. When Kacey reached the main stairway, they heard, "You upstairs?" then a murmured, "This place needs a freakin'

intercom." Raising her voice again: "David?"

David turned toward the door, then spun back. "Stay!" he

whispered, with an emphatic downward stab of one finger. Sarrinah

battled against the desire to obey his command and the need to

flee. She stood immobile as he crept toward the door to the

hallway, and peered around it. After a moment, he returned to

stand before her again.

"She's gone upstairs. I should go before she starts looking

for me. But *we* need to talk." His finger flashed back and forth,

pointing first at his own chest, then at hers. "We need–" She

wordlessly interrupted with a slow, sad shake of her head. David

exhaled a loud gust of breath, closed his eyes and dropped his chin

to his chest.

Sarrinah's hand twitched up, then back down as she

stopped herself in the act of reaching to lift his chin with her

fingers. "I don't wish us to part enemies."

Her statement had the desired effect. His head snapped

upward and she smiled at the vehemence with which he said,

"We'll never be enemies!" Seeing her expression and the humor in her eyes, his mouth stretched in a lopsided grin.

"I'm pleased to hear you say so," smile widening as his grin became a true smile. "I wish to thank you, before I depart, for the months we were…" She trailed off, unsure how to finish the sentence. *Together?* "For your friendship and affection, for… for… everything, David." Noticing the gathering moisture in his eyes, she hurried to finish. "Despite my circumstance, you have made my 'life' pleasant. More than pleasant. I…" She faltered, her vision blurred by unshed tears, then gathered her courage to say, "I care for you deeply. I will carry you in my heart always." Turning away as the first tear fell, she walked to the door.

"Sarrinah, wait," he said, voice rough with emotion. She stopped but did not turn toward him. "If it's possible, take your sculpture. The one in the salon. And remember me."

She wiped away her tears, and hoping her smile contained all the tenderness she felt, she turned and said, "I shall think of you always. Goodbye, David."

CHAPTER 23

DAVID

DAVID CLENCHED HIS JAWS, rocked his head back and stared at the library ceiling, unseeing. *She's gone. She just walked away.* He sucked a long breath in through his nose and blinked to clear his eyes of moisture. *Why? She seemed so happy…* Lowering his gaze to the open doorway, his mind leapt to finish the thought. *…before Kacey moved in.* His indignation and self-pity drained away with the realization. *Fair. I stole her home and her freedom, and I've done nothing to fix that. She was fair to leave.* He took a shuddering breath. *You can't have your cake and eat it too. But I do wish she'd given me more time to work on Kacey.* His mind churned with curiosity about where she had gone (was going?), and how, and if she would ever come back, if she…

"Daaaaaaavid."

Jerked from his musings by Kacey's call, he hurried into the hall, surprised by the shakiness in his legs. Kacey stood at the bottom of the stairs, hands coming up to cup her mouth for another yell. "Here. Sorry," he said.

Kacey startled, puffed out a breath and spun toward him. "I was actually starting to worry." She hurried to him, wrapped her arms around his chest, and clung to him.

"Sorry," he repeated.

Without releasing him, she backed a step and smiled up at him indulgently. "Lost in a book again?" she asked. David nodded, and she stepped to his side, one arm still holding to his waist. He flung an arm around her shoulder and gave her squeeze, allowing her to propel him forward.

"How long you been home, Baby?" she asked.

"Not long." As they reached the bottom of the stairs, he released her and said, "Before we go up, I just want to check something in the salon."

Kacey huffed out a breath. "For? It can't wait 'til morning?" Exasperation tinged her voice.

Well, honey, I just want to check if a certain ghost took her sculpture before she did her poof trick. He flashed a tight smile and gestured up the stairs. "You're right. Sorry."

She stepped up the first stair, then turned toward him. "Must have been a long bank meeting to keep you so long." Reaching up to muss his hair, she said, "And can't have been a good one to have ruffled your feathers so much." She took his hand and they began ascending.

"It wasn't bad. Afterward, I wandered around the MoMA and grabbed some lunch before heading back." The split-second decision not to mention Simon surprised him, but with his thoughts swirling around Sarrinah's abrupt and unexpected departure, he wasn't really focused on the conversation.

"That's cool," she said. "Any new exhibits at MoMA?"

"A couple," he responded.

Several more steps in silence until, on reaching the landing, she laughed, grabbed his shoulders and shook him. "What's up with you? Getting a sentence from you usually isn't like pulling teeth." She laughed again.

"Sorry."

"And no more sorrys!" She gave him a playful slap. "Come on. I got you a present. That'll cheer you up." She spun away from him to continue up.

Geez, so you got the wind knocked out of your sails. Pull yourself together! For years, all you've wanted was Kacey, and now you've got her. Don't blow it by making her wonder if you're okay. Taking a deep breath, he hurried the two steps to catch up with her. "So, how'd your day go? I'm actually kind of surprised you're home so early."

"Just wanted to be with you, Baby." She lifted herself to her toes for a kiss. "Ran some quick errands and then hooked up with Sheila and Terry for shopping, lunch, more shopping. You're gonna love your present. I've kept in touch with Sheila, but haven't seen her in, gosh, probably two years now. She hasn't changed a bit. Terry, now – whoa – she's gotten kind of frumpy, but she still tells the most wicked jokes, and no, don't ask. They'd only make you blush." She giggled, topped the stairs, and said, "Now, wait right here until I call you. You're going to looooove it!" She ran down the hallway in the direction of their bedroom.

David stared after her, stunned and a little sickened by Kacey's deliberate exclusion of her meeting with Simon. What did she have to hide? On the other hand, he hadn't mentioned that Simon had been his lunch partner. On the other-other hand, it wouldn't be strange for him to see Simon on a trip to the City. For Kacey to do so, however...

"Ready!" Kacey's voice was filled with excitement.

David paced with steady steps toward the bedroom, for once hoping Kacey's present was not another negligee. He definitely appreciated her collection of "naughties" as she called them but, with his sadness over Sarrinah's departure and the newly added confusion about Kacey's visit to Simon, he wasn't sure he'd be up for the occasion. If anything, he wanted to cuddle, comfortable and secure in the arms of the woman he loved, talking long into the night.

And she'll tell me about Simon, and why she went there. I'm just feeling vulnerable, so I'm getting melodramatic.

Just outside the door to the bedroom, he stopped and said, "Ready?"

"Double ready!"

He stepped into the room, sucked in a breath and laughed out loud. The large box Kacey had brought into the house was on

265

the bed. She sat on the floor, her back against the cushion-topped storage bench at the foot of their bed, a fuzzy-haired golden retriever puppy squirming in her lap.

"Get over here. This little love bug wants to meet her daddy."

David rushed forward and dropped to sit cross-legged in front of Kacey. He lifted the puppy and tried to cradle it, but once in his arms, it lifted its paws to his chest and bathed his chin with its tongue, its tail wagging so ferociously the little body swung back and forth with the motion. David made muffled noises under the onslaught, then lowered the puppy to his lap. Running his hand along the downy fur, he said, "What's your name, princess? Huh? Huh? Ouch!" The little nip to his finger had surprised him more than hurt him. He chuckled and went back to petting the creature in an effort to calm it down.

Kacey laughed and leant her efforts to corralling the excited puppy. "She doesn't have a name yet."

"Princess it is, then." David rolled backward, bringing Princess with him, clutched to his chest. Lying on his back, he let go, and brought both hands up to the back of his head, pulling it forward to watch the puppy. It frolicked on his chest for only a moment before missing its footing and sliding off. Crawling through the triangle opening of David's bent arm, it ambushed David's ear and the side of his face with licks and snuffles and puppy squeals, until David was consumed by giggles. In self-defense, he captured the little thing and sat up again.

Kacey reached around the side of the storage bench, and carefully brought forward a double dog bowl containing food and water. She placed it between them, and David put Princess down, nudging her toward the dish. He watching the little tongue lapping at the water, then looked up at Kacey, his cheeks almost aching from smiling and laughing.

Kacey beamed at him, her eyes sparkling with laughter. "You like her?"

"Yeah." He glanced down and ran his fingers over Princess' head and back. "Yeah, I like her." Raising his head to meet Kacey's eyes he said, "I love her. You know that I always wanted–"

Kacey nodded her head vigorously, smile splitting her face. "Uh-huh. That's why I *knew* you'd love your present."

LOVE WHISPERS THROUGH THE VEIL

David gestured for Kacey to come closer and she rose to her knees. He pulled her into an awkward embrace, both leaning over the puppy between them. "I love her a lot." He kissed Kacey then leaned further to whisper in her ear, "But not nearly as much as I love you."

***

David sat in his office making notes for updates to the schedules for the cleaning crew and chef; Kacey wanted both to come more often. With Sarrinah gone (he suppressed the stab of regret that came with the acknowledgement), he had no reason not to accommodate Kacey. She had also made noises about adding other staff, maybe a butler/valet or servants who could serve their meals, but he had quashed that idea. Sure, he had the money to afford such "luxuries" (as Kacey called them), but absolutely no desire for them.

Hand resting on the large receiver of the rotary phone that had come with the house – he could not bring himself to replace it – he searched through his papers for the phone number to the cleaning agency. The phone rang under his hand.

"David here," he answered.

"John Willard calling."

David took a moment to make the connection, but then he remembered the historian. "I've been meaning to call you." Sarrinah had been gone for days when his calendar pinged him to contact the man for an update and he had wrestled with the idea of calling to cancel the search. Finding the answer — even if the answer was the one he hoped for — could no longer help Sarrinah. If it ever could have. In the end, he decided to let the search continue, if only to appease the curiosity which had been his impetus for hiring the man.

"I tried your cell, but you didn't answer. I hope it's all right that I called this numb—"

"It's fine." Willard did occasionally call David for updates in an effort to show that he was earning the money David had paid, but this time David thought he detected a note of urgency in the man's voice. "You've found something?"

"Yes, I have." The excitement was evident in his words. *"I've…"* Willard broke off and chuckled in a self-deprecating manner before continuing. *"It's really not the sort of thing a non-historian*

would find all that exciting. It's not world changing stuff. But, by my standards anyway, I've hit the jackpot."

"So, you know what happened?"

"I certainly think I do. I'll leave it to you to decide."

"I'm ready. Hit me with it." Thoughts flashing to how Sarrinah would tease him for the slang, he could not resist resorting to one of her expressions. "I'm 'all agog,' as my friend would say."

"I'm waiting for one last piece of information, and then I'll drop the full report – with copies of all the documentation – in the mail. Really, you need to read what I've found. I could summarize, but I'd rather you looked at the evidence with an untainted mind. After that, I'll be more than pleased to discuss it with you, or answer any questions."

"You're killing me here!"

Willard laughed in response. *"I'm glad you're so excited – especially given the money spent. I didn't expect you'd want the news in any rush. After all, it's all ancient history at this point. Another couple of days or weeks isn't going to change anything, right?"*

David's enthusiasm broke and dissipated. "Unfortunately not." He sighed. "Can you at least give me a hint?" Then worried that the answer would only add to his disappointment, he quickly amended, "No. Don't."

"I'm not often in a position to say this — most people aren't as generous as you've been — but I do have unspent funds left. How do you want me to return the balance?" Willard was positively cheerful.

"Keep it." In answer to the silence on the other end of the phone, he said, "At least for now. You said I might have questions. There might be more for you to do."

"I see, yes. I look forward to your call."

David hung up and, inexplicably in need of comfort, he rose and crossed to the sunny spot on the floor where Princess lay curled. He sat, and as gently as he could transferred the sleeping puppy to his lap. Stroking the soft fur, his thoughts turned — as they had so many times in the recent days — to Sarrinah, where she was, how she was doing. At least she had managed to take the sculpture from the salon. That she had done so both relieved him and gave him a nostalgic pleasure. His mind turned to memories of their time together, dancing, talking, reading, laughing. *She had a gorgeous laugh. I hope she's laughing a lot now, wherever she is.*

His thoughts were interrupted by a gentle knock. He looked up to see Kacey peeking around the door frame.

"Thousand dollars for your thoughts?" she said, stepping slowly into the room as if unsure of herself. He sighed at her unfortunate choice of words. His irritation at her constant reference to money lately was probably exacerbated by his melancholy over Sarrinah's disappearance.

When he did not answer, she brandished his phone and said, "Your phone rang. Didn't know if it was important."

"Thanks." He took the proffered phone.

"Can I join you?" she asked, folding to the floor to sit opposite him. When he only continued stroking Princess, she said, "Something the matter, Baby? You look sad." She reached out and he took her hand.

"Do you believe in ghosts?" he asked without thinking.

"Ghosts?"

David raised his gaze to look at her. She was no longer smiling, but cocking her head with a puzzled expression. Then her mouth hardened, and she dropped her hand from his. "Is this about the baby?"

Surprised at the question, he said, "No." When her expression did not change, he said, "What if it is? I've tried to talk about her. I think we *need* to talk about what happened, but you…" He sputtered to a stop as Kacey jerked to standing and walked toward the door. Reaching the door, she turned toward him, her arms lifted to either side of her, hands bracing the frame.

"It's done. And I don't like thinking about it. I don't know why you insist on wallowing."

"*She*" – he emphasized the pronoun – "was our baby and–"

She stopped him with a palm shoved toward him, like a policeman calling "halt." She spun away, anger evident in her movements, then flipped an answer at him over her shoulder before stalking away. "No. I don't believe in ghosts."

CHAPTER 24

SARRINAH

SARRINAH HELD A CANDLE before her as she crept down the servants' stairs leading to the billiard room. While she preferred the stairs toward the back of the house – they were wider – they were too close to the residential wing for safe use during her midnight forays. Once upon a time, when her only desire was to rid the house of David, she might have enjoyed causing the stairs to creak late at night. (She had not thought of doing so then – nor did she have the ability.) However, she did not now want to alert David to the fact that she remained in residence. He seemed to have accepted her deception that she had discovered a way to "leave." He had left no further notes in the writing desk in the salon, nor called out to her on the two occasions Kacey had left the house since Sarrinah's "departure."

Since then, Sarrinah rarely ventured from the attic during the daylight hours. The few times she had, she had been so overwhelmed with anxiety that David might unexpectedly appear around the next corner that the benefit of traversing the house in sunlight had hardly seemed worth the effort. The deciding event had taken place just over two weeks ago. She had peeked into the hall in advance of dashing across it when she saw David emerge from the kitchen with a breakfast tray. Apparently having less modesty with only Kacey in the house, he had been wearing naught but his undershorts. Sarrinah had been frozen in mortification at seeing him in such a state of undress, and – though she was loath to admit it – in fascination at his near-nudity and in admiration of his well-formed chest and arms.

Since then, she had only ventured forth after the house quieted when she was certain David and Kacey were well into their slumbers. Even these forays were limited as she could not be certain the candles in the third floor storage room would be restocked once she had used them all. Nor did she want to cause David to question why such a replenishment was needed. Thus, despite wishing for the freedom to wander her beloved home, she limited her excursions to late-night foraging missions to the library for replacement books.

Reaching the bottom of the stairs, she hitched her cloth sack full of books more securely over her shoulder, and gently pushed the door open. Much to her astonishment, the billiard room was not dark, but obliquely lit by the hallway light. Nearly dropping her load, she backed quickly and extinguished the candle with a panicked huff of breath.

Perhaps they simply forgot to put out the light?

She lowered the sack and candlestick to the floor and eased into the billiard room, all senses alert. Staying close to the wall, she crept toward the door into the hallway, then froze at the unmistakable sound of a voice speaking quietly in the corridor. *Kacey?* She spun away with the intention of returning to the attic, but curiosity overcame her. Moving slowly, she stole toward the hallway. As she approached the open door, Kacey meandered past, telephone pressed to her ear. Sarrinah sucked in a breath to suppress a squeal – she had been in plain view if Kacey had glanced her way! – and slid behind the door. For several seconds, she could not distinguish Kacey's words over the turmoil of panic that suffused her mind. After several deep breaths to calm herself, she listened to the half-whispered voice.

In a tone of mild irritation, Kacey said, "Look, I try, okay? But you know me. Once I'm asleep, I'm out for the night. Can't exactly set an alarm, can I?" A pause, apparently listening to the other party's response. "Yes, that's what I did. Laid there for a freakin' hour just to make sure he was asleep. I nodded off twice but managed–" Another pause, and the indistinct sound of feet padding across carpet near Sarrinah's hidden form. Voice now smoothed to gentleness, Kacey said, "Yeah, I know, Baby. I know." A longer pause, and when Kacey spoke again, she had moved too far down the hall and Sarrinah could barely make out the words. "You know I do… Yes… I know… Yes…" Just as the indistinguishable murmur faded to nothing, the light in the hallway extinguished.

For an immeasurable length of time, Sarrinah kept her hidden position, too shaken by the near encounter to risk any movement. With the eventual realization that she could not remain downstairs until morning, she summoned the courage to slip around the door to peer down the hall. Detecting no one in the pallid moonlight, she crept back to retrieve her sack and candlestick, but did not mount the stairs to the attic. *Kacey must surely have returned to bed by now.* Not daring to relight her candle, she reentered the billiard room. At the door, she checked the hallway again before dashing across it to the salon. Her subsequent progress through the connecting rooms to the library and back took longer than usual in the moonlit darkness. She had to force herself not to run up the stairs to her attic alcove.

Near breathless with relief as she settled in her chair, she absently stacked her new books on the side table, her thoughts only now turning to what she could remember of Kacey's words. Unable to truly make sense of what she'd heard, she nonetheless believed one thing with certainty: Kacey had waited until David was asleep to engage in what was obviously meant to be a secret conversation. She was less certain about Kacey's use of the word "Baby" when speaking to the other party. Until tonight, she had assumed the word to be an affectionate (if unfitting) moniker for David. *And now Kacey is using the term with another?*

With a sigh, Sarrinah tried to shake off the rising feeling of outrage. *I have no right to judge. Perhaps I misunderstood the significance of the conversation.* She inhaled deeply and released another long breath. Despite an earnest effort to refrain from disliking Kacey, she was finding the endeavor more difficult with each passing week.

She stood and walked the short distance to the sculpture she had taken – with David's permission – from the salon. Running her fingers lightly along the familiar curves, she closed her eyes. *This is the only part of David that is – and ever will be – truly mine. Oh my beloved!* She raised her gaze to the rafters above her and delivered a heartfelt prayer that she was wrong in her recent suspicions regarding Kacey. *Please don't let her break his heart again! He deserves to be happy.*

Sarrinah returned to her chair, first reaching for the playing cards, then the topmost book on the stack, but in her newfound concern for David, she could not so easily distract herself.

And yet I must, and for many, many years to come. Even if Kacey loves another, even if she leaves him, his heart will heal. He is a kind and gracious man and will find love again – hopefully with someone who returns his affection. Mercilessly quelling the hopeful impulse that followed, she dashed tears from her cheeks with two savage swipes of her hands and spoke aloud.

LOVE WHISPERS THROUGH THE VEIL

"And that person will never be me."

***

With the bright morning light came a new determination not to devolve into the sad, pathetic creature she had once been. *David taught me the true meaning of love and awoke me to the joyful person I was in life. I would diminish his gift by allowing myself to become a creature of misery again.*

She cast her eye to her side table with books and playing cards, then walked to the edge of the carpet to survey the jumble of furnishings and effects in the rest of the attic, thinking to explore yet again. Suddenly realizing the source of at least some of her melancholy, she said aloud, "I am weary of this small realm. My mind and my body demand more. How am I to relish my days when they consist of unrelieved tedium?" Walking slow circles about her alcove, she chased her thoughts toward a solution. Having returned for the fourth time to the fervent wish that she at least had the benefit of the entire house with its various artworks, views of the landscape — *even so little as a different chair on which to place my derriere!* — she stopped her pacing and laughed aloud.

"And why not? How many times did I tell David we could easily avoid each other in the vastness of this house? Certainly I know more now than I ever did about how to best accomplish quiet and safe passage from one area of the house to another." Enchanted with the idea, she clapped her hands in delight. "But only with extreme caution. I cannot risk discovery. David would… David would…"

David would be hurt. Or worse, hopeful. Her exuberance melted into self-chastisement. *No. I cannot be selfish where his happiness is at stake.* With a heavy sigh, she lifted the playing cards, and sank to the threadbare carpet to deal the cards for a game of Patience. As she leaned forward, a bit of lace at the hem of her dress tore under one knee. Surprised, she sat back to examine the cloth. Until now, her clothing had been a part of her ghostliness, as impervious to change (or the elements) as she. Now, on close investigation, her dress, and even her slippers, were showing obvious signs of wear. Did her substantiality now extend to her clothing? Experimentally, she unlaced one slipper – then after a moment of hesitation – removed it to study it in the sunlight from the window. Yes, the brocade showed fraying at the heel. This concerned Sarrinah – *in a century, I shall be left in rags!* – but also excited her. *I am no longer all of a piece. I can remove my shoes. The better for creeping about* – here in the attic, or *on the stairs!* This thought was quickly amended to add: *At night. Only at night.*

Not long after this discovery, during one of her midnight adventures, she was transfixed by the glow of the full moon through the French doors of the living room, and drawn to the splash of silver light across the terrace. *It looks like snow – so beautiful!* Looking down at her bare toes where they peeked from under her gown, a thought occurred. *My clothes are no longer a part of my ghostliness… perhaps neither am I trapped indoors!* Her excitement rose as she carefully opened a French door. *I shall dance in the moonlight!*

Her feverish hopes were soon dashed. Despite efforts to move across the threshold – whether slowly or at a dash – she was repelled as surely as if the house were encased in transparent metal. The barrier did not prevent a cool night breeze from caressing her skin and ruffling her skirt, but she, nonetheless, could not pass through.

She stood in the open doorway for many minutes before make one final attempt to push through to the terrace, then sighed her disappointment, closed the door and proceeded to the library.

After her failed venture to go out of doors, the idea of quitting her attic prison (for that is how she began to feel about her alcove) during the daylight hours returned again and again. At first, she mounted heartfelt resistance to the impulse, but as time passed, her idle mind turned more to how the deed could be safely accomplished.

Only ever barefoot, the better to maintain silence, she cautioned herself.

And slowly. Listening from behind each door to determine which rooms David and Kacey occupy.

And no more than once a week. Predictably, she did not adhere to this last admonition beyond the first week.

Sarrinah did learn much about the habits of David and Kacey during her outings. David maintained his custom of walking about the house. He played billiards (once with Kacey), worked in the office, labored in his studio, read in the library, dined in the dining room (always with Kacey), and enjoyed the secret garden in fair weather. He seemed to genuinely enjoy the house, often strolling without apparent destination to savor the artwork (the foyer was still a favorite) or the ambiance of a room. On one particularly hair-raising day when Sarrinah was spending a pleasant moment in the salon, she heard David's distinctive footfall and threw herself to the floor behind a couch. Heart beating in her throat, she had been struck with terror when David sat on the couch behind which she was hiding. He stretched his arms across the back, hummed, and drummed his fingers idly, his hand so near she could have touched it with her nose.

Please, oh please, don't let Kacey join him! If David remained in the room for any length of time – which he likely would if Kacey joined him – she was sure to be discovered! *Why, why have I been so foolish?!*

David stopped his tune and his drumming fingers, then stood and walked to the door. "I miss you," he said before she heard his retreating footsteps. The fear in her heart melted into an aching fondness that kept her on her knees for some long minutes afterward.

Kacey did not share David's habits. (In point of fact, she did not seem to share much of her time with him. While this would have been normal in Sarrinah's time when men's and women's lives were lived quite separately, this certainly had not been the case between she and David before Kacey's arrival.) Yes, Kacey always accompanied him to the dining room for meals, and occasionally walked with him on his excursions of the house, but seemed mostly to restrict herself to the residential wing and her "laptop" – whatever that may be.

On the one occasion Kacey had ventured into the secret garden, Sarrinah had been appalled by what she witnessed. From her hiding place peeking at the garden from the morning room, she had seen Kacey chase the puppy, Princess, from the dining room into the garden. She watched helpless as Kacey jerked what appeared to be a shoe from the dog's mouth, then kicked at the dear little thing. Sarrinah brooded for hours afterward that David could love such a woman, and ended by convincing herself that he could not possibly be aware of this side of the woman's nature.

The combination of her near-brush with David in the salon and her depression and concern over Kacey's treatment of the puppy once again doused Sarrinah's enthusiasm for daylight forays. She retreated to her custom of only leaving the attic late at night. She knew her reticence would not last, but for now at least, she contented herself with the austere comforts of her alcove.

Some two weeks into her renewed self-banishment to the attic, and having finished the last of the books she had borrowed from the library, she languidly roused herself from the simple entertainment of watching dust motes float in the rays of the rising sun. She began placing each of her borrowed books carefully into the cloth sac in preparation for another excursion to the library that night when she heard an unmistakable tread on the attic stairs.

She lowered the last book into the bag as quickly and noiselessly as she could, then leapt toward the window to pull the heavy curtain to block the sunlight. Tiptoeing – and glad as ever that she wore no shoes – she crept to a hidden vantage point behind a draped chest of drawers at the edge of her alcove.

While she did not hear the attic door open (she kept it well oiled), she knew when David entered because the light of an electric torch flashed about the gloom. Although the light did not penetrate to her far corner, her breathing came in quick bursts.

Am I to have no safe haven? Recognizing the thought as ungenerous, she immediately repented of it. *I have caused my own dilemma. David does not deserve my pique.*

Much to her relief, David did not stay long, and did not conduct any lengthy search of the attic. He directly approached a stack of portraits where they leaned against the wall. Putting the top portrait to one side – the portrait of she and William, she remembered – he continued through the others, then murmured something inaudible and pulled another out. She could not make out the subject of the portrait, but he examined it for some time, flicking the light of the torch over the surface of it, then took it with him when he departed.

Huffing out a breath she hadn't known she was holding, Sarrinah collapsed back onto the carpet, relieved that David had not discovered her hiding place. When the sound of his footsteps faded to nothing, she sighed loudly. He had been so near – alone, here, in the attic, the only realm left her – yet even then, he remained impossibly far away.

CHAPTER 25

DAVID

DAVID WAS HALFWAY DOWN the attic stairs, portrait in hand, when he stopped, sat down, and held it out at arm's length to look at it.

What the hell am I doing?

The artistry was fantastic, but the subject of the portrait was… *Go ahead. You can admit it: She's the most beautiful woman in the world. Or she was.*

He stood and climbed several steps toward the attic to return the portrait to the darkness, then stopped again, and descended.

She was my friend. She's gone. I want to remember her. There's nothing wrong with that.

With a resolute stride, David carried the portrait to his studio, took down the landscape hanging over the fireplace, and hung the portrait of Sarrinah. Unable to tear his eyes away, he stepped backward several steps, then leaned against the table saw, smiling, pleased by the thought that she would be "watching" him while he worked.

He had gone to the attic to get the portrait of her and William. On a whim, he had decided to look through the remaining portraits on the off chance he found another, better one. And he had. This painting featured Sarrinah's head and shoulders only, with the barest suggestion of lace at the edge of her off-the-shoulder dress. Her hair was pulled up in an elegant evening style, with only ringlets framing her face. The artist had been expert enough to give the impression that she stared out of the portrait at the viewer, and her tender smile seemed directed at David.

"Pretty girl." Kacey's muzzy voice broke his reverie.

Without turning toward her, he said, "Yeah. I found this in the attic."

She spoke through a yawn. "You're up early."

David turned with a smile and made a show of glancing at his wrist watch. "Actually, *you're* up early."

Kacey pushed herself off from her position leaning against the entry, and shuffled toward David, wrapping her arms around his waist and pressing against him. Speaking with a muffled voice into his chest, she asked, "Had breakfast?"

"I'm not really hungry. But I can fix you something."

Kacey raised herself to her toes for a kiss then pressed herself against him, moving sinuously. "If you come back to bed, I promise to help you work up an appetite." She lifted his shirt and kissed his chest. Lowering the shirt, she gave him come-hither eyes and pulled at his wrist. "Come on, Baby. Kacey's hungry." He let her lead him down the hall.

In the aftermath of their lovemaking, Kacey slept again. David watched her sleep, physically satisfied but worried at the lack of fulfillment he felt with their relationship in general.

I'm not being fair. Kacey's a city girl, and for months now, she has selflessly accommodated my desire to be in the country – probably bored out of her mind. I can't expect her to sparkle when I've taken her from the shine and glitz of her natural environment.

He rolled away from her, slipped out of bed, and dressed. Calling to Princess in a whisper and smiling at the dog's enthusiastic willingness to follow him, he went to the kitchen to see what he could drum up for breakfast.

***

Using a slice of sourdough toast to sop up the remains of eggs-over-easy, he glanced at Kacey's plate. She hadn't eaten half what he'd served, but twiddled with her fork as she flipped the page on the magazine she was reading.

"Weren't hungry after all, huh?" he asked.

Kacey smiled and looked up from her magazine. Winking at him, she said, "You're all the sustenance I need, Baby." Then with a crooked grin, "Well… almost." She scooped egg onto her toast, topped it with a slice of bacon, then folded the toast over, making a sandwich. "As always, you fixed the eggs perfectly." She rolled her eyes in appreciation as she chewed, then turned back to the magazine.

"What would you think about a night out?" he asked. Kacey's gaze returned to his, and he continued. "We could go into the City, drinks, dinner, dancing – the whole deal – then stay in the loft overnight. If you want, we'll even stay the next day. Go to MoMA, or shopping, or whatever."

291

Instead of the expected excitement, in a tone of incredulity, she said, "Really? I mean, what's the occasion?"

See what you've done to her? She's afraid to get excited because you've kept her cooped up here for way too long. "You are." He reached across the space between them to take her hand.

She remained silent for a moment as if doubtful of his sincerity. When he raised his eyebrows and nodded, she leapt from her chair and squeezed into his lap, eyes sparkling. "Yes please!" She kissed him. "I just knew if I was a really good girl I'd get everything I wanted!"

David chuckled. "Is tonight too soon?"

"No sir, it is not!" Kacey wriggled from his lap and returned to her seat. "I've got to finish my breakfast! I'm gonna need my strength." Taking another bite of her sandwich, she leaned toward him to slap at his shoulder and mumbled, "And so are you, Baby!"

David watched as she ate with renewed energy, happy to have awakened the Kacey he knew, and sorry that he had let things get this far.

She wriggled in her seat again, happy as a child going to the circus. "After I'm finished here, I'll get to packing. I know, I know, not much, but we can't go shopping tomorrow in dancing shoes!"

Just as she grabbed the last slice of bacon, the doorbell rang. "Mail," David said in explanation. "It can wait."

"Go. You don't have to stand on ceremony with me. I'll pour us more coffee?"

"Sure."

David whistled as he strode the long hallway to the front entrance, enthusiastic about the upcoming evening. He hadn't gone out in a long time and he looked forward to being with Kacey in her element. As he stepped outside, he was surprised to see an unfamiliar car approaching up the long drive. He turned to the lockbox and retrieved the mail, then walked down the steps to greet the visitor. *Probably somebody who's gotten lost.*

He approached the car as it came to a stop. The driver, instead of rolling down the window, reached to get something from the passenger seat, then got out of the still-idling car holding what appeared to be a large colorful brochure. The man extended his arm to shake hands as he approached and David reached out to

293

reciprocate. *At least he left the car running, so he's not planning a long-winded sales presentation. I like him already.*

"David Cartell?" the man asked as they shook hands, his smile broad and ingratiating.

David stifled his surprised at being identified by name. *So this is no random drive-by salesman.* "Yes, I'm David Cartell."

The man lifted the brochure featuring a sleek red car on the front. David suppressed a groan and reached out to accept it. Instead of pressing the brochure into David's hand, the man opened it and extracted a stapled stack of papers from within.

As David took them, the man smiled again but the expression now contained a hint of self-satisfaction.

"What's this—?" David began, but the man spun away from him.

Slipping swiftly into the driver's seat, he turned to David and said, "You've been served," then slammed the car door and sped down the driveway.

"Served?" David watched the car until it turned from his view, then looked down at the papers he held. He read the caption:

COMPLAINT FOR DIVORCE/DISSOLUTION BASED ON

IRRECONCILABLE DIFFERENCES. "What…?" he murmured, eyes darting in disbelief to the other words that caught his immediate attention: KACEY ELAINE CARTELL, PLAINTIFF. Mouth falling open, he reread the caption then jerked toward the house, gaze falling on the open door and the hall beyond.

At the end of that hall is the dining room, and in the dining room sits Kacey, innocently pouring us more coffee.

His skin prickled and his stomach gave a sudden nauseous twist as the mixture of betrayal, heartbreak, and incredulity buffeted him in waves. He began walking toward the house with slow plodding steps that increased in speed with each stride. As he entered the foyer, he flung the unopened mail toward his office. One large manila envelope slid all the way across the carpet of the office until it disappeared under his desk, while the other envelopes and magazines fluttered and spun haphazardly toward the floor of the foyer or office. Looking once more at the legal document he held, he loped down the long hallway toward the dining room.

He skidded to a halt just inside the dining room, staring at Kacey as if she had suddenly become a stranger to him. She had allowed the shoulder of her loose top to slide down to her elbow, leaving her back and shoulder completely bare, as if emphasizing her underlying nudity. She finishing sipping her coffee, and turned her head to David with a smile as she heard his precipitous entry. Her skin blanched and her eyes widened at the expression on his face but she said nothing.

"What the hell is this, Kacey?" he asked, shaking the divorce complaint.

Tilting her head coyly and turning toward him in her chair, she giggled and said, "How would I know, Baby? What is it?"

Her flippancy struck a blow that added exasperation to the confusion of feelings within him. He strode forward and slapped the pages to the table. Glancing down, she spoke quietly, as if to herself. "Wow, and they told me these probably wouldn't be served until next week." She met his eye again. "Sit down, David." Her voice was saccharine with pity. When he only gaped at her, she repeated her request with more force in her tone.

David stood for a moment more, then slammed himself into his chair. "Why Kacey? Why are you doing this? Why, after all this time? Why this…" he gestured between them, "this… charade?"

Kacey stood with slow, measured movements, then pulled the shoulder of her blouse up to cover herself. Turning away, she walked to the door of the dining room, then turned back to face him. When she spoke, her voice was devoid of all soft coyness, all flirtatiousness. "I'm going to stand over here while we talk. I want you to stay there, okay?"

"Is this a joke?" Anger rising at her insinuation, he said, "Like I'm going to hit you, or something? Seriously Kacey?"

"My attorney told me to take precautions."

David shook his head, pulled his glasses off, then pressed his fingers to his eyelids. "I can't believe this."

"To answer your question, David," she said, her tone didactic, the words coming out as a well-prepared speech, "the 'why' is easy. We have nothing in common and haven't for a long time – if we ever did."

David sucked in a shuddering breath, mind turning over the well-worn memories of their earlier years together. Had she always felt this way? Or had time – and her other relationships – colored her perceptions of those years? He shook his head again and kept his fingers pressed to his eyes, unwilling to look at her, afraid to see the expression that accompanied her emotionless words.

"Why now?" she continued. "Because for years, you've been becoming more and more successful, *wealthier*, although you don't seem to like that word. Why would I divorce you then when you might be twice as rich in another year or two? Then I heard you retired. Retirement sounds like 'no more money coming in' – not good for my plans, if the rumors about your retirement were true. I thought it'd be a good idea to see if you'd really quit, or if this was just some publicity stunt. I went to New York but couldn't find you. Took me six months. When I did find you, you showed me that crap you're working on now." Spiteful irritation colored her next words. "Crap, David. Simon says no one's interested. You'd save a lot of money on fancy woods and great big tools if you took up crocheting doilies for the local farmer's market."

Simon. Everything Simon said about her is true. With a moan, *Why didn't I see it?* He heard Kacey inhale sharply as if trying to regain control of herself. After a moment of silence, she continued, smug now in her perceived victory.

298

"What else was I going to say? Let's see. Oh yeah." David could picture her ticking her checklist off on her fingers. "I want this house. After all, I spent the best years of my marriage here."

David roused himself to say, "You can't have the house, Kacey."

"We'll see about that," she answered crisply.

David sighed and said, "Princess stays with me." *What am I doing, dickering with her like this is some twisted auction?* But, with the pain that was coursing through him, the comfort of Princess curled against him seemed a life-saving necessity.

Kacey laughed. "Keep the bitch. All she ever does is chew on my shoes." She made a disgusted sound in her throat, and said, "God David, you always were a sap. Here's one for you. Might make you feel better. Our '*baby*' that you keep moaning about? I didn't have a miscarriage. I aborted it. I wasn't raising a child in that slum we used to live in. And I have no idea if it would have been a girl – but you kept asking."

All the muscles in David's body went limp and he slid from his chair to the floor, then curled away from where Kacey stood, eyes gazing unblinking along the long stretch of carpet, the forest of table and chair legs. He did not have the energy to voice his thoughts. *Go away. Please, just go away, Kacey.*

"I'm going to grab some clothes and leave now, David. Sorry to have cancel our hot date tonight – who knew? My attorney will be in touch." He could picture her waggling her fingers toward his back as she walked away.

David closed and then opened his eyes in a long, languid blink, but did not otherwise move. *Tears… where are the tears? Everything I thought I knew about Kacey, about the baby, about my* life *is in shambles, and I'm just lying here. I think… I think…* but the shock of the encounter had left his mind strangely blank. *I think I'm going to lie here forever.*

***

For a long time, David did not stir from his position other than to blink his eyes. His breathing remained strangely even, especially considering the turmoil of his thoughts.

Did I ever know that woman? Ever? Was there anything honest about our relationship at all?

His mind ran through a slide show of the last six months, beginning with the shocked moment when he first saw her standing on his front door stoop, the many times they'd made love, their picnics and funny conversations, the day she gave him Princess.

A lie. All of it a lie.

He stopped breathing mid-inhale as another realization came to him.

I've spent years blaming myself for the death of our daughter... our child, he corrected himself, reminding himself that Kacey had even lied about knowing the sex of the child. *Now I know I didn't.* He exhaled a shaky breath. *Even worse than it just being an accident, Kacey finally admitted the truth. She "disposed of" our child.*

That thought circled and repeated itself for long minutes before allowing him to move past it. *I should be crying. Or angry.* Instead, realizing how much and how long he had suffered under Kacey's hypocrisy and falsehoods left him too numb to move from his position.

What a fool I've been. What a damned fool. He took a deep breath and let it out with a moan.

Well, no more. Even though Kacey spent her last minutes in this house trying to hurt me (what did I ever do to her to deserve her nastiness?), instead she's set me free. Liberated me from the dark burden of guilt and self-

doubt. He inhaled again deeply and this time the exhalation came

with a feeling of release.

CHAPTER 26

SARRINAH

FROM HER ATTIC ALCOVE, Sarrinah peered through the high window and watched the taxi came to a stop. She stepped onto the stool beneath the window in the hopes of being able to see who entered the vehicle. If David and Kacey were leaving, she would have the freedom to wander the house without fear of discovery. Pressing her forehead to the glass, she caught a bare glimpse of Kacey throwing a bag across the seat and entering the taxi with some haste.

David remains. Very well, I shall stay in my domain.

She returned to her reading but could not sustain her concentration. Going once again to the stack of portraits David had investigated that morning, she went through them for a third time since his visit, trying to determine which he had taken. A flush of excitement heated her cheeks as she suddenly recalled which was missing.

My portrait that William commissioned to hang in the atrium!

She tried to quell the thrill of delight – *he wanted my portrait!* – with the somber reiteration of her oath never to show herself to David, but she could not resist the temptation to leave the attic in clandestine search to discover where he had placed the portrait. *Perhaps in the salon, in memoriam to the ghost who once dwelled there?*

Not wanting to be burdened in any way during her visit below, she left her borrowed books for a midnight exchange and crept down the attic stairs, ears strained for any sounds of David. She could hear nothing, even when passing the residential wing, no music, no whine of tools in the atrium. *If not here, he could be anywhere in the house. I must be cautious.*

After confirming that he was not in the billiard room, nor in his office, she crept guardedly into the salon. David was (thankfully) not there but, surprisingly, neither was the portrait. She passed through the living room, ears alert to the sound of his tread in the outer hallway or on the main stairs, then paused at the library door. *If he is reading here, it would explain the silence in the house.* Warily, she peered into the library, ready to retreat if he was in occupancy. He was not.

Her curiosity about where David might have hung her portrait was now overcome by her wonder about his whereabouts. *The secret garden?* In her bare feet, she padded across the morning room toward the arcade and a view of the garden, nonetheless pausing at the door to the dining room. She saw nobody, although the breakfast dishes remained on the table. As she dashed across the open doorway toward the garden, she heard a low moan. She froze and pressed her back against the wall near the door she had just passed. *I saw no one! But the sound emanated from the dining room, I am sure of it!* She stayed motionless, breathless with alarm that she should be discovered, but as the silence stretched for minutes, she began to believe she had imagined the sound. Inching toward the door, she peeked into the dining room then jerked her head back. Nothing and nobody. Allowing herself a longer glance, she still saw no one. Just as she was about to turn away, a small movement on the floor caught her attention.

Sarrinah dodged behind the cover of the doorframe, hands flying to her mouth to muffle a shout.

LOVE WHISPERS THROUGH THE VEIL

David! Why is he lying on the floor? Is he ill? Injured? Dead? This last thought brought her close to howling and rushing to him, but then she reminded herself: *He cannot be dead. It was his movement that caught my attention.* Frantic with worry, she paced the length of the wall, toward the arcade and back again to peer once again around the edge of the door. *What shall I do? I cannot go to him…* Her mind turned once again to Kacey's precipitous departure. *Was she fleeing? Has she harmed him? If she wounded him mortally, I must do something!*

She had advanced three tip-toed steps into the dining room when the musical tones of David's personal telephone sounded. Freezing mid-step, she waited for any reaction, praying for any indication of life or consciousness from her beloved.

With a heavy sigh and a groan, David rolled to his back and reached for his pocket. Sarrinah suppressed a squeal caused by equal measures of relief and fright, spun and dashed into the morning room. The phone sounded again before she heard David's voice.

"Hello… yes… yes… That'll be fine. Yeah. Okay." If she had not been so delighted to hear his voice, she might have been bothered by the dull tones in which he spoke.

In the ensuing silence, she could not resist another glance toward where David lay. His telephone sat on his chest, rising and falling with each breath. His eyes were open and directed toward the ceiling. After a long sigh, he slipped the telephone into his pocket and jerked himself into a sitting position. Shaking his head as if denial of something, he then shrugged with a single twitch of his shoulders and said, "Well, there you have it. Move along, folks. Nothing to see here. Please go about your business." With surprising energy, he rose and began stacking the breakfast dishes.

Confused and curious, Sarrinah nonetheless did not feel brave enough to continue eavesdropping. When David took the dishes to the kitchen, she ran down the main hallway, ducked into the billiard room and escaped to the solace of her attic aerie.

***

Against expectations, Kacey did not return that night. Knowing David was still alone in the house, and especially after the extraordinary discovery of him lying on the dining room floor, Sarrinah could suppress neither her worry for him, nor her own inquisitiveness. Determined to discover the reason for the strange occurrence, she spent hours daily exploring the house and watching David for signs of illness or injury.

On the day after the "event" (as Sarrinah had come to think of it), David collected all the framed pictures of Kacey and placed them in a black plastic garbage sack. He then added in the box of Kacey's photographs that he had so often looked through when he first came to this house. After placing the bag where it would be collected for disposal, he took a glass and a large bottle of whiskey – a substance Sarrinah had never seen David imbibe – to his bedroom for the night. That night, during her late night meanderings, she discovered where David had hung her portrait; she would have been more pleased had she not been so terribly anxious for the dear man.

Over the following days, David assiduously inspected every room of the house to gather any of Kacey's personal belongings. These he packed into several brown cardboard boxes which he then carefully labeled with her name and stacked in the foyer near the entry door. He even went so far as to remove the bowl of decorated glass balls from the living room which Kacey had once declared she thought attractive. After wrapping each ball with care and placing them in yet another box, he paused, shook his head and pulled them out again. He opened the front door, and dropped to sit in the middle of the open doorframe. Looking every bit the part of a young boy playing marbles, David then unwrapped each ball, and rolled it across the front stoop toward the driveway. From her spot just inside the salon, Sarrinah could hear the crash and tinkle of each ball as it broke on the stairs, some breaking on the first step, others lasting through the first drop only to shatter on the second.

Under other circumstances, Sarrinah would have been appalled at such willful and meaningless destruction, but having arrived at the inescapable conclusion that Kacey had – once again – abandoned David, she silently cheered for this symbolic acceptance that reconciliation would not occur.

For an entire week after Kacey's departure, David passed through his days with uncharacteristic silence, neither playing his music nor talking to himself as was his wont. He even eschewed the movies he usually enjoyed in the evenings. He spoke on the telephone several times a day, but otherwise maintained a monk-like muteness. Sarrinah at first worried over this unusual desire for silence, but soon noticed that he did not at all behave as though depressed. Instead, he delved into his woodwork, twice working through the night.

The sculptures he produced – three in that first week – were astounding. The first was a broken, jagged, rough-surfaced twist of wood, highlighted by smooth rivulets running in crooked, variably spaced lines from top to bottom. At the sight of it during one of her midnight excursions (for there was no truly safe location from which to watch David work during the day), she was at once saddened and awed. She reached toward the only part of the sculpture that welcomed touching – the polished lines – and felt she was tracing the tracks of tears flowing across a ruined landscape.

The second sculpture seemed sister to the first, with rough parts and smooth, but with a greater ratio of polished wood. Of the polished areas, the rivulets no longer seemed representative of tears but of flowing and merging rivers, and the curious extrusions and swirling carved areas spoke to her of renewal, growth, hope and springtime.

The final sculpture sent Sarrinah into near rapture, speaking so clearly to her of strength and renewal. All three works were of a similar size and shape, yet this third contained no roughness at all. Most of the wood had been carved away, leaving an airy and ethereal structure that brought to mind leaping and dancing and exuberant joy. Sarrinah wept for the beauty of it. Later that night, once again ensconced in the attic, she shed tears of thankfulness for such a palpable indication that Kacey had not destroyed David. Not at all. Whatever had passed between the two, instead of wounding David further, it had cured the illusions surrounding their relationship and cleared the way for true healing.

David, my beloved, you will yet love again. I pray your new love is worthy of the greatness of your heart.

***

When the doorbell rang, Sarrinah raced through the connecting rooms to see who had called. If Kacey had finally returned, Sarrinah was determined to witness whatever confrontation was to come.

"Simon, so glad you could make it!" David's ebullient greeting was followed by, "Come in, come in. You're probably soaked to the skin."

"Nonsense, I nearly parked on your entry stair and dashed to the door." Sarrinah smiled at the pleasant voice, and peeked out to see Simon setting down his wet umbrella and removing his coat.

"Sorry about the weather."

"Yes, do something about that, would you?" Simon pulled a handkerchief from a pocket and used it to mop at his face.

David laughed, and gestured down the hall, but Simon cocked his head and squinted as he examined David's face. "Are you really as healthy and happy as you look? I must admit, I fully expected to be greeted by a gloomy and miserable man in desperate need of cheering."

"I'm fine. Yeah, I have occasional bouts of anger, directed at Kacey as well as myself, but—"

"More at Kacey, I hope," Simon interrupted.

"Definitely," David answered, some of the good humor leaving his voice.

"Good man," Simon answered with a sharp nod of his head, then with a smile, imitated David's gesture toward the hallway.

David's excitement was obvious as he led Simon away from the entry. "I've got some new pieces I want you to see. I need a fresh eye to tell me if they're any good or if I've just lost it completely. I mean, *I* like them, but–"

"David!" Simon stopped so abruptly that David had to pace back several steps to meet him. "Don't get me wrong. I'm not leaving before I've seen what you've been working on, but I've been worried sick about you. You call with a scant two-word statement that 'Kacey left' and ask if I can come see you." Simon huffed before continuing. "At the risk of prying or of touching an open wound – which you do *not* appear to have, by the by – *what the hell happened?*"

David chuckled at his friend's vehemence. "Sorry, I've been preoccupied lately." He ignored Simon's guffaw and led him toward the large formal living room. "Let's sit down. This is a great room to watch the rain from…"

"I've seen enough rain."

"…and I'll tell you what went down."

"That's more like it."

Sarrinah shared with Simon a desire to understand what had transpired between David and Kacey, and blessed her good luck in having a vantage from which to hear the explanation. She hurried across the salon to take up a post at the side door into the library in time to hear Simon say, "Good Lord, I'd forgotten the fabulous views you have from your palazzo… even in the rain."

"Can I get you something to drink?"

"Later. Right now, it is my thirst for knowledge that needs quenching."

Sarrinah could hear the men settling into chairs. After a lengthy stillness, David cleared his throat and spoke, voice devoid of the ebullience with which he had greeted Simon.

"There's not much to tell, actually. You were right about Kacey all along, and I won't blame you for saying so. In short, money is all she wanted, from the start of our relationship. She delayed divorcing me until she thought I'd accumulated enough. When she showed up here, it was to make sure she didn't have any competition for my wealth, and to confirm I was really all washed up. Now she's filed for divorce."

Silence stretched for several seconds before Simon spoke, voice full of sympathy. "David… I don't know what to say. I'm so very sorry."

"That's not all," David added. Sarrinah could hear fingers drumming a sharp staccato rhythm on wood, a clear sign of David's agitation. "She didn't miscarry. She…" – the sound of David clearing his throat again – "She aborted my child."

Sarrinah's hands flew to her mouth, and she blinked against suddenly over-full eyes. *That evil, evil woman! She not only purposely destroyed David's child, but confessed her crime to him? Oh David, oh my poor, precious David. I worried that she had wounded him that awful day, and she had done worse than I could imagine!* Tears of vicarious hurt and compassion flowed freely down her cheeks.

Simon murmured, "Merciless hell." Then in disbelief, "She *told* you this?"

David did not answer, but she could picture him nodding, perhaps unable for the moment to speak.

Outrage apparent, Simon said, "Well, she bloody well will not get a thing out of you. You haven't been together for years. She's been here mere months, so she can't claim she's become accustomed to this style of living. With a half-decent lawyer, you should be able to argue—"

"I'm settling, Simon." David paused for a beat and said, "I'm keeping this house, my dog, and any future rights to my wood sculpture or any income from it. I'm giving her everything else."

Simon groaned. "Not everything, David. You've millions. And I still have two of your metal sculptures that are probably worth—"

"She can have them. They're not worth anything or you wouldn't still have them." Sarrinah could hear the grin in David's voice when he said, "In fact, once we get everything settled, I want you to deliver them to her front yard."

Simon barked out a startled laugh and David joined him. "David, they're enormous. What on earth would she do with them?"

"Won't be my problem, will it?" David answered, still laughing. Sarrinah stifled the giggle David's laughter provoked, then quickly sobered. *How can I even dream of laughing knowing how much David must be suffering for Kacey's unforgiveable act?*

Simon's laugh reduced to a chuckle, then dissipated. "David, why give her anything? I know people say that money can't buy happiness, but–"

David barked out a bitter laugh and said, "The person who said that never had the pleasure of paying for a divorce." He chuckled at Simon's loud guffaw, then continued, in a serious voice. "I just want her gone. No arguments. No long, drawn-out legal proceedings. Just gone."

Simon, speaking cautiously: "Okay, David. But how are you going to live? Are you planning to sell this monstrosity of a house, and–"

"I'm never, *never* selling this house." Vehemence. Determination. Then in more congenial tones, "But that does bring me to one of the reasons I asked you here. My wood sculpture."

"Aaahhh. Do I sense the blessedly beautiful prospect of an upcoming show?"

"Once everything is signed and settled. Maybe. If you think they're worth anything at all."

317

Sarrinah heard the happy sound of a sharp hand clap. "Very well, lead on, boy wonder. Despite your unhappy news, I say: Good riddance to the worthless wench." A low chuckle and then, "This may turn out to be an extraordinarily good day after all!"

CHAPTER 27

DAVID

DAVID PULLED BACK AND secured the heavy crimson curtains and sheer drapes so he could enjoy the spectacular view from the pavilion; thankfully the wind was minimal and the rain fell straight down, rather than blowing in upon him. He poured himself a cup of coffee, pulled the blanket tightly around his shoulders, and settled in the seat that would afford the best perspective of the misty panorama.

It looks like another world entirely. And tomorrow, it will change yet again, becoming greener and fresher than it was before the rain. Life is change.

This immutable fact had been elevated to the fore of his thoughts over the last three months. His dreams for the future had changed, no longer including Kacey. His art form had changed. And, after settling with Kacey, his financial situation would change.

No, it probably didn't have to change as drastically as it was going to, but he wanted this house. He needed to keep this house.

He had argued with his confused and unwilling lawyer about the plan for settling things with Kacey, but finally managed to convince the reluctant woman into making the more-than-generous settlement offer he wanted. Kacey initially argued – no doubt against the advice of *her* lawyer – that she wanted the house, but in the end, had accepted David's offering, relinquishing his dog and his wood sculpture without disagreement. The only matter remaining was the formality of putting the offer to paper in the appropriate officialese. No doubt there would be further arguments between the lawyers about the specific phrasing of "paragraph F(1)(c)(iii)" or whatever, but once the agreement was completed and signed, the final step of court approval would be simple.

Kacey only argued for the house out of spite. She didn't really want it. She hated being away from the hustle and bustle of city life. The spark of anger this thought aroused sputtered and quickly washed away in the indifference that suffused him when he thought of Kacey. *My Kacey never existed. My Kacey was an illusion I created and nurtured – a dream I've now awoken from.*

A gust of wind and the accompanying splatter of rain roused David from his musings. Shivering, he finished his coffee and hurried from the pavilion with the tray of dishes. As he began to pour the remaining coffee into the kitchen sink, an alluring and fragrant steam rose from the pot, and he poured himself another cup instead, hoping to ward off the chill that still enveloped him. Despite his intention to go up to his studio to begin his work for the day, he wandered the dark and quiet main floor hall, peering into each room he passed with an indefinable feeling of looking for something. When he reached the salon, the impression sharpened and he sighed in sudden understanding.

"If I missed you when Kacey was here, you can imagine that I think of little else now. Despite the rainy day gloom, you would have brightened the whole house." He smiled as he remembered the day he had complained to Sarrinah of the malaise that sometimes overcame him on wet and overcast days. She had *literally* brightened the whole house, turning on every light in every room, from the basement to the third floor. *Can't afford to do that now, though. Especially as the bill for such extravagance probably won't come in until after the settlement.*

Thankfully, rather than giving Kacey every last dime (which had been David's original flippant intention), David's attorney had insisted on two things: that her fees be deducted from the settlement amount, and that David retain enough for "living expenses." The woman had originally suggested half a million dollars, but David would not agree to more than $100,000. While this would have seemed a fortune in David's youth, he'd be lucky if that lasted a year with the expenses of maintaining this house. He had caved to the necessity of canceling his cleaning contract, and releasing the gardening crew and chef. He had been pleased when the head groundskeeper, Finn, and Alexandre, the chef, had both indicated a desire to return in the future if his circumstances changed.

And on that note, I'd better get busy. This is my do-or-die moment. And I promised Simon at least five more pieces for the show. David couldn't suppress his excitement – and concurrent anxiety – at the thought of reentering the art scene with an entirely different form of sculpture. Yes, he would likely have some initial interest by the sole virtue of already being a well-celebrated sculptor. *But that doesn't guarantee I won't fall on my face when I defy public expectations by presenting something new.*

Simon had no such qualms. The man was giddy with anticipation, and effusive in his reassurances that David's wood sculpture would quickly gain ground. "The pieces are smaller, and can be appreciated by more individuals for display in their homes. That's more sales. And if you get me a couple of outrageously large pieces, you'll still get hotels, restaurants and office buildings. Besides, I'm going to suggest exorbitant prices! You are, after all, David Cartell."

Simon had approached several prospective galleries for the opening show, insisting on signed confidentiality agreements before showing samples of David's new work. Weeks later, unwilling to deliver the news over the phone, he drove out to tell David that two of the most prestigious galleries were vying for the honor of hosting the opening. "All we have to do is pick a date – so tell your lawyer to get on with it. Tagliaboo is so enthusiastic about your sculpture that even if they've booked something else, I won't be surprised if they boot them just to get you in." With a long familiar gleam in his eye, he rubbed his chin and said, "Now to start working on your worldwide tour…"

David laughed. "You've always been my biggest fan, Simon. But do me a favor and wait on the tour until we know whether the opening is a success?"

Adopting a wounded expression, Simon said, "Oh, but it will be, David." Then, with a clap to David's shoulder, "Show me what you've been working on. Do you have anything more completed for me? If so, I'll have it picked up post haste so we can get it photographed for the brochure. Lord, the layout they did for your trio – 'The Agony and the Ecstasy' – is fantastic. That'll be our cover and announcement poster."

Simon had since accompanied every delivery van and – in the case of one big daddy of a sculpture – the truck that had come to the house for completed items, ostensibly to ensure the safety of the transfer. David suspected the real reason was to make sure his "favorite artist" was not sliding into a depression over Kacey. Whatever the reason, David was always thankful to see his friend; with a new show to prepare for, he appreciated the man's infectious enthusiasm.

Even with the gloom of the rainy morning still hanging over him, thoughts of Simon cheered him and quickened his step. He entered the studio and, as had been his habit since Kacey's departure, greeted Sarrinah's portrait.

"Good morning." Then, circling the room to flip all the lights on, "Lots to do today. What should I start with? The final coat of varnish on that one, or finish up the detail work on this one?" He waited a beat as he imagined her response and said, "Yeah, you're right. Finishing the varnish will mean one more done and ready for pick up." He got out the superfine sandpaper and the chamois cloth he would use for dusting the wood after sanding. As he began gently stroking the wood with the sandpaper, he continued the one-sided conversation.

"So what are you reading?" He posed the question in what he hoped was a tone of airy innocence. Pausing in his work, he listened with anticipation. When there was no response, he blew a puff of air at the nearly invisible dust he had raised and resumed sanding, careful to follow the wood grain. "I've just finished *The Oracle Glass*. It's a modern book – written about ten years ago – but I think you'd like it. It's set in 17th Century France. Now, I think I'll start one of Alexandre Dumas' books next. Maybe *Count of Monte Cristo?*" Again he stopped sanding and listened for a response, then sighed when he heard nothing.

The truth was, *The Count of Monte Cristo* was missing from his library. More importantly, it had not been missing two days ago.

David first noticed several books missing from the library shortly after Kacey had gone, including *Emma* which he wanted to reread. At the time, he had assumed (with considerable annoyance) that Kacey had taken the books when she left, although he puzzled over her reasoning; to his knowledge, her choice of reading material had never tended toward the classics. When, two weeks later, he found *Emma* on the shelf, he assumed that he had overlooked it in his earlier search. The other possibility – that Sarrinah was somehow taking and returning the books – did not occur to him until, during one of his one-sided conversations, he mentioned the incident.

Since then, he had kept a careful and almost daily inventory of the books in the classics section of his library. Yesterday, much to his excitement, he noticed certain "returns" and several different books missing. Uncertain how she was accomplishing the feat –

after all, he knew nothing about where she had "gone" or how – he was certain of one thing: Sarrinah was, in some extraordinary way, still visiting the house.

Now, confounded in his attempt to coax her into speaking to him, he said, "I miss you. I wish you'd never gone," and then could think of nothing more to say. He worked for hours in silence, mind groping toward anything else he could do to bring her back.

***

David leaned back in his office chair and stretched luxuriously, then pulled his glasses off and pinched at the bridge of his nose. The settlement agreement had been signed two months ago, and his attorney had called this morning to tell him of the court's expedited approval of the agreement. Despite her obvious chagrin at the terms David had insisted on, she managed to congratulate him on a successful divorce and to wish him the best of luck in the future. Suddenly faced with the reality of his financial circumstances, he had spent the hours since putting together yet another budget with the goal of being able to maintain the house for as long as possible.

If my opening flops, I'll... I'll have to... With a sigh, he said in a raised voice, "I won't let this house go, Sarrinah. I swear I won't."

The day of his mention of *The Count of Monte Cristo*, all the missing books had reappeared in the library. Rather than accept this as a rejection of his desire for her presence, he had – in the months since – redoubled his efforts to tempt her return. He had searched the house from top to bottom, even taking a brief poke around the attic. He had wheedled and cajoled her through conversations, strolls and lunches in the secret garden, playing her favorite music, and reading aloud in the library. As yet, while he sometimes thought he heard noises in the night, and even once the sound of muffled footsteps hurrying away during the day, he had no real evidence that these were not figments of his imagination. This did not shake his certainty that she was somehow still attached to the house, that she could somehow return to him. So, while knowing that selling the house made the most financial sense, he vowed silently – once more – never to do so.

He yawned as he raised his arms over his head, and stretched his legs out under the desk. When his foot, instead of rubbing against carpet, slid over something smooth, he bent to peer into the darkness there. "What's this?" Dropping to his knees and crawling under the huge desk, he retrieved a large manila envelope. "How did this…?" he began, puzzled because he ordinarily kept a neat and organized office. In a flash of memory, he recalled the one day his office had not been orderly: the day he'd been served with the divorce papers and had flung the mail through the door. Suddenly realizing how long this bit of mail had gone unnoticed, he flipped the envelope over to look for the addressee. *John Willard, Genealogy and Historical Records Research.*

"Holy moly!" In the chaos of the time since his last conversation with the historian, David had been so preoccupied with the divorce and all that had entailed, as well as preparing non-stop for the upcoming opening show, he had completely forgotten about the promised information. The man was probably devastated (or annoyed) not to have received a phone call regarding the results of his months of research.

David pulled the stack of paper from the envelope and read the cover letter, which – rather than reflecting the excitement of their last conversation – clinically reported that no certain conclusion could be reached, although "certain findings are suggestive that events did not proceed as reported in the newspapers of the time." There followed a list of the attached materials and a statement that Willard would be happy to entertain questions, further discussion or additional research. With a quickening heartbeat, David slid the papers back into the envelope.

"This calls for a glass of wine, and a more comfortable chair." He pulled a spiral notebook from a drawer, clipped a pen to its cover, and tucking the envelope and notebook under one arm, left his office.

***

Entering the library, David turned on the subtle accent lighting and the reading lamp above his favorite chair, thus achieving an appropriately mysterious ambiance. Comfortably ensconced, a glass of wine on the table beside him, he pulled the papers from the envelope and read the cover letter again, looking over the list of attachments. The attachments included newspaper articles as well as birth, marriage and death statistics for both William and Sarrinah with supporting documentation. (William had apparently remarried. David wondered if that information would hurt or help Sarrinah's guilt and heartache.) There were also

330

employment records (incomplete) for staff employed at the house at the time (*where on earth did he come up with those?*); and the most enigmatic entry, "Excerpts from the Diary of Minnie Sebastian, ca. 1900-1903, with appended explanatory notations."

I know what I'm starting with. I can look at newspapers and other records later!

Pushing the cover letter aside, David flipped to the tab labeled "Diary." The header at the top of the first page read, "Explanatory Notations," and contained a bulleted list of sentences. He almost flipped past it to the diary, but the first item caught his eye. "Minnie Sebastian was the only witness to Sarrinah Bladeswell's death."

Whoa! She must be the maid who testified about Sarrinah's "dark moods" as well as swearing to the suicide! David hadn't recalled the name from the archived records he'd found online, but he remembered there had been a maid involved. He quickly read on.

> • *Minnie Sebastian was employed by William Bladeswell until her unexplained departure approximately three months after Sarrinah Bladeswell's death.*

- *Minnie Sebastian thereafter entered*
employment at nearby Nesilik Manor, where she
remained until her death.
- *The attached excerpts are from the self-styled*
"Dairy of Minnie Sebastian," kept in the
historical memorabilia of Nesilik Manor. The
document has long been considered either a
contemporaneously penned "fiction" or a faked
artifact due to the fact that the events described
within the "diary" never took place at Nesilik
Manor.

With a trembling hand, David turned the page. The top of the following page consisted of a copy of a handwritten document written in a nearly illegible script. Thankfully, the bottom of the page appeared to be a typewritten translation. As he read the first words, he released a choked croak and brought a fist to his mouth.

Today I kilt a woman. This declarashin is not
strickly true as I did not do it today, but the gilt
rides me each day as if newly born, and so I say:
Today I kilt a woman.

Transfixed, David read on, not stopping for food, nor even to refill his wine glass until the conclusion of the sometimes repetitive and often circuitous account. When he finished, he understood why the historian had stated that "no certain conclusion could be reached." The diary never mentioned Sarrinah by name – referring only to "m'lady" – nor did it contain details of the house that could help in a positive identification of this, the Bladeswell estate. On the other hand, there were no particulars about the house or circumstances that could unequivocally eliminate Sarrinah as the subject of the confession.

And David was certain beyond question that the document was a confession. Yes, it contained an agonized lament of guilt, but it was nonetheless an admission of Sarrinah's murder.

I was right. She didn't kill herself. The thought was not accompanied by any feeling of satisfaction. Instead, his mind swirled with an acute regret for everything she had lost – *and at such a young age!* – as well as all the suffering she had endured as a trapped and tortured soul in the more-than-century since.

In an attempt to clear his mind, he flipped back to the first tab to read the newspaper clippings. Unfortunately, righteous anger entered his mix of emotions as he read the eyewitness accounts as related by "Minnie Sebastian, maid to the deceased woman." He lifted the manila envelope from the floor beside his chair and slid the stack of papers into it. After refilling his glass, he returned to his chair, put his head back, and closed his eyes.

I've got to tell Sarrinah. She's not a ghost because she killed herself. She's been trapped here because of the trauma of her death. Or because she needed the truth discovered. Or something. If I explain what really happened, she'll be able to... David sat forward, and braced his elbows on his knees, his hanging head cupped in his hands. *She'll be able to go. Really go. And forever.*

And I'm not sure I can stand that thought.

CHAPTER 28

SARRINAH

AFTER KACEY'S DEPARTURE, SARRINAH could not resist the draw to leave the attic to ensure David's wellbeing. When he abandoned his unusual silence and returned to his more natural behavior, playing music, watching movies, and talking aloud to both himself and his puppy, Princess, she would have forsaken her frequent forays to check on him and once more retired to her attic lodgings, except for one thing: He also began speaking to her again, engaging in imagined conversations as he had when he had first come to the house. She found listening irresistible because his discourse was now more intimate and familiar, including references to their previous activities and discussions, as well as lamentations that she had gone.

One particular conversation did bring Sarrinah close to panic. While discussing books, David mentioned the desire to read a book she had recently taken from the library. Without listening to another word, she dashed to the attic and retrieved the entire stack she had taken, stealthily returning them to the library while he continued his work in the upstairs atrium. After that incident, and in addition to vowing anew never to appear to David, she added the oath never to take another book from the library.

As the days went by, she abandoned her attic refuge and began staying in one of the guest rooms on third floor. David rarely frequented that area of the house. She certainly preferred the sunlit room and the comforts available, as well as the easier access to the remainder of the house. Her one regret was that she could not display her sculpture there. She was thankful of her decision not to do so on the day David searched the entire house for some unknown purpose or item – including the rooms on the third floor and the attic. She initially worried that he might discover her sculpture in the attic, but he did not remain there long enough to have reached her far corner alcove. With a cheerfulness she wished she could share with David, she pretended they were engaged in a game of seek-and-find, and kept away from where he was searching.

Quiet, pleasant weeks and months passed, and David finished the woodwork projects needed for his gallery exhibition. During his months of preparation, he had so entrenched himself in his atrium studio, she knew she could reliably find him there. The sounds of saw, hammer and chisel further informed her of his location. However, since his completion of the final sculpture, she learned to exercise more caution, as he had returned to his habit of wandering the house, enjoying the various rooms for their distinct purposes and individual décor.

He seemed happy, but so alone. Her fervent wish for him, now that he was no longer so focused on his art, was that he had another companion – more worthy than Kacey – with whom to share the house. *After all, he is the most wonderful, loving and deserving man I've known.*

***

Sarrinah sighed with pleasure as she enjoyed the spectacular vista from the window of her third-floor room. The tops of the trees, swathed in the yellow, orange and crimson leaves of autumn, had just begun to glow in the light from the rising sun. Even though unable to stroll at her leisure under the brilliant foliage, she still delighted in the jewel-toned hues of her favorite season.

She was startled from her quiet enjoyment by a shout from the floor below. As she crept toward the door of her room, the shout came again. David's voice, she was certain. She could not discern his words, but the tenor of his voice did not portray pain or anger. Nonetheless, she entered the hall outside her room in an attempt to discover the direction from which the bellow came. She knew multiple exits from the third floor, and felt certain she could escape detection if David was once again engaged in a peculiar game of seek-and-find.

The shout came again, and despite now being in the hall where it should have been clearer, it seemed to come from farther away. *Why would David be walking through the house repeatedly crying out?*

Sarrinah descended the nearest servants' stair to the second floor, and stopped to listen at the door. The shout came again from some distance. She pushed the door open and listened. When David next yelled, she knew he had now descended to the first floor and was moving toward the front of the house. As fast as she could safely manage, she scurried through the servants' passages and stairways to the downstairs billiard room to listen again from behind the door.

"Sarrinah!" The shock of her name being bellowed from the foyer down the main hallway almost sent her racing back up the stairs. "Come to the library. It's important!" David repeated the call just outside the billiard room and, suddenly frightened, she ran on tiptoes up several steps, breath coming in gasps. His next call came from further down the hall.

What is the meaning of this? This is no imagined conversation, but rather a summons. Why does he believe I can hear him? I am certain I returned the books before he discovered they were missing. Has he caught a glimpse of me despite all my cautions?

She crept down the stairs and pressed her ear to the door. The shouts continued as he traversed to the rear of the house, and then subsided.

I should return to the third floor. Or perhaps as far as the attic. Despite knowing the wisdom of this, she could not bring herself to mount the stairs. *Is he in the library now?* After another moment of indecision, she pushed the door open and crept across the billiard room. *I will not show myself to him, but I must know what he will say!*

After daring to dash across the hallway, she slipped through the salon to the living room and took up a post where she could hear him if he spoke in the library. After long minutes of silence she began to fear he was not in the library after all. *What if this is a ruse he has concocted? What if he enters the living room and sees me here?* Screwing up her courage, she peeked into the library.

David stood at the south windows looking out toward Randish Lake, hands clasped behind his back. In a low voice that barely carried to her ears he murmured, "Well, I've yelled myself hoarse. I don't know what else I can do." Then raising his voice, he said, "I'm turning around now, Sarrinah. I hope to see you standing there when I do."

Sarrinah jerked her head back as he turned to face the open, empty room, then heard his disappointed sigh. She felt a pang in her heart to know she had injured his expectations. Clenching her fists painfully and pulling them to her chest, her answer howled through her mind. *I do this for you, David, for you! To do as you ask would be selfish of me — it being my greatest desire — and would only bring you unhappiness in the end!*

She heard the sound of his footsteps, and believing he was leaving the room, she could not resist another quick glance. David had advanced to the middle of the room and with arms outstretched and his gaze directed upward, he spoke again.

"I am in love with you, Sarrinah."

Sarrinah puffed out a breath in disbelief. Tears of sublime joy and crushing heartbreak cascaded down her cheeks as she braced herself against the wall to keep from collapsing.

"I've loved you since before Kacey came here and screwed everything up. I admit, I kept telling myself that I loved you as a friend – the best friend I've ever had – but just as a friend, because… well, because that's all we ever could be. I don't mean I didn't want to touch you, to kiss you, to hold you in my arms. You had to have noticed how hard it was for me."

And for me, dear, dear David, to force myself to flinch away from your touch. Sarrinah's tears continued to flow and she swallowed against a sob. *Please, stop! You cannot know how difficult it is not to run to you!* Despite the vehemence of her plea, the ecstasy of hearing his declaration kept her from fleeing as she knew she should.

"I think you loved me, too – I hope you still do, wherever you are." His voice was rough with emotion when he continued. "So, please, come back to me." He cleared his throat and released a husky sigh.

Hands pressed to her mouth, Sarrinah rocked against the agony of ignoring his pleas, especially in the face of her passionate desire to succumb to them.

She heard the rustle of movement, and then: "On my knees, Sarrinah, I'm begging you. Come back to me."

Sarrinah could no longer fight his entreaties and her own heart. After lifting her hands from her mouth to wipe away her tears, she stepped into the library. As her movement caught his eye, he turned his head toward her, his mouth open in surprise. His shocked expression transformed slowly into a smile and Sarrinah's smile grew to match his.

David rose from his kneeling position, but did not move toward her. "Sarrinah." His voice was low and reverent, as if he spoke her name as a prayer.

"David." Her cheeks ached from the fullness of her smile, and her eyes sparkled with renewed tears. She said aloud the words she had repeated so often in her mind. "David, my love."

"Wow," he murmured, then shook his head as if attempting to break a spell. "I've missed you so much." He stepped toward her, holding a hand out toward her. "I know," he said, "I know I shouldn't, but I don't care. I want to touch you." He stopped before her, hand outstretched. Hoping she was correct in her beliefs about the changes she had undergone, she lifted her hand and placed it in his.

As their palms met, David flinched in expectation of what he would feel, then closed his warm fingers around her hand. The sensation of his skin against hers was everything she imagined and Sarrinah nearly swooned. His eyes widened and his mouth opened in surprise. "What...? How...?" He brought his other hand up to trap her hand between them.

Sarrinah laughed. "With the strength of your life force, I seem to have become quite substantial. Quite 'thick' as you used to say."

David pulled her into his arms almost violently, his strong arms crushing her body against his. As she wrapped her arms around him, renewed tears flowed along with her laughter. He spoke over her shoulder, seemingly unwilling to relinquish the embrace.

"Are you...? Are you human? Real?"

Lifting her head to speak into his ear, she said, "I am what I am, David. Thicker, yes, more able to affect my environment. But I cannot leave the house. I have no need of food. I don't believe I've aged in the time you have been here."

He released her, but only back far enough to hold her at arm's length as he gazed at her. His smile did not falter, but to her surprise, she saw agony as well as joy reflected in the glitter that moistened his eyes. "This is almost too much. I mean, I wanted so much to see you one last time, but I never expected..." His words trailed off as he brought a finger to brush against her cheek.

Sarrinah froze in the act of stepping once again into his arms and her smile faltered as terror slashed through her heart. "Last time...?"

He went on as if she hadn't spoken. "Now, I want more than anything to kiss you, but if I do, I *know* I won't be able to go through with it." He pulled her into another embrace, this time holding her gently and entwining his fingers in her hair. "I love you, Sarrinah," he murmured. "I wish I could be with you always."

The agony and confusion these words brought Sarrinah kept her from being able to return his caresses.

He released her, and backed slowly from her, one step and then another, eyes roving over her face as if memorizing every detail of her features. When his legs bumped into his chair, he gestured and said, "Please, sit down. I've something to tell you. Something important. God help me, at this moment, it's the last thing I want to do, but…" When Sarrinah did not move from where she stood, he gestured again. Expression now solemn and pained, he swallowed. "Please."

The effort to move from her locked position, to place one foot before the other, brought her to trembling. She fell more than sat once she reached the chair he indicated.

David took a deep breath, then leaned forward, supporting his upper body with elbows to his knees. "Much as I want you to stay with me, I love you too much to deny you the possibility of going" – he lifted one hand and gestured with a vague motion toward the ceiling – "home, or wherever it is you should have gone when you died."

"David, I–" she began, lip quivering as she blinked to clear the sudden cloudiness of her vision.

"You didn't kill yourself. You *didn't*. I know what actually happened."

Sarrinah opened her mouth but could not utter any words.

"Your maid. Do you remember her name?"

"M-M-Minnie," she stuttered, surprise by the question.

"Minnie Sebastian, right?" Sarrinah nodded and David plunged on, as if frantic to get the words out. "You argued with her the day you died, something trivial, and she was angry."

Memories of that morning flooded into her mind. Closing her eyes to capture the details, she said, "Minnie had just returned from a week-long hiatus to care for her ailing sister. Of course, there was no question of the necessity and we allowed her to go, and for as long as needed. But that morning, only four days after her return, she asked if she could leave off her afternoon and evening duties to go to a fair with a man who was courting her. I…" Sarrinah opened her eyes, and with a rush of guilt at being so ungenerous, she said, "I denied her, saying there was too much to be done in the wake of her recent absence." Sarrinah wrung her hands together. "In retrospect, her chores could have waited another day."

David dismissed her words with a wave of his hand. "So she was angry with you." Sarrinah nodded and David rushed on. "She wanted to exact revenge, and when she saw her opportunity, she took it. She spilled soapy water at the top of the main staircase" – he spread his hands and bobbed his head to make sure she understood the significance – "*the main staircase*, then told you that you were needed downstairs."

Sarrinah gasped as her missing memories of that day crowded into her mind. David's next words seemed to come from far away until they faded away entirely. "In her dairy, she claims she only meant to injure your pride, but instead, you…"

Sarrinah strode from her bedchamber still pulling up her gloves. As she entered the atrium, Minnie approached.

"Pardon, m'lady. You've a visitor, a Mrs. Fairlane. Simpson asked her to wait in the salon."

"Mrs. Fairlane? At this hour...?"

Minnie curtsied and said, "She indicated to Simpson that she hoped to see you urgently."

"Oh. Well, then." Sarrinah stepped away, then turned back. "Minnie, I am sorry about this afternoon. I hope you aren't too disappointed. The guest rooms are in abominable condition and with the Westerfields coming next week…"

"I understand m'lady."

"Thank you."

Sarrinah lifted her skirts as she approached the marble stairs. Just as she reached the top, her foot went out from under her. Instead of simply falling to her bottom, she twisted in an effort to catch hold of the rail, and was suddenly tumbling… Screams, screams and excruciating pain as her arm connected with a riser, shock and hurt as her leg contorted into an unnatural position, another scream as she realized she was going to hit her head… blackness.

Sarrinah threw her head back and inhaled sharply, her body rigid, her arms flung out to her sides. Then David's voice, blurred and muffled at first, then coming clear.

"…solved. We know the truth now. I'll publish it, clear your name, and…"

Even through closed eyes, she was aware of a brightness, a light that suffused and warmed her, clung to her, called to her.

David's voice, diminishing as though he were speeding away from her. "Yes, that's it. Go home… I love you, Sarrin…"

David! My beloved! My dearest one! David! The words screamed in her mind, even as she felt herself dissolving, lightening, floating… *David!*

CHAPTER 29

DAVID

DAVID KNEW THE MOMENT the memories returned to Sarrinah. As he battered her with the barest facts he had gleaned from Minnie's diary, she moaned, and he could see rapid and jerking movements of her eyes beneath her closed lids.

It's working!

Leaning closer to her, he shouted, "You slipped, and you fell down the stairs. You didn't throw yourself. You didn't kill yourself. This was a petty act of vengeance that–"

Sarrinah screamed, then screamed again, the sound tearing at her throat, and startling David to momentary silence. Then she convulsively jerked out of her chair and into a standing position, eyes closed, back arched, arms stiff and stretched out to her sides.

David's mouth hung open in shock as he blinked and tried to regain traction. *Snap out of it, you idiot! It's working!* He stood and shouted, "Yes, that's right. The mystery's solved. We know the truth now. I'll publish it, clear your name, and…" He sputtered to a stop as a sudden glow of warm yellow light enveloped her, then began pulsating with the rhythm of his rapid heartbeat.

"Yes, that's it. Go home, or to heaven, or…" The exhilaration of success at achieving her release, crashed against the realization that she would be gone. He swallowed against a tight throat and barked out a noise that was part groan, part sob. "I love you, Sarrinah!"

He blinked against the moisture in his eyes, unable to tear them away from the vision of the radiant woman before him. *How will it happen? Will she fade away? Burst into fireworks of light? Just disappear?*

The light brightened as he watched. Backing away from Sarrinah, he raised one arm to shield his eyes, then screwed his lids closed as the incandescence increased to a blinding luminosity. A sudden flash made him cry out, and then he could see nothing behind his closed eyes except blackness highlighted by sparks and red amorphous blotches. Blinking against the spots in his vision, he lowered his arm.

"David." Sarrinah still stood where he had last seen her, but instead of agony marring her lovely features, she wore a tender smile.

"Wha... what...?" David stammered.

She stepped into his arms and pressed her cheek to his. He returned the embrace, but then stepped back.

"What... What happened? I saw you. I saw the" – bringing both hands up, he gestured amorphously around her – "the glow thing. I thought... I thought you were going into the light or... whatever."

Sarrinah laughed lightly. "I saw the way. But I chose to stay."

David's mouth opened and closed again before he could speak. "So... does that mean that you're... What does that mean?"

"I am as you have known me. I cannot leave the house, I need not eat, I will not age. If I am not sustained by a life force, I will once more fade."

Anger flooded David that she would do such a thing. "What!? Why? Why on earth did you... I was *trying* to save you. Why?"

She dropped her gaze and smiled shyly. "Being with you, having your love… that is heaven to me." When he could only groan in response, she stepped toward him and lifted his chin until their eyes met. "I will never – *can* never – bind you. If you regret the words you said, if you–"

David pulled her to him, and their lips came together in a long and lingering kiss. "I love you, and I want to spend the rest of my life with you. That's the truth. But I can't tie you here to this half life." He held up a hand when she opened her mouth to interject. "So, for my own peace of mind, please. Go to where you belong." He kissed her again. "Please, before I change my mind."

"I no longer know the way, David."

David closed his eyes, groaned, then pulled her into a tight embrace. He spoke into her hair. "And you remember everything now. There's no awakening the memories again, right? No second chance?"

"You are not wrong. But, I say again David, if you–"

He backed from her, stuck his tongue out and made a raspberry sound. "Don't say it again." He kissed her forehead, and said, "Okay, so I'm stuck with you. Bummer. I tried to do the right thing, and instead I get everything I could possibly want, and I don't even have to feel like the bad guy. I can live with that."

Sarrinah's laughter was a magical sound in his ears. He lifted her and spun around as he laughed with her. Lowering her to the floor, he leaned in and kissed her again, tenderly, slowly.

When they separated, Sarrinah said, "If you intend to continue kissing me like that, we'll have to marry…"

"I thought you'd never ask. I'm ready to exchange our vows now, but can you wait until Simon can be here?"

"Of course, my love." She pulled his head forward to kiss him again.

When she released him, he stepped to her side, and keeping an arm around her, he led her from the room. As they stepped into the hallway, he pointed first in one direction, then in the other. "So, what do you want to do?"

Sarrinah brought a finger to her chin, and tilted her head to the side in thought. Then raising the finger into the air, she said, "Ah! I'd like to retrieve the sculpture you gave me."

"Where is it?"

"In the attic."

"The attic!" When he turned to her, she wore an expression of wide-eyed innocence. Chuckling, he began to lead her to the back stairs she favored. "You've got a lot of explaining to do."

Sarrinah stopped him, and pointed in the opposite direction down the hallway. "And I'd like to take the main staircase."

***

As the day for David's gallery opening approached, his growing anxiety became more and more difficult to mask. He felt so much pride in the work he'd done, it was as if he had birthed them instead of carved them. Simon's enthusiasm never flagged, and Sarrinah's praises were unending.

But that's really not the point, is it. I need sales. I need money. I need this to work.

Over the last several months, his life with Sarrinah had been everything he could wish for, but no matter how many times he tried to rework his budget – and even postponing every bit of necessary maintenance to the house – if the show did not go well, it would not be many years before the house fell to pieces around his head. The thought brought him close to despair because he loved the house as he had loved nowhere else he'd ever lived. *But I love Sarrinah more. I've got to come up with a plan if everything goes to hell.*

His options were few, and all unattractive. He could keep one section of the house in repair, and let the rest rot away. He could tear the whole thing down and build a modest house in its place. *Or can I destroy it without hurting Sarrinah? And would she ever forgive me?*

"I thought you might need a glass of wine, David."

He glanced up to watch Sarrinah approach. She held a glass of wine in one hand, while the other held the long swishing skirt of a jewel-toned multicolor maxi-dress. (For reasons he could well understand, she favored longer skirts, and certainly she had the perfect figure for the fitted bodice and flowing skirt of the modern maxi-dress.)

She smiled as she placed the stemmed glass within his reach. "You've been growling and moaning for at least half an hour. Troubles?"

David reached for her and when she rounded his desk, he pulled her into his lap. "Never when you're with me." He meant the comment as a trifling flattery, but his thoughts darkened. *Which is what I'm trying to ensure without worrying you about it.*

His expression must have clouded with the thought because Sarrinah's smooth brow crinkled with concern. "What is it, David?"

He let out an explosive gust of breath, shook his head in an effort to clear his mind, and pulled her into a kiss. "I'm just worried about the show."

"But Simon says–"

"Simon says, 'Touch your nose.'" He put a finger to the tip of her nose. "Simon says, 'Take a sip of wine.'" He sipped and replaced the glass. "Kiss your man." When Sarrinah leaned toward him with pursed lips, he stopped her with a wagging finger. "Simon didn't say it." She laughed, having only recently learned the game reference, then pulled his finger out of the way and kissed him.

He gently nudged her from his lap, rose and took her hand. Lifting the glass, he said, "I know, I know. I need to chill. How about a movie…?"

***

The day of the opening arrived faster than David thought possible. He woke expecting anxiety to keep his stomach churning all day; instead the adrenaline and excitement left him heady and full of energy.

When Simon's limousine arrived in early afternoon to take him to the City, Sarrinah walked David to the door, straightened the bowtie of his tuxedo, and kissed him. "You look very handsome, my dear."

David brought a hand to his waist, gyrated his hips, and struck a pose. In his best Elvis imitation, he said, "'Hank you, 'hank you very much."

They both laughed, and then he pulled Sarrinah close and leaned his forehead against hers. He whispered, "I'm a little nervous."

"You'll be wonderful," she whispered in return.

The trip to the City seemed interminable, despite David's efforts to distract himself with comical YouTube videos. The show, on the other hand, sped by, leaving David with only an impression of chic young up-and-comings; serious-faced, well-dressed executive types; one elderly woman in an outlandish hat; and an endless array of handshakes, back slaps, and congratulations. When he excused himself, Simon was ensconced in a crowd at the other side of the room, but smiled, winked and raised a hand to David in farewell. Drained from the experience, David slept for the long ride back to his home.

The following morning, David awoke later than usual, and rolled toward Sarrinah. She lay facing him, propped up on one elbow.

"Morning, gorgeous," he said, sleep burring his voice.

She rolled toward him for a kiss, then smiling, produced a newspaper from behind her back.

David groaned and covered his head with a pillow. "No, no, I can't read reviews before coffee."

Sarrinah laughed, pulled the pillow away and threw it to the floor. "This is yesterday's paper, so new reviews."

"Oh. Okay." David sat up, and propped himself against the headboard. "What is it that has so interested my wife?"

Sarrinah opened the paper and folded it to the appropriate page, then dropped the paper to his lap. It was open to the Local News section. David scanned the top headline, then moved to the next. "Aaah," he said, smile growing. He read the headline aloud. "120-Year-Old Mystery Solved." He scanned quickly through the article, already knowing its contents, then said, "We're framing this. In the end, I guess it wasn't necessary to get it published, but I like seeing it just the same." Somehow feeling a weight had been lifted from his shoulders, David sighed luxuriously, stretched, and said "Coffee. Must. Have. Coffee."

As he rolled out of bed, his cell phone buzzed on the nightstand. "Simon," he answered, "I can't handle reviews this early. I haven't had coffee yet."

"Still in bed, you lazy git? Well, I'm fifteen minutes out. Put some clothes on. Oh, and I'll join you for coffee."

David and Sarrinah greeted Simon at the door when he arrived some twenty minutes later. Simon swept into the foyer, kissed Sarrinah on both cheeks, and said, "Good morning, my dear."

"Lovely to see you again, Simon."

Then Simon turned to David, propped his hands on his waist in a posture of scolding, and said, "And you, my boy."

"After coffee," David said, trepidatious yet bursting with need-to-know. "That's the same suit you were wearing last night. Didn't you get any sleep?"

"Who needs sleep?"

"Coffee's in the morning room. I needed the exercise."

Simon shook a stack of newspapers at David as the three began the trek to the opposite end of the house. "I must tell you, David–"

David brought his hands to his ears. "No reviews before coffee!"

Simon raised his right hand, and said, "No reviews before coffee, I swear." After several more steps, he said, "But how would you feel about just a general overall impression?"

"Only if it's good."

"It's not good, David," Simon said. Despite Simon's cheerful tone, David's stomach twisted with dread. "It's bloody fantastic!"

David stopped and turned to Simon, whose face – despite obvious indications of fatigue – stretched in a gargantuan smile. "Seriously?"

"David, I'm a genius. Or, I should say you're a genius. Yeah, we're a pair of geniuses." Simon threw back his head in laughter, then said, "We have a bidding war over 'The Agony and the Ecstasy,' we have requests for more, more, and more, and if you have a single piece that wasn't sold from the entire exhibit, I can't remember which it is."

David felt his face flush, but could not think how to respond to such incredible news. Simon stepped closer and put his hands on David's shoulders. "In short, you're going to be rich. You are going to be wildly, and – quite predictably, if you ask me – very, very rich!"

CHAPTER 30

FORTY YEARS LATER

SARRINAH SAT AT THE bedside and held David's hand while he slept. Her heart overflowed with love as she gazed through misty tears at his time-worn face, her thumb sliding back and forth over the soft, crepe-paper skin of his hand. The monitoring machines burbled a background chorus in the darkened room which she was able to ignore.

Not long now, dearest one. I cannot join you on your next great adventure, but I have no regrets.

David's fingers tightened around hers as if in response to her thoughts, as if consoling her or reassuring her that he remained with her.

I retract that statement. I do regret how very much I will miss you when you are gone.

LOVE WHISPERS THROUGH THE VEIL

Forty years. Four decades of a happiness so sublime she could not have imagined the breadth of it when yet living. In those years, much had changed, yet much had remained the same. David had changed, aged, as was natural to every living soul, and had done so with grace and humor. Sarrinah had physically remained the same, yet had grown to understand the times in which they lived. Together they had nurtured a deepening of the love they shared.

They tended toward a life of privacy, both by necessity and proclivity. David achieved unheard of successes with his wood sculpture, yet enjoyed and cultivated an air of mystique which only added to his reputation. However, in celebration of their tremendous home which they maintained and improved with passionate dedication, once a year they hosted a grand ball in the lavish style typical of such affairs during Sarrinah's youth, with entertainments, feasting and dancing. If anyone noticed that the hostess (who, over the years was presented first as wife, then daughter, and granddaughter of the host) never ate during the festivities, no comment was made.

Simon, alone of their few friends, was fully aware of Sarrinah's nature. For this reason, when the house was placed in trust for perpetuity, Simon served as the first trustee, fully understanding the reason for the faithful maintenance of the home and the enigmatic "relative" who would continue to dwell there.

Sarrinah sighed in resignation, knowing that the time for such necessities was close at hand. She was torn by twin desires: That the house be abandoned so that she could fade into forgetful oblivion, and that some living soul remained so that she could remember the fullness of her life and love with David.

"Sarrinah." Her name came as a rasp as David opened his eyes.

"I'm here David." Sarrinah leaned closer to be sure to hear his words.

"I want you to stay with me always, Sarrinah."

"You will forever be in my heart, my love. Forever." Pushing aside thoughts of the long, lonely time ahead of her, Sarrinah blinked back tears, and pressed a smile to her face.

"Come closer, Darling. Kiss me."

LOVE WHISPERS THROUGH THE VEIL

Sarrinah stood from the chair and bent to press her lips to his. As their mouths parted, she felt David's hands grip her shoulders. "I'm here, David."

David pulled her closer and wrapped his arms around her, embracing her with a startling strength. Whispering into her ear, he said, "It's time Sarrinah."

Clenching her lips against a sob of grief, she could only nod her head in response.

"Don't let go, Sarrinah." As she slid her hands further under his shoulders and squeezed him to her as firmly as she dared, she heard his final words. "Don't let go. *I can show you the way.*"

Sarrinah sucked in a breath as a warmth enveloped her. "David, I love you." His grip tightened and her eyelids fluttered. "David!" she exclaimed in surprise as the warmth transformed into a brightness that seemed to wrap and surround them both. She sucked in another breath, then relaxed.

"Forever," Sarrinah murmured as she floated, wrapped in David's arms, into the light.

***
**
*

Thank you for taking the time to read

Love Whispers Through the Veil!

Nothing helps an author (or a future reader) more than an honest review… it's true! Think about it: If you were looking at a book and it had two reviews, you'd be less likely to read it than if it had ten thousand!

I read every review so that I can figure out what worked, and what didn't, and how to improve as a writer. (Improvement is a life-long job, or it should be!) I'd love to hear your thoughts!

So, if you enjoyed **Love Whispers Through the Veil**, please do your part to spread the word by leaving a review on Amazon!

Thanks a bunch!

If you want more from Davyne DeSye…

HISTORICAL ROMANCE

For Love of the Phantom, Book #1 in the Phantom Rising Series

Skeletons in the Closet, Book #2 in the Phantom Rising Series

Phantom Rising, Book #3 in the Phantom Rising Series

SCIENCE FICTION

Carapace

Soap Bubble Dreams and Other Distortions

Made in the USA
Las Vegas, NV
04 January 2022

40378771R10218